T0131773

The sweetest revenge . . .

He's the Swift brother who got left behind, the son abandoned by his father. Now Kyle Swift is a man determined to destroy the whitewater rafting empire built by the half brothers he never knew, the Swift sons who got the life—and the love—he was denied. Seducing Fisher Jones isn't part of his revenge, but sharing a bed with the beautiful whitewater instructor is the one bright spot in his otherwise dark plan. That is, if he manages not to fall for the sad-eyed beauty...

Fearless when it comes to facing even the most daunting river rapids, Fisher never takes chances with her love life—until the night she gets swept away by a sexy stranger. But when her one-night stand unexpectedly shows up in her whitewater class, Fisher faces her greatest challenge yet: keeping her heart safe from a man determined to put an end to the family business—and the life—she holds dear....

Books by Kristina Mathews

More Than a Game Series
Better Than Perfect
Worth the Trade
Making a Comeback
Earning a Ring

Swift River Romance Series
Swept Away
In Too Deep
Diving In

Published by Kensington Publishing Corporation

Diving In

A Swift River Romance

Kristina Mathews

LYRICAL PRESS
Kensington Publishing Corp.
www.kensingtonbooks.com

Lyrical Press books are published by
Kensington Publishing Corp. 119 West 40th Street New York, NY 10018

All Kensington titles, imprints, and distributed lines are available at special quantity discounts for bulk purchases for sales promotion, premiums, fund-raising, and educational or institutional use.

Special book excerpts or customized printings can also be created to fit specific needs. For details, write or phone the office of the Kensington Special Sales Manager:
Kensington Publishing Corp.
119 West 40th Street
New York, NY 10018
Attn. Special Sales Department. Phone: 1-800-221-2647.

Kensington and the K logo Reg. U.S. Pat. & TM Off.
LYRICAL PRESS Reg. U.S. Pat. & TM Off.
Lyrical Press and the L logo are trademarks of Kensington Publishing Corp.

First Electronic Edition: September 2017
eISBN-13: 978-1-60183-924-4
eISBN-10: 1-60183-924-3

First Print Edition: September 2017
ISBN-13: 978-1-60183-927-5
ISBN-10: 1-60183-927-8

Printed in the United States of America

To my readers, thank you for keeping my dream alive.

Chapter 1

Life is good.

At least that's what it said on the front of Fisher Jones's T-shirt. Standing in the parking lot of the American River Grill—the Argo to the locals—she accepted congratulations and hugs from her friends and coworkers. They had been celebrating her recent promotion to river operations manager. She'd be in charge of the rafting part of the Swift River Adventure Company and Resort.

No one knew she'd been crafting a letter of resignation. One she'd been working on for weeks. No, months. But she didn't have the courage to hand it in. She loved life on the American River. Taking visitors down the river was always a thrill. Whether it was their first time or they were return customers, they always had a blast. She especially enjoyed helping people rise to the challenge of stepping outside their comfort zones.

Fisher loved her job. That wasn't the problem.

The problem was she loved her boss. Her married, with children, boss. Four years ago, at this very bar, Cody Swift had hit on her. It being her first night in Prospector Springs, she had brushed him off. A good thing, since the very next morning she'd started her first day as his assistant guide.

Although she'd seen dozens of women floating in and out of his bed, she'd come to know the real Cody. The man behind the fun-loving, life-of-the-party persona. They'd developed a friendship. And somewhere along the line, her feelings had deepened.

She had hoped, after his twin brother, Carson, met and married Lily, Cody might consider settling down and sticking with one woman.

And that's exactly what he did. Only it was Miranda who had managed to capture his heart. And then she gave him two beautiful, perfect twin daughters, Ava and Addy.

Fisher had never been one of those women who went all gaga over babies. But damn, those two girls were adorable. She watched Cody lovingly strap them into their infant seats and she could almost feel her ovaries explode.

She reached for her sunglasses to hide the glisten of tears that would come if she watched him another minute. But they weren't perched on the top of her head, where she normally kept them when she wasn't squinting into the bright sunshine.

"I think I left my sunglasses inside," she said to Brooke, a fellow guide and the woman she shared a room with at the guides' house back at the resort. "Can you give me a minute to go look for them?"

"Sure." Brooke had ridden over in Fisher's Jeep. Cody had, of course, driven with his wife and daughters. Carson had come down from Hidden Creek with Lily and their baby boy, Brandon. Gavin, Jake, and Aubrey had all piled in Jake's old Honda. Tyler had been working the store, so he'd met them there after closing out the register.

"If you want to ride back with me, I don't mind." Tyler flashed Brooke a hopeful smile.

"You guys go ahead." Fisher almost preferred driving by herself. As much as she appreciated everyone coming out to help her celebrate, she needed some space. And that was hard to get when she lived with all the guides.

"You sure?" Brooke asked. "You're okay to drive, right?"

"Oh yeah. I only had one beer." She didn't trust herself to have any more than that around Cody. The last thing she needed was to loosen up too much and let her feelings show. "Heck, I may even go back and have one more, maybe stay for the band."

"Do you want me to hang out with you?" Brooke offered, but Fisher could tell she'd rather go with Tyler. Something had been developing between them, and maybe with Fisher out of the way…

"No. I'm fine. I'll text and let you know when I'm on my way home. So you don't worry." Fisher gave Brooke a wink, letting her know that she'd hold back, give them time to…whatever.

Brooke blushed and then darted toward Tyler's pickup.

Fisher walked back into the bar, but the tables they'd been sitting at were already cleared. Hopefully the waitress had handed her sunglasses over to the bartender.

The crowd had picked up even though the sun hadn't gone down yet. Of course, it was Friday night in June. The weather was fine, the food fabulous, and live music would keep the place rocking into the night.

Fisher pushed her way to the bar, but Randy, the bartender, was slammed. She wasn't in a hurry. Her friends had left, and now that she didn't have to watch Cody kissing his babies and his wife, she didn't really need her sunglasses. Wouldn't need them until noon tomorrow when she'd meet her students for whitewater school orientation. Mostly college kids, eager for a summer job of adventure, they'd learn more than just how to read a current and maneuver a raft. She'd be teaching whitewater safety, wilderness camping, environmental awareness, and gourmet outdoor cooking skills.

She'd been guiding for Swift River Adventure Company for four years. She'd been an instructor for two years, but this would be her first year in charge of the school. Cody had been the one to really put himself into the instruction, but he'd be a little busy being a hands-on dad wrangling two four-month-old babies.

Since she'd start work a good three hours later than normal, Fisher figured she might go ahead and have a second beer. If she did end up feeling tipsy, there was a well-maintained bike path, and she could walk home.

"Here you go, a Strong Blonde for the strong blonde." Randy set a glass of the local craft brew in front of her. It wasn't her usual drink choice. She preferred a pale ale or an IPA after a long day on the river.

"I didn't order this," Fisher said with a smile.

"No. He did." Randy nodded toward the guy on the end of the bar, who lifted a glass and flashed a killer set of dimples.

"Oh, okay." Fisher felt heat creep across her cheeks. She took a sip and smiled at the stranger. He was kind of cute. No, he was very cute. *Hot*, actually. And he was walking toward her.

"Hi. I'm Kyle." He offered a firm handshake. Warm, strong. Kind of tingly.

"Fisher." She held up her glass. "Thanks for the drink."

"Well, I wasn't sure what to order, but then I saw you walk in and decided I was in the mood for a strong blonde." He glanced down at her bare arms, well sculpted from her years on the river. "And then I thought I'd try the beer."

"Well, be careful," Fisher warned. "Strong blondes can knock you flat on your back if you're not used to them."

"That's what I was hoping for." He grinned at her, lifted his glass, and took a long sip, not taking his eyes off her.

Flirting. Something she'd given up on in recent years. Not that she'd been completely celibate since the night she'd turned Cody down. No, she'd hooked up with an old boyfriend here and there. She'd even tried dating this guy who lived over in Auburn, but he didn't get her excited enough to keep making the twenty-mile commute.

What the hell? Kyle was good looking. His hair a little darker than Cody's, a little longer, too, but not long enough for a ponytail or man bun. He had a nice smile. His eyes were startlingly blue, and presently focused on her chest.

"Life is good?" He was just reading her shirt. No need to get too excited. "What's good about your life right now?"

"Besides not having to pay for beer?" Fisher took another drink to lubricate her very rusty flirting gears. "I guess getting a promotion today was pretty good."

"Oh yeah? Congratulations." He held his glass up in a toast and she dutifully tapped it.

"Thanks. It's weird, though." She took another swallow and found the glass nearly empty. "I was going to quit."

"Really?" He flagged the bartender and held up two fingers. "Tell me about it."

She should tell him to slow down, these beers were strong. Hence the name. But she'd felt so numb lately, she welcomed the buzzed feeling. And the novel sensation of having a guy interested in her.

"It's complicated." She lifted her glass again. Probably not a good idea, but neither was spilling her guts about her sad crush on her boss.

"I like complicated women." He matched her swallow for swallow. "Especially when they look as good as you."

She laughed, sputtering the last of her beer.

"What? Don't tell me you don't realize how hot you are?" His eyes filled with longing. Lust.

"It is rather warm in here." She fanned herself. Was it the beer or the way he looked at her?

He paid for the two fresh pints and grabbed both glasses. "Why don't we check out the deck? I think the band is about to start."

"Yeah. Sure." Fisher's legs felt a little wobbly. But she also felt a sense of exhilaration. She took the beer he offered and gave him what she hoped was an encouraging smile.

He held the door open for her and she scooted past him onto the deck. It was a perfect night. Warm, but with enough of a breeze that it wasn't stuffy. The sun was just setting, painting the sky in orange, pink, and purple.

Kyle placed his hand on the small of her back and she had to admit, it felt nice. Sexy, yet comforting. He guided her to the edge of the deck, where they could set their drinks on the wide ledge.

"Wow. Beautiful." But he wasn't looking at the sunset or the river below them.

"How many of those have you had?" Fisher wasn't used to the attention. She was used to being one of the guys. Used to teasing, of the brotherly love kind. "And have you eaten dinner?"

"This is my second. And yes. I've had my dinner." He continued to look at her as if he hoped she was on the menu.

"Good. I mean, it's just that these are kind of potent."

"I don't know about the beer, but I'm definitely feeling the effects of a certain strong blonde."

"And what effect is that?" She tried to sound sexy, sure of herself, but she was really bad at flirting.

"I think you know." He lowered his voice, making her insides quiver.

"Why don't you enlighten me." He made her nervous, but not in a creeped-out way. No, it was more how she felt when approaching a big rapid. Full of excitement, tension, anticipation. But the river was familiar, something she'd come to understand, and respect. Could she respect this man, or herself, if she took this flirtation to the next level?

"You're beautiful."

"Oh please." Her cheeks heated and she glanced up at the outdoor TV where the baseball game was playing. The Giants had two on and no one out. Good, she needed a distraction. But she could hardly focus on the game. She could still feel his eyes on her.

"You a baseball fan?" The intensity in his voice eased, just enough to help her relax a little.

"Sure. You?"

"A little. I catch an Angels' game now and again."

"So, you're a Southern California guy?" She turned toward him, and yeah, he was definitely one hot guy.

"Guilty." He leaned closer, lowering his voice. "Is that a deal-breaker for you?"

"No." Were they negotiating here?

"So what is a deal-breaker for you?"

"Are you married? Involved with someone?"

"No. I'm not married." His voice slid over her, as smooth as the river gliding over a flat boulder. "But I am hoping to get involved, at least for tonight."

"Why?" She sipped her beer, hiding behind the glass. "I mean, why me?"

"You really have to ask?"

"Yeah. Because…" She sank back against the railing. She was blowing it. Big-time.

"Someone hurt you." He reached for the hand that wasn't holding her beer. His grip was soft, warm, and steady. "Recently, I'd say."

"No." She sighed, leaning her head back and letting her eyes flutter closed briefly.

"He's an idiot. Whoever he is." He stroked her hand gently with his thumb.

"He's married." She didn't mean to let it out. Yet, it felt somewhat freeing. "And my boss."

"Married, huh?" His eyebrow shot up. "The bastard."

"No. It's not like that." Fisher tried to stand tall. "He's totally faithful. And I'm just pathetic."

"You don't look pathetic to me." He sounded sincere, like he cared or something. "In fact you look like the kind of woman who is usually ready for adventure. Why not take a chance on someone who is equally up for the challenge?"

He was still interested in her for some reason. And she was standing here telling him about her stupid crush on Cody. It was stupid. She knew it. She just didn't know how to move past it.

So here was a guy—a hot guy—who was interested in helping her move on. Sure, he wouldn't be around tomorrow or the next day or the day after that. But he was here. Now. And he was willing. She just had to have the courage to jump on it. To jump on him.

"Would you like to dance?"

She set her beer down, hoping he'd get the hint that she was ready to give him a chance.

"Absolutely."

He shot her a wicked grin and took her hand. She expected him to lead her over to where others were dancing, but there was plenty of room where they stood. He placed his other hand on her waist and pulled her close. Fisher circled her arms around his neck and leaned against his shoulder. She closed her eyes, focused on the sensation of having a man hold her, hips gently swaying with the music.

His heart beat steadily against hers, and her whole body flooded with emotion. Desire. Heat. Connection.

The song ended and the band started playing a livelier tune. Fisher pulled away, but Kyle kept his hands on her hips.

"You feel so good," he murmured. "I want to hold you a little longer."

And she couldn't think of one reason to argue. Sure, there were people around. Some of them probably people she knew, but she didn't care if they were staring at them. She couldn't let go.

"Just one question?" Fisher's heartbeat quickened.

"Anything." He kept his hands right where they were.

"How do you feel about the designated hitter?" Because she couldn't ask him not to hurt her.

"I have a feeling this is important to you." He pulled her even closer, so he could whisper in her ear. "Since my team is in the American League, I'm kind of for it. But… I can see why some people feel it interferes with the integrity of the game."

"True." Fisher liked the way he was humoring her. "Besides, there's nothing better than pitchers who rake."

"Wow. That is the sexiest thing I have ever heard." He brushed his lips against the delicate skin behind her ear. "Can I kiss you?"

She nodded, feeling a little lightheaded.

Slowly, carefully, he lowered his mouth to hers. Just a whisper of kiss, and she sighed. He pressed his lips more firmly against hers and slipped his tongue into her mouth. Slow, yet sweet, playing her until she opened to him.

One of his hands slid into her hair, gently stroking her long silky strands, and the other pulled her hips closer. Pressing her against him, so she could feel just how turned on he was.

Amazingly, she was even more turned on.

"Wow." She finally came up for air. "That was…just…wow."

"Yes, you are pretty spectacular." Kyle's eyes blazed with desire.

"There's just one problem." Fisher had to regain some control. "I don't think I should drive."

A wicked smile spread across his lips, lips that were slightly swollen from their kiss. "You think you can walk? My RV is just on the other side of the parking lot."

"Yeah. That sounds good." Fisher reached for her glass and downed the rest of it. She shouldn't feel this drunk. And she wasn't. Not really. Just tipsy enough that she could let herself be seduced by a handsome stranger. But not so much that she would regret it in the morning.

She wanted this. No. She needed this. She needed to forget about Cody, even if it was only for one night.

* * * *

Steady. Kyle led the hot blonde—no, the *strong* blonde—across the parking lot to his RV. She was intoxicating, that's for sure. He knew better than to mix business with pleasure, but as he was perusing the beer menu, he'd looked up and there she was.

Tall, not quite six feet, and strong. She looked like she worked out, but not with a personal trainer. No, she was one of those outdoorsy-type girls. She could be a triathlete or something. Tan and blond, but not like the women he knew in Southern California. This one was all-natural. She didn't wear so much as mascara. No, the closest thing to makeup she wore was lip balm, the kind with SPF to protect her luscious lips from the sun.

She had an air about her that said she was comfortable here. Comfortable in her skin. She'd given the bartender a friendly smile, not the kind designed to flirt or get served more quickly. She kind of stood there, content to just wait her turn, and maybe look around a bit. But she wasn't on the prowl. Something else that made her stand out.

"It's nothing fancy." He pulled out his keys when they reached the RV, suddenly a little nervous. "But the bed is big enough for two."

"Sure. No big deal." She sounded nervous, too. "I have to tell you: I don't do this kind of thing. Like, ever."

"If you change your mind, that's okay." He didn't want to pressure her. "The dining table converts into an extra bed. I can sleep there."

"Huh? Why would you sleep on the dining table?"

"Well, you said you shouldn't drive, and if you've changed your mind, you can have the comfortable bed." He was sounding like someone who didn't do this sort of thing very often. Or, like, ever.

"No, I haven't changed my mind." She tucked a strand of sun-kissed blond hair behind her ear. "It's just that... I'm not a virgin or anything, but it's been a really long time, and I don't want to disappoint you."

"You won't disappoint me." He cupped her cheek, looked into her bright yet somewhat distant blue eyes. "You've already made my night. Anything from here on out is just a bonus."

She blinked; her eyes sparkled a little too much. No, he couldn't have her cry. That would make her just a little too vulnerable.

"Kyle?" She tilted her head just slightly, a smile warming on her lips. "Are we going to go inside, or what?"

"Yeah." He fumbled with the keys and finally got the door unlocked. He was off his game somehow. Maybe he should mention that this RV had once belonged to... No, he had a feeling she wouldn't give a damn about the movie star who had owned it. And now that he thought about it, it was kind of weird that he seduced women by bringing them to an RV that had been owned by a celebrity, especially when he knew at least half of them were picturing making love to that movie star and not him.

But there was still a chance that Fisher would be thinking about her married boss. He'd have to make sure that didn't happen. Not tonight.

"Do you live here, or is this a vacation thing?" Fisher stepped inside, and he could tell she was impressed by the luxuriousness of the camper. He'd been in fancier, but the wood floors, maple cabinets, flat-screen TV, and mosaic tile backsplash were a far cry from the Formica table tops and indoor/outdoor carpeting of the old-school travel trailers he'd seen growing up. And lived in for a short time.

"I'm just passing through." He didn't want to go into too much detail about why he was here in Prospector Springs. Basically, he was a spy. But not of the James Bond variety. His company had sent him here to get a feel for a small business they were interested in buying. "Taking some time to figure out what I want to be when I grow up."

"Well, this is as good a place as any to find yourself." She surveyed the interior and her gaze traveled toward the back of the RV, where the queen-size bed was.

"Can I get you anything? Another beer?" Not that he wanted to delay things, but he wanted to make her more comfortable.

"Some water?" She smoothed the hem of her short denim skirt down her strong, sexy thighs.

"Good idea." He pulled two bottles of water from the fridge, opened one, and handed it to her before opening his own.

He watched her down half the bottle, impressed by her toned arms, her sexy shoulders. "You're like a cougar."

"Wait. How old are you?" Her eyes grew wide and she set the water on the counter.

"Not that kind of cougar." He laughed. "I mean, that's what it is about you. You're like a mountain lion. Strong. Sleek. Powerful."

"Are you worried I'm going to maul you?" She bit her lower lip and it was just about the sexiest thing he'd ever seen.

"I can only hope." He moved toward her, placing his hands on her impressive shoulders. "You could tear me limb from limb, but I have a feeling it will be worth it."

"Kiss me." She looked up at him with a fierce hunger in her eyes.

He brushed his lips against hers. For some reason, he felt like he had to be gentle with her. Not move too fast. But she forced her tongue into his mouth. And she devoured him. Her lips were every bit as strong as the rest of her. He reached up to gently touch her face, but she grabbed his ass, pressing him against her. Against the one part of her body that would be soft.

Her leg snaked up around his thigh, and her skirt inched up as she rubbed up against him. He dropped his hand to her rear, under her skirt, expecting to find a bare cheek. But instead of a thong, she wore thin cotton panties. He didn't think he could get any harder, but boy, was he wrong.

He slipped his finger beneath the elastic, finding her soft, warm center. She groaned in pleasure. Oh how he wanted to make her cry out in ecstasy, but the angle wasn't quite right. He stepped back enough to slide her panties down her hips, down her legs, until she stepped out of them completely.

Then he moved his hands back up her legs and shoved her skirt out of the way.

She was a natural blonde. He placed a gentle kiss on the golden curls at the apex of her thighs. A soft moan escaped her lips and he was tempted to deepen the kiss, but she was leaning against the counter. He wanted to give her the royal treatment. "The bed is this way." He growled as he tugged her toward the back of the trailer.

"You have condoms?" Her plea was desperate, and he was so glad he could produce them for her.

"Come." He lifted her up and she wrapped her legs around his waist. "And then I'm going to make you come and come and—"

She stuck her tongue down his throat and by some miracle he was able to carry her the ten steps or so to the bed. He laid her on the mattress and dropped to his knees. He needed to taste her like he needed to breathe.

Spreading her thighs apart, he lowered his head and buried himself in her blond curls. He slid his tongue into her silky sweetness. God, she was so wet. So delicious. He devoured her, coaxing her toward a climax.

"Kyle! Oh my God, please…" A guttural moan cut off the rest of her words.

"Please stop?" He was 99 percent sure she meant the opposite, so he gave her one more slow slide of his tongue.

"No." She panted, lifting her hips, pressing against his mouth, showing him that she wanted him to continue. "Wait. Oh, God. Kyle."

She shuddered.

"I want you inside me." She lifted her head; her eyes were glossy, shimmering with passion, not sadness. "Please. Now."

"Well, since you said 'please.'" He tore off his shirt and shoved his pants and boxer briefs out of the way. He took two steps toward the side table where he kept a supply of condoms and grabbed a package, tore it open, and sheathed himself in record time.

"You are so beautiful." He unbuttoned her skirt and slid it down her hips; then he moved her tank top out of the way and reached for her bra, but her nipples showed through the thin white cotton of her bra. "Oh God."

He sucked her breast through the simple garment.

"I know, they're a little on the small side." Vulnerability sounded in her voice, making him want to do everything he could to make this a night she'd never forget.

"No. They're perfect." He pulled down the soft cup, and took her damp nipple into his mouth. "You're perfect."

He suckled her breast, scraping his teeth ever so gently against the pebbled flesh. "Fisher…"

He lifted his head and looked her in the eye. She was absolutely gorgeous, her lips swollen from his kisses, her eyes glazed over with passion, her breath coming in ragged gasps. He needed to be inside her. He needed to possess her. To please her. He slid his hand between her thighs, stroking her sweetly, bringing her closer, closer to the edge. When her breathing quickened and she lifted her hips, he positioned himself over her.

"Open your eyes," he insisted. "I want to see you when I enter you."

"Kyle." She looked up at him. Their eyes locked in a blaze of passion that was hotter than anything he'd ever experienced before.

Then he thrust, gently at first, watching her eyes widen in pleasure. She welcomed him, lifting her hips, taking him deeper.

He closed his eyes. Couldn't handle the intense emotions he saw in her eyes. Wonder. Passion. Complete surrender.

He couldn't handle it, because her eyes mirrored his own feelings.

She wrapped her legs around his waist, clenched her inner muscles, and cried out his name as she succumbed to another orgasm.

His was more powerful than anything he'd ever felt.

Chapter 2

Shortly after dawn, Fisher slipped out of Kyle's bed. She hadn't quite regrown her bones, but they were solid enough for her to stand and search the floor for her clothes. She found her tank top, bra, and skirt rather quickly, but her panties weren't near the bed.

She shook the fog from her head and remembered drinking bottled water toward the front of the camper, closer to the door. Right. He'd removed her panties and she'd left her leather flip-flops in the kitchen area of his luxury RV.

As quietly as possible, she searched for her missing undergarments. There they were, on the floor, next to her shoes and her small handbag that she must have dropped when he'd kissed her.

Slipping on her underwear and sandals, she cast one last, longing glance at the man in the bed.

Had she really had wild, wanton sex with a total stranger? She didn't even know his last name. But what did it matter? She was never going to see him again. And she'd accomplished her goal.

One whole night where she didn't ache for Cody.

Kyle would never know the gift he'd given her last night. But it wasn't just the physical satisfaction that she'd always remember. She'd had orgasms before. Usually with the help of Buzz—her trusted vibrator. No. It was the way he made her feel like the sexiest woman in the world. Like she was beautiful, and interesting, and worthy of, if not love, at least sex.

And why not? She was a healthy twenty-six-year-old single woman. Saving herself for a man who'd moved on years ago wasn't getting her anywhere. And as much as she'd wanted him, she would never, ever, in a million years break up a marriage. Especially when there were children involved.

It was time for her to move on. Get a life. And getting laid was a good way to start.

Quietly, she let herself out of the RV. The early morning sun reminded her that she'd never found her sunglasses. And the Argo wouldn't open until eleven. So she'd have to drive home in the bright sunlight and hope she could find a spare pair before she met her whitewater school students.

Fisher climbed into her Jeep and checked the glove box. No such luck. She felt around under the seat and found a baseball hat. She gathered her hair into a loose ponytail and threaded it through the hole in the back of the cap. Better than nothing.

At least it was a short drive to the resort. Not too much time for her to think about what she'd done. She pulled into the driveway, right next to Cody's truck. His door opened and he stepped out just as she shut off her engine. He took a few steps to lean on the open window of her passenger side door.

"Just getting home?" He knew. It was clear from the tone of his voice that he knew exactly what she'd been up to.

"Yeah." Of all the people she had to run into first thing this morning.

"Good. I'm glad you continued to celebrate." He flashed a heartbreaking smile. "I'd hate for you to let us old married folks slow you down."

Like she needed a reminder that he was married. It was like a tick biting her heart, burying itself deeper and deeper each day.

"I hope you had a good time." He sounded sincere enough, as if he meant it. As if he wanted her to be happy.

"I did." She tried to keep her voice cheerful. To act like this was just a conversation between two friends. "You're here awfully early."

"Babies make a really effective alarm clock." His grin showed how much he adored his children. "Addy went back to sleep, but Ava is raring to go. I don't even want to think about when she starts walking."

"She'll give you a run for your money." Fisher couldn't help but picture him chasing his kids as toddlers. He'd have his hands full, for sure.

"I'd better start saving up my energy." He stood, perhaps realizing that she might not want to stay and chat. "Well, I'll let you go. You ready for your guide school? They should start coming in around noon."

"I'll be ready." After breakfast, a shower, and maybe a nap. "Aren't I always?"

"Of course. I don't know what we'd do around here without you."

"You'd manage."

"No. Seriously, we should have given you a raise a long time ago." He leaned on the door again. Did he not know what he was doing to her? Obviously not. But maybe that was a good thing.

"Well, it's not like I have a lot of expenses." The rent was super cheap on the room she shared, and her Jeep was paid for.

"Well, you might want to save up for a place of your own."

"Maybe." But she couldn't imagine living alone.

"Well, I'd better get going. Miranda is going to need me this afternoon." Cody stood again. Maybe this time he meant it. "She's working on her second book. Can you believe it? The first one comes out in September."

"Yeah, that's so cool." The last thing she wanted was to read a romance novel written by the woman who was married to the man she couldn't have. "I can't wait to get an autographed copy."

"So, let me know if you need anything. I'll be around."

"Yeah, sure." Until his wife called him home.

Fisher opened the driver's side door and stepped out of her Jeep. She gave Cody a wave and made her way to the guides' house. She hoped someone had made coffee, a task that often fell to her since she was usually the first one up.

Ross was there, sitting at the kitchen table, wearing board shorts and his guitar.

"Look at you, doing the walk of shame." He strummed his guitar for dramatic effect.

"What? Shame?" She rolled her eyes. "Why is it that when one of you guys gets laid, you brag about it? High-five each other. You never call it shameful. But when a woman does it…"

"You're right." Ross set his guitar down and stood up. "Put 'er there." He held up his hand and she smacked it. Hard.

"So?" He waggled his eyebrows, looking for details. "How was it?"

"A lady never tells." She smiled coyly. "At least not before coffee."

"There's coffee and bacon, but you'll have to scramble your own eggs." Ross picked up his mug and chuckled softly. "Unless they've already been scrambled."

"Oh, grow up." Fisher made her way toward the coffeepot. She poured a steaming mug and inhaled.

"Hey, you wanna play with the boys?" Ross shrugged.

"I sent the boys home and found myself a man." Fisher had always been able to fit in with the guys. She'd listened to their bragging and banter and bullshitting. But she'd been a little on the outside. Until Brooke had joined the team last summer, she'd been the only woman who lived here full-time. Lily had come along a few weeks before Brooke, but she wasn't one of the guys. She'd become a friend, and as far as Fisher knew, she was the only one who knew about her feelings for Cody.

"I'm happy for you." Ross started strumming a soulful tune on his guitar.

"Thanks." Was it that obvious to everyone that she'd lived like a nun in some ways?

"No, really." Ross gave her a genuine smile.

"Am I that pathetic?" She suddenly felt very tired. She couldn't decide if she needed food or sleep.

"No. Just selective, I guess."

She grabbed a couple pieces of bacon from the oven and sat down at the table. Food. Nap. Shower. Then she could face the day.

"So who was he?" Ross asked.

"I don't really know. He's a SoCal guy, so…" She shrugged. How did they do it? How did they just hook up with random people and act like it was no big deal?

"So what was it about him that made you, you know?"

"I don't know. I guess he was interested at a time when I needed to feel…"

"Wanted?" Ross played another few notes on his guitar.

"Something like that." Fisher polished off the bacon and licked her fingers. "What? Are you going to write a song about it?"

"You never know." Ross turned his attention to his guitar. He hummed along, a sign that he was, indeed, working on a new song.

Fisher took the rest of her coffee up to her room and encountered Tyler in the hallway. He had a goofy grin on his face.

"You just getting home?" he asked, raking his hand through his hair.

"Yeah. So did you keep Brooke from worrying about me all night?"

"I did my best." Tyler shrugged and headed down to the kitchen.

Thankfully, Brooke was in the bathroom when Fisher got to the room.

Suddenly very weary, she collapsed on her bed. Her body still hummed, but her mind started racing.

What had she done? And why did something that had been so good last night only make her feel even worse this morning? It was supposed to be meaningless sex. It didn't matter, though. She'd never see him again. She hadn't given him the chance to offer anything more. Or to disappoint her when he didn't.

* * * *

Kyle woke to an empty bed. It wasn't the first time, but it was the first time in a long time he'd been disappointed by his companion's early departure.

His strong blonde. Strong. Sexy. And so damned responsive.

He felt pretty good about helping her forget her boss for the night.

But he needed to remember why he was here. What *his* boss expected of him. And what he owed the man who'd given him a shot to make something of himself even without a college education.

Time to get moving. Shake off the fog of last night and go over his reports one last time before getting into the character of a whitewater guide-in-training. He was in good shape physically but had never actually been down a river in a raft. Except for the one at Disney's California Adventure. At least he was a strong swimmer. He imagined that the years he'd spent boogie boarding and bodysurfing would help prepare him for the experience of being thrown into the water.

He read over the introductory e-mail, which included a list of gear and personal items he'd need, a glossary of terms he would learn, and a general outline of what to expect for each day of the course. The first day would consist of introductions, safety instructions, and setting up camp. He had a small tent, but he planned on sleeping in the RV except for the two nights they would be in the wilderness camps.

Sleeping in dirt wasn't the most appealing idea to him, but he could fake it for a few days. Especially if it helped him fit in and be accepted as one of the guys. And once he gained their trust, he'd be in a position to take down the company. Or rather, buy them out. Well, he would just be the deal maker. His boss would write the check.

They'd make a nice profit when they sold to a larger company, and if he stuck it to his big brothers, that would be even better. It would serve them right for taking his father away from him when he was just ten. For sending him back when they got their inheritance. He would have been better off if his father had stayed gone. And his mother would have been much better off without having her heart broken time and again by a man who was too good for his youngest son but not good enough for his oldest sons.

Chapter 3

Kyle pulled the trailer into the Swift River campground. He parked in his spot, hooked up the RV, and slipped into his swim trunks, a faded T-shirt from his favorite surf shop, and his new river sandals. A pair of dark sunglasses had transformed him into the character of a disenchanted car salesman looking for a change of pace.

He basically was a salesman. He just dealt in companies, not cars. His role wasn't always easy to explain. Mostly it was to check out small companies, find out in what areas they needed to take their business to the next level, and then present his findings to his boss, mentor, and the man who'd been more of a positive influence on his life than Joe Swift ever even tried to be.

JP Wilson had given Kyle his first job: mowing Wilson's lawn and hauling trash to the dump. It took him several months before Kyle realized that Mr. Wilson had a full gardening crew, but he must have felt sorry for the kid who'd gone door-to-door looking for work, trying to support his mother in any way he could.

Time to explore his new home for the week. The next few months, if he got hired on after the course ended.

Kyle walked through the campground. The RV spaces were tucked away on one end of the property. Some were close to the river and some more inland. He'd managed to reserve a prime spot only a short distance from the water. From there, he followed a trail past the volleyball court and a group picnic area to where the whitewater school would convene.

He had to admit, it was a beautiful location. Towering pines, steady oaks, and several other trees shaded the campground. Tangles of blackberries sprawled across the ground, along with ferns and grasses and wildflowers.

The individual tent sites were tucked away, offering privacy and a sense of seclusion. There were a few group campsites that were more open, with space for kids to run around and play tag, toss a Frisbee or a ball. Most of the whitewater school students would camp at one of these sites. He could see a few of them already setting up their tents and staking their claim on the large lawn area.

He approached the group, ready to get to know his fellow guides-in-training. He expected to meet mostly college students, and perhaps a few people in their midtwenties, hoping for one last stab at a life of adventure outside the corporate world.

What he didn't expect was to find *her*. His strong blonde. She stood with a couple of the students, chatting and laughing with them. She wore a blue Swift River Adventures T-shirt, flowered board shorts, and river sandals. Her hair was in two long braids, and her smile was infectious. When she looked over his direction, her cheeks darkened to a deep pink and her smile faded.

For one brief moment, he thought he might have made a mistake last night. She could become a distraction. A complication he didn't need.

But then he remembered the way she had responded to his touch. The way she had called out his name. And the way she'd writhed in ecstasy beneath him.

He took two long strides toward her, his smile broadening as he got closer.

"Hi." He nodded and held his hand out. "Are you one of the instructors?"

"Yes." She took his hand for a brief shake, but he wouldn't let go. He couldn't. "I'm one of the instructors."

"That makes my day." He finally released her hand, but not before sliding his middle finger across her palm, making her shiver. Was she remembering all the other places he'd stroked her? He hoped so.

"Well…" She took a step back. "You should meet everyone. This is, um…"

"Nolan." One of the guys she was talking to stepped forward and offered a quick handshake.

"Brett." Someone else stepped up.

He was introduced to Dana, Leia, and Chad, but he kept his attention on Fisher. She was even prettier in the light of day. He could tell she'd been surprised to see him. Maybe even a little bit flustered, but she recovered quickly.

"Well, we're still waiting for a few out-of-town arrivals," she announced. "We can start with one of the important tasks you'll be responsible for on every trip. Lunch."

That got a few chuckles.

"We've got deli meats, cheese, and fruit in the cooler here." She indicated the white ice chest at the end of one of the picnic tables. "And breads, trail mix, and chips are in the ammo can. Could I get one of you to help me haul it up here?"

Kyle rushed to be the first one to get to the table.

He'd always tried to be the best in any situation. He might not be the smartest or most educated guy, but he could be the hardest working. And now he had extra incentive.

He wanted Fisher. One night wasn't enough. Not with her. Especially now that he realized that her boss, the one she was trying to forget, was one of his brothers.

"What do you need me to do first?" He lifted the metal box to the middle of the table.

"You can start on the sandwiches." Fisher flipped open the latches on the army surplus ammo can. Inside it was neatly organized with two loaves of bread, a large bag of trail mix, dried fruit, crackers, cutting boards, knives, and oatmeal cookies. There was also a jar of peanut butter, strawberry jam, and a roll of paper towels.

She opened the cooler and someone else stepped up. Dana or Leia, he wasn't sure which one, pulled out sliced cheese, deli meats, and bunches of red and green grapes. She also pulled out a selection of fresh apple cider.

Soon the rest of them gathered around and started helping themselves to sandwiches, snacks, and juice.

Kyle had made himself a ham and cheese sandwich, then grabbed a handful of trail mix and some red grapes. But then he noticed Fisher didn't have anything to eat yet.

"What can I make for you?" He came up beside her as she was surveying the group.

"Oh, I'll just throw together a PB&J." She moved toward the table.

"I'll get it for you." He reached for the peanut butter. "White or wheat?"

"Wheat. But I can do it." She tried to take the knife from him.

"I don't mind." He leaned in close. "Besides, I didn't get a chance to make you breakfast this morning."

Her cheeks flamed.

"Don't worry, no one heard," Kyle whispered. "But I was sorry you didn't stick around."

"Can we not do this here?"

"Okay. My RV is parked in spot six. Come find me when you want to continue this."

He spread peanut butter and strawberry jam on the bread. He sliced the sandwich diagonally, like his mama used to do, and placed the halves on a paper towel.

"Thank you." She took the sandwich and met his eyes with a look of thanks, and longing.

He watched her eat quickly and start cleaning up. The two women jumped in to help, and Kyle made sure to be one of the first of the guys to step up.

* * * *

The remaining guide school students arrived just as they'd started cleaning up the lunch. Good. The last thing she needed was to stand around listening to her one-night stand telling her how disappointed he was that she'd left before he woke up. In front of people. Especially her students.

She appreciated the sandwich and the fact that he'd been one of the first to pitch in and help get lunch set up. She liked to start with something simple, just to get a feel for everyone's comfort zone. See who was more than willing to jump right into the middle of things and who hung back, needing a bit more direction. She had a feeling Kyle was going to be the worst kind. Too eager. And with their added history, albeit a short one, it could get complicated.

Exactly what she didn't need.

Especially with Cody marching over, probably to check on her. Not that he didn't trust her, but… She had no idea if he knew how she felt about him and felt bad about it. Or if he had no clue that every time he showed up just to chat, a small piece of her heart eroded away like the granite rocks, slowly being turned into dust.

Either way, she'd have to paste on a smile and do what she always did…her job.

"Hi, I'm Cody Swift." He greeted their guests, no, their students. Some would become part of the family and stay on for the summer. "Welcome to Swift River Adventures. You'll work hard, get wet, get dirty, have fun, and learn a lot about the river, including safety, how to read a current, right a flipped raft, and retrieve a swimmer. You'll also learn a lot about yourselves."

He got a few chuckles, and he smiled, making eye contact with each of them.

"Listen to Fisher. She's one of the best. No. I take that back. She is the best." He looked directly at her, with respect, admiration, and friendship showing in his gaze. Nothing more.

She looked away and noticed that Kyle was watching her. The way he looked at her was something else entirely. It was the way he looked at her last night, at the bar. Only more intense.

Her cheeks heated, and she shifted uncomfortably, wondering if everyone could see the desire in Kyle's eyes. Why wasn't he wearing those expensive sunglasses he had hanging from the front of his shirt?

"As I was saying," Cody continued, "Fisher will be your main instructor. Tyler and Brooke will assist her. And if there's anything else you need, my twin brother, Carson, and I are usually around."

He smiled at her and then went around, shaking hands and chatting with each of the newcomers. Except Kyle, who was now standing next to her.

"Are you okay?" He glanced at Cody long enough for her to realize he remembered her mentioning her feelings for her boss.

"Yeah. Everyone's always a little nervous the first day of school. That's why I like to start with feeding you."

"No, I mean him." He jerked his head in Cody's direction. "He's your boss, right?"

"Yes." She couldn't look at him. Not when he knew too much about her. Not the least of which was what she looked like naked.

"I can see what you like about him."

"Can we just drop it?" She did not need two men tormenting her.

"I thought maybe last night helped." He kept his voice low, the conversation private even in a crowd. "But I can see I've got more work to do."

"Yes. If you could gather up the last of the recycling. There's a bin right outside the store." She moved away from him, toward some of the others.

It was going to be a long week. A long week indeed.

* * * *

So that was Cody. His big brother. One of them, anyway. Kyle wasn't sure how he'd feel upon meeting him. Just because he shared half their DNA didn't mean they would automatically be connected. And as far as he was concerned, the half they shared wasn't the better half.

So Kyle watched, trying to scope him out, not getting too friendly, but he knew he couldn't be too standoffish, either.

And then there was Fisher.

He moved closer, placing a hand on her shoulder. She sighed before pulling away.

"The recycling." Her voice was somewhat strained as she nodded in the direction of the picnic table, where someone else had already collected the empty juice containers into a bag.

"Looks like it's under control." He wanted to touch her again. Taste her. Get tangled up in her long blond hair. A smart man would back off. Let her go. Obviously, her heart belonged to another man. She could never give him more than her body.

But what a body. He let out a low whistle, just loud enough for her to hear.

Kyle smiled, offering her a smoldering look. He wanted her to know that he thought she was sexy as hell, and he was just about to say something when Cody stepped forward.

"Hi, we haven't met yet. I'm Cody." His brother extended a hand and Kyle reluctantly shook it.

"Kyle." He left off his last name, for now. "This is a great place you've got here."

"Thanks." Cody glanced between him and Fisher and a small, knowing smile spread across his face. "I see you've become acquainted with our Fisher."

Our Fisher?

"We have actually met before." Fisher blushed deeply.

"Good." He nodded then eyed Kyle suspiciously. "Well, you do what she says and you'll be all right. This one knows her stuff. You go against her, and you'll be sorry."

Was that a threat?

"On the river, Fisher is the best there is."

"Stop." Fisher shoved Cody in a playful, almost sisterly way. "You've practically guaranteed I'm going to make a big mistake. I'm not infallible, you know."

"I know, it's just that you're the most trusted, most faithful of all of my guides." Cody seemed oblivious to the fact that Fisher had a thing for him. Or maybe he knew damn well and was playing her. "You're in good hands."

"Just go." Fisher shoved Cody again. "Miranda probably needs your help with the babies. Isn't it getting close to naptime?"

"Yeah." Cody got a goofy grin on his face. Miranda must be his wife. "It is almost naptime. My favorite time of the day."

Kyle watched Fisher watch Cody walk away. He definitely had his work cut out for him, but he was up for the challenge. He would enjoy distracting Fisher. Taking her mind off Cody as he took her body to new heights. The guy wouldn't know what hit him. His brother obviously didn't appreciate Fisher. And he'd really miss her when his company slipped away as well.

Chapter 4

"Welcome to the boat barn. This is where the magic happens. Actually, this is where the work begins to make the magic happen on the river." Fisher led the group into the warehouse where all the equipment was kept. Each of the shelves was neatly organized and labeled. She started by pointing to the large whiteboard just inside the door. "Here is where you'll find just about everything you need to know."

She pointed to the section that listed the trip schedules, including which boats were assigned, and the names of the guides that would be working each day. There was a standard checklist, listing all the equipment and supplies needed for each trip. Another section of the board listed equipment failures, down to which tubes or valves to check for leaks. There was a place to request supplies, such as bandages for the first aid kit, patches for the rafts, and hand sanitizer for those times when soap and water weren't easily accessible.

"There's also an online calendar that we e-mail to all our guides, but we've found it's a good idea to have a low-tech option, for those times when someone forgets to take their phones out of their pockets before taking a swim." The group chuckled at that, but when it happened to them, they wouldn't laugh.

"And here are the rafts." She pointed to the row of low shelves that held the rolled-up rafts. They had a couple of older Avon rafts that had been in use since Cody and Carson were first learning the river, and the new Hyside boats they had bought when Lily found the money their former bookkeeper had attempted to embezzle. "They're heavy, so it's recommended to use the buddy system when lifting them."

Fisher looked at the group, knowing Kyle would be more than happy to help demonstrate proper lifting technique.

"Dana, why don't you come over here and stand on that side. Here, take my hands." She held her arms out and the petite young woman followed directions. "Okay, now rock the raft into position."

With her shoulder, Fisher guided the heavy raft into their outstretched arms. "Now lift with your legs. Perfect."

With teamwork, the raft wasn't as bulky and heavy.

Next she showed them how to unroll the boat, and they took turns rolling it back up and securing it. "Some companies leave the rafts inflated for the season, and store them on trailers, but we like to keep ours inside, out of the sunlight, when not in use."

"We'll be meeting Tyler and Brooke as they come off an upper trip." Fisher had a lot of details to go over before they got on the river. "The river is basically divided into two stretches of about ten miles each. The upper starts at Chili Bar and ends here at the camp. And the lower stretch, which we'll start on today, starts here and ends at the upper end of Folsom Lake at the Salmon Falls Bridge."

For the most part, her students were interested and attentive. Kyle was a little too attentive. Every time she looked in his direction, he was staring at her. Smiling in that knowing way. But he'd behaved himself. He hadn't made his interest too obvious and as far as she could tell, the others hadn't picked up on it.

Cody had. But maybe that was only because he'd caught her coming home this morning instead of last night. Or maybe it was because he knew her so well, he picked up on her feelings.

No. He didn't know her all that well. Not since Miranda had captured his attention. And his heart.

Maybe it would have been easier if Fisher didn't like Miranda. If Cody's wife wasn't so cool. The two women weren't exactly close, but they got along okay. Probably because Miranda was so secure in her relationship with Cody. They'd met on another river, when Cody had been impersonating Carson. But then Miranda showed up looking for the man she'd met, and Cody wouldn't let her get away.

She led the group over to where the life jackets were hung up.

"Guest safety is a number-one priority." She made a point of making eye contact with each of them. "Life jackets are to be worn at all times on the river."

She handed each of them a personal floatation device, or PFD.

"Proper fit is important. Make sure your vest is snug, and then I want you to take turns lifting up on the shoulder straps. There shouldn't be any movement." She went around to each student, checking both their individual fit and that they were checking each other. "But you don't want it so tight that it's hard to breathe."

When she got to Kyle, she found it hard to breathe, and she hadn't even put her life jacket on yet. He looked at her with smoldering eyes. Memories of the night before flooded her thoughts and made the barn uncomfortably warm.

"Is this a good fit?" Kyle flexed his biceps as he gripped the straps on his vest.

Fisher had never had a problem concentrating before. Even when she was with Cody, she was able to keep her focus on her job. On the river.

"I think we should head down to the river." She took a step back, away from Kyle. "We'll use the boats already down there, but I do need everyone to grab a paddle and follow me."

Fisher grabbed her paddle and swung her life jacket over one shoulder. She already knew it was properly adjusted, since no one else ever wore it.

"Even with a life jacket, the river can be dangerous." She needed to keep their attention, but not make it too terrifying. "It's important to plan for the unexpected. On the river, the three hazards you're likely to encounter are lightning sand, fire spurts, and rodents of unusual size."

Kyle laughed, but the others didn't seem to get the reference to *The Princess Bride*.

"In all seriousness, the most common dangers are ejection, wraps, and flips." She was somehow comforted by Kyle's presence. Weird. "Ejections happen most frequently. So it's important that your passengers know what to do if they find themselves out of the boat unexpectedly. The important things to remember are to keep your feet downstream, butts up, and don't fight the current."

More nods from her students.

"If they can hang on to their paddle, even better." She offered an encouraging smile. "Assure them that you will come to them once you get through the rapid and make it to calmer water. That's when they can swim toward the raft as you maneuver toward them. The paddle can be used to close the distance, if they still have it. Once they get to the boat, you or one of the fellow passengers will grab the shoulders of the life jacket and pull the swimmer into the boat.

"Don't worry, we'll have plenty of chances to practice before you get your first passengers. Both as a swimmer and a rescuer." She made a point to look directly at the petite female guides. "And you'd be surprised at how easily you can lift someone even twice your size, if you let gravity and momentum be your friend."

Just as they reached the sandy bank, three rafts came into view. Jake,

Tyler, and Brooke were bringing their passengers ashore with smiles on their faces and stories to tell when they got back home.

Jake would finish the posttrip debriefing, informing the passengers where they could purchase their photos that were taken as they went through the biggest rapid, giving them recommendations for grabbing a bite to eat on the way home, and inviting them to leave a review. He would also collect any tips and distribute the money to his fellow guides later.

Tyler and Brooke stayed behind to take their students down the lower stretch. It would be a long day for them, but business was booming, and with Cody and Carson shifting their focus to the business side of things as well as helping with their babies, everyone was getting a lot of extra work. Fisher was salary, but the others would get extra pay for the extra work.

The group was split up to about four students per raft. Kyle, not surprisingly, managed to make his way into Fisher's boat.

"We've talked about what to do if you fall out"—Fisher addressed Kyle, Nolan, Leia, and Brett—"and now it's quiz time. Anyone?"

"Feet downstream," Nolan answered.

"On your back," Kyle added, his voice dripping with innuendo.

"Don't panic," Leia suggested.

"And don't fight the current."

"Good." Fisher smiled. "You were paying attention. And we'll all get plenty of opportunities to take a swim a little later."

"Now let's practice a few strokes." Why did she have to look directly at Kyle when she said that? His smile indicated that he was well aware how awkward it was for her. Especially with him sitting practically on her lap. "Actually, let's move around a bit, to better distribute weight and strength. Leia, I'm going to have you move back to where Brett is. Kyle, take Leia's spot at the front on the left, and Brett you can sit right in front of me."

"Where should I go?" Nolan asked.

"You're fine up front on the right." Fisher needed to put some space between her and Kyle, but she also wanted to keep an eye on him. "Now Kyle, you're in the hot seat. It will be your stroke that your teammates will follow."

Leia giggled quietly behind him.

"Nolan, you'll want to match Kyle's rhythm." That was a better word than stroke, but still, she couldn't help but recall his rhythms and strokes from last night. Why couldn't she just let it go?

Because she wanted more.

* * * *

She was killing him. Each command dripped with sexual innuendo. *Stroke, harder, deeper, faster.* But even when she was talking about how to identify poison oak, he was turned on. Not that he had any fantasies involving calamine lotion, but he liked her confidence, her sense of humor, and the way she didn't let his presence disrupt her class.

She was a little rattled, maybe, by him being there, when they'd both expected to go their separate ways after last night. But now that he had a chance to spend more time with her, he was going to take every advantage he could.

The hard part would be getting her alone.

They made it through the first rapid, Fisher giving commands and the others following his lead in paddling through the current.

"Now who wants to go for a swim?" Fisher asked.

"I'll go." Kyle stood up, ready to jump in. He needed to cool off.

"Good. Just stick your paddle under the tube and slide on in." Was she doing it on purpose? No. He didn't think so. He was just so charged up he read too much into everything she said.

He tucked his paddle securely under the middle tube and did a little backflip into the river. The cold water was refreshing.

"Be sure to stay away from the front of the raft," Fisher called from the boat.

He kept his feet downstream, as instructed. Arms out to the side, head back, he looked up into the blue sky. Gorgeous. And the exact color of Fisher's eyes.

So much for cooling himself off. He never got this worked up over a woman. Not unless he'd gone a really long time without getting laid. It had been little more than twelve hours, yet he couldn't shake his lust. And the water wasn't quite cold enough.

"Now swim on over to the side." His instructor wouldn't let him get too far away. He hoped that was a good thing.

She reached down and grabbed the shoulder straps on his life jacket. He was almost in the boat when she pushed him back in. Maybe she wasn't as interested as he'd hoped.

"Okay, Leia. Now your turn. Bring him in." Fisher moved out of the way and let her smallest student try to fish the biggest guy out of the water. The girl wasn't tiny, but she wasn't as strong as Fisher.

"Like this?" Leia grabbed him and he threw his weight toward the boat. Somehow, it worked. He was about a foot taller than her, and probably outweighed her by close to a hundred pounds, but she had managed to get him back into the raft.

Next, the rest of them took turns jumping out and pulling each other back on board.

"Now that you know how to get your passengers back in the boat, what should you do if you're the one to fall out?" Fisher quizzed her students.

"Hopefully, you've gone over how to retrieve swimmers," Leia said.

"Yes. And while you assure your passengers that if they fall out, you'll bring the boat to them," Fisher said, "if you're the one to fall out, you'll want to get yourself back to the raft as quickly and as safely as possible."

Fisher stood up abruptly and let herself fall into the river.

Kyle's first instinct was to dive in after her. But he'd been given the task of leading his fellow passengers, so he figured the first thing he should do was to act calm. Just like he'd done before he jumped overboard, he secured his own paddle, and stood ready to haul her in once she swam toward the raft.

He grabbed her outstretched paddle and pulled her right up to the side of the raft. He tossed the paddle aboard and reached for her shoulder straps. He pulled her in with enough force that they both fell into the middle of the raft. He was flat on the inflated floor of the boat and she was sprawled on top of him.

Without thinking, he grabbed her hips, pulling her close to him. His heart hammered beneath the thick padding of his life jacket and he wondered if hers was pounding a similar beat.

"You can let go of me." She sounded a little out of breath.

"Yeah." He knew what he should do. But he couldn't quite get his hands to agree. She felt so good.

"Kyle," she pleaded. They weren't alone. In a bed. They were on the river, with three others in the raft with them. He finally released her and she scrambled to the back of the raft where she picked up her paddle and gave the command to "forward paddle."

Kyle found his spot and the crew got back into a steady rhythm. Fisher complimented them on their ability to paddle in sync with each other and follow commands. She warned them that every crew was different. Sometimes they would encounter a group of ten-year-olds who would be more interested in splashing each other than maneuvering the raft downstream. Other times they would get that one guy who thought he was stronger, smarter, and more experienced than everyone else, the guide included, and he would try to do things his own way. With experience and practice, they would learn how to deal with all kinds of situations.

They each took turns paddle captaining, which was the official term for leading a group of paddlers down the river in a raft. Fisher pointed out things like how to position the raft before a rapid, how to read the current, and how to correct a bad angle with one or two strokes from the guide.

Kyle was feeling confident by the time his turn came along. Leia had gone first, taking a cautious yet competent approach. Next, Brett managed to bounce off a few rocks, but with no major damage. Then Nolan got the raft stuck on a rock, but one of the other boats came along and bounced them off.

When it was his turn, Kyle was determined to make a good impression. On his fellow students, but mostly on his instructor. He wouldn't be too cautious or too cocky. He would show that he'd been paying attention, soaking in Fisher's words of encouragement and instruction.

He gave the commands. "Forward paddle. Stop. Left back."

His crew did exactly as he instructed. The raft was perfectly positioned. Except the current was faster than he anticipated. They were headed straight toward the rock in the middle of the rapid. He used his paddle to make a correction, but he dug in a little too deep and he managed to spin them 360 degrees around. They hit the rock dead on, and the front of the boat lifted in the air, almost vertical, and everyone went flying into the river.

Well, not everyone. Kyle felt himself being jerked backward and tossed to the floor of the boat like a fish. He scrambled to a sitting position and found Fisher was maneuvering the raft through the rapid.

"I'm sorry. I guess I screwed up." Kyle couldn't remember the last time he'd admitted to a mistake. He'd made plenty, but never admitted them. But for some reason, he knew Fisher already knew he was in over his head, and she'd call bullshit if he tried to deny it.

"Help pull the crew back in," she commanded as they came alongside the swimmers. "We'll talk about it when everyone can benefit."

Leia was the closest and Kyle was able to get her aboard; then she helped pull Brett into the raft while Fisher grabbed Nolan.

"Well, that was interesting." Nolan shook his head and ran his fingers through his wet hair.

"Kyle has just demonstrated the dump truck move." Somehow, Fisher kept her cool. Made it almost seem normal. "And the important thing is that he was able to account for all the passengers."

What a loser. Instead of impressing her, he nearly drowned his fellow students.

Chapter 5

Somehow they had made it to the end of the river without losing any more passengers and Fisher had managed to keep from losing her mind.

Kyle wasn't making it easier. Not with his muscles flexing with each stroke of his paddle. Or his overeager enthusiasm to do the extra work. But by the end of the trip, she realized he wasn't the only one. Leia tried to overcompensate for her size, digging her paddle in with more force than was necessary or even useful. And Brett and Nolan seemed to be in competition over who could play it cooler.

What she had to realize was that they were all at least somewhat out of their element. And she could include herself in that group. She wasn't used to spending the night with a stranger, only to have that stranger show up in her class the next day.

Now she'd just have to get through take-out, making dinner, and getting her students settled in camp.

They pulled up to the riverbank, and Fisher instructed everyone to stack their paddles in a neat pile, take any loose items out of the raft, and help her carry the raft up the boat ramp to the staging area.

"Leia, could you grab the paddles and carry them up?" Fisher hoped she wouldn't think it was a sexism thing, but being a foot shorter than the rest of them would make it awkward for her to help carry the boat. "The rest of us are going to take the raft. Lift together."

The three guys lifted the heavy boat at the same time she grabbed the back end. "Now balance on top of our heads and we'll walk up in unison. Anyone here ever do a potato sack race?"

"No." Brett shook his head and then reached up to grab the raft as it started to slip.

"The important thing is that we move together. As one." Shit. Her cheeks flamed as she thought of how well she and Kyle had moved as one last night. He didn't say anything, but she noticed him stand a little taller, a little straighter.

Had the others noticed? Or had they noticed that so many terms she used every day had sexual undertones? Every time she gave the command to stroke, dig in, go deeper, harder, or with more power.

Or was she just hyperalert to the double meaning of these words due to her long-suppressed sexuality?

They reached the paved area of the commercial take-out. "Leia, prop a couple of those paddles underneath the raft here, so it can dry. The rest of you go back and gather any gear, personal items, or garbage left behind."

Nolan and Brett hustled down to the river, but not surprisingly, Kyle lingered.

"Is there something you need?" Damn, more innuendo.

"I was just going to ask you the same thing." He leaned in, occupying her space. Fortunately, Leia had followed the others down to the river, determined to work harder than any of the guys. Fisher understood. She'd been there. Lived most of her life trying to prove herself as capable, if not more so, than any man. She'd made her mark here, at Swift River Adventures. She no longer had to work twice as long and three times as hard to get the same recognition as a guy.

To be fair, she'd never had to prove herself to Carson or Cody. It had been more for her own needs and occasionally for some of the passengers who hadn't taken her seriously. But usually by the end of the trip, if a guy couldn't be won over after ten miles in a raft with her, that was his problem. Not hers.

"You know what would be helpful?" Fisher tried to focus on the problem at hand. "If you could act like you don't know me. I mean, you don't, not really. But you know what I mean?"

"You think that because I'm from Southern California I must be an actor? That I can just pretend like we've never met? Or that you didn't rock my world?"

"No. It's just that…" She looked up to see the Swift River van pulling into the parking lot. Maybe it was a sign that her heart didn't jump into her throat at the idea of seeing Cody after a long trip. "I don't think it's a good idea to make our prior connection known to everyone else."

"Does he know?" Kyle moved in closer as the van pulled to a stop.

"Who?" She feigned innocence.

"Your boss," he whispered into her ear, his breath doing funny things to her equilibrium.

"You mean Carson?" She realized, once he got out of the van, that it wasn't Cody driving after all. But for the first time in a long time, she didn't care. "I'm sure he couldn't care less, unless it interfered with the business. I am working here, you know."

Fisher stepped away from Kyle. It wasn't because she was worried what Carson would think, but she needed space. Kyle was too close. And she was woman enough to admit it scared her a little.

Maybe that was part of the reason she'd held on to her crush on Cody for so long. It was safe. She didn't have to get involved with anyone else if she continued to hold out for someone she had always known deep down wasn't interested in her.

She'd worked with Cody for four years. And she'd been able to put her feelings aside for at least half of that time. Surely, she could go a whole week without letting her feelings for Kyle—which were purely physical— get in the way.

Rafters from the other two boats were unloading and packing up. Tyler and Brooke led their students in much the same way she instructed hers. Everyone had the look of a river rat, waterlogged, sun kissed, and gloriously spent.

Even if they stayed up too late talking about their experiences of the day, they'd sleep well. And then they'd get up and do it again tomorrow.

"How'd your pretty boy do?" Tyler came up to Fisher and nodded to where Kyle was loading the rest of the gear into the back of the van.

"Fine." She tried to play it cool. "All my students did fine."

"I saw him dump truck on his first rapid."

"It's something we've all done, and not just on our first day."

"True, but I think he's trying to impress you." Tyler was talking about Kyle, but his eyes were on Brooke. "I think he's hot for you."

"He was last night." She might as well admit it. Then maybe she could just do her damn job.

"So he's the guy, huh?" Tyler nodded. "Was it a little weird when he showed up here?"

"A little. But I'm a professional." That didn't come out right. "I'm a professional guide, that is. I'm not going to let my personal life interfere with my work. Like you won't let your personal life interfere with your work. None of us would, right?"

"Right." Tyler stopped watching Brooke and faced Fisher. "What happens on the river stays on the river, and what happens back on dry land…"

He shrugged and walked toward his crew, making sure everything was loaded before he herded them into the van. Brooke did the same with her crew and Fisher did one last check to see that nothing was left behind.

Kyle was the only one still waiting to get in the van. "After you." He motioned for her to enter before him.

"You go ahead; I'll sit up front." She gave him a quick smile and then went to the front passenger door and slid in beside Carson. Yet she could feel Kyle's eyes on her. If she turned around, she'd surely catch him watching her.

Once the van was on the two-lane highway, the students started chatting in the back. She just sank back against the seat. Even though it had been a short trip, she was wiped. But they still had to set up the camp kitchen, make dinner, and assign kitchen duty for the rest of the week.

Once they got back to the resort, Fisher jumped out and directed the students to begin unloading and putting the gear away. Then they all headed back to the campsite.

"What do you think about keeping our crews together one more day?" Fisher asked Brooke and Tyler as they walked from the boat barn.

"Sounds good to me," Brooke said.

"No problemo," Tyler added.

"And I was thinking the first kitchen shifts would be the same crews, at least until we decide to mix things up on Monday."

"So who gets the first shift?" Brooke asked.

"Doesn't matter, everyone will get a chance to run a breakfast, lunch, and dinner shift." Fisher wouldn't mind if either of them volunteered their crew, but she was fine with letting hers start. She was curious to see if Kyle's eagerness extended to cooking and cleaning, or if he was only the first to volunteer if it was a physical task.

"I could have my guys start," she said.

"Sounds good." Tyler shrugged. "Mine can take breakfast tomorrow and that would leave lunch for Brooke's team."

"Alrighty then, we'll get started on dinner." Fisher quickened her steps and caught up with the students who were starting to mill about, uncertain of what to do next.

"I'm going to need Leia, Brett, Nolan, and Kyle to come over here and make dinner. The rest of you can take a shower, hang out in your tents, or just sit back and relax a bit. We should be ready to eat in about forty-five minutes."

Her crew gathered around the picnic table. "So, we've prepacked everything for you. By the end of the week, you'll know how to pack a camp kitchen, plan for meals, and be able to set up, cook, and clean up. We'll practice as if we're in a wilderness camp, no running to the store if you forget something or drop the meat in the dirt."

That got some nervous chuckles.

"First thing is setting up the kitchen. Step one would have been unloading everything from the rafts." Fisher pointed at the table, coolers, and the dry box that contained the camp stove, pots, pans, dish tubs, dishes, and dry goods. "You'll want to set up the cooktop on a sturdy surface, as level as possible. It's pretty easy to set up here and at our camp downriver. But on some of the more remote rivers, finding a good spot can be more challenging. So you'll want to make sure you set up the kitchen before anyone starts staking out their tent locations."

She felt like she was talking too much, but there was a lot more to guiding than just getting the passengers down the river. At Swift River Adventures, it was about the whole experience, not just the rafting.

"Now, some people are fine with beans and weenies for camp fare, but we like to take it up a notch." She took a breath. "Tonight, we'll be making fajitas. Steak and chicken. But first, we need to get the stove set up and the clean-up station. Who has cooked on a propane camp stove before?"

* * * *

"I've used camp stoves plenty of times." Kyle stepped forward. He wasn't just sucking up; he really did have experience. Too much experience. He'd lived in a camper for almost a year. It wasn't right after his dad left. His mom had held on for nearly two years. Until Kyle came down with mono. His mother missed too much work and lost her job. Then without a job and no savings, they couldn't keep up with rent. A friend of a friend had a small camper that they'd used until they got back on their feet. It took eleven months.

"Good." Fisher stepped aside and watched him hook up the propane canister. She didn't know that for those eleven months it had been their only way of cooking since the stove in the camper hadn't worked. The refrigerator hadn't been all that great, either.

"So let's divvy up the tasks, shall we?" Fisher didn't exactly avoid him, but she seemed to be trying not to pay too much attention to him. "Let's set up the rest of the kitchen. There is always a menu for each trip, specifying ingredients to be used for each meal. Brett, can you grab the notebook right on top?"

Brett reached into the large metal container and picked up a spiral-bound laminated notebook.

"Good, now open it up. You'll notice the first two pages are the shopping list for the whole week. Flip to dinner number one." Fisher was a good leader. Hands on, but she didn't try to do everything for them. "Read the ingredients for tonight's meal and the rest of you can start unloading the stuff from the cooler."

Brett read off the list: *chicken, beef, bell peppers, onions, limes, cilantro, garlic.*

Leia reached into the cooler and pulled out the ingredients, Nolan stood back. Either he didn't want to get in the way or he was content letting the woman handle the cooking.

"What about tortillas?" Kyle asked.

"They're in the dry box, along with cans of salsa and the spices." Fisher stepped aside so Kyle could find what they needed to get the meal started. He pulled out a cutting board, chef's knife, and a large skillet.

It wasn't long before they had found a system. Leia made the marinade, while Kyle sliced onions and peppers and the meat. Nolan worked at grating the cheese while Brett opened a couple of small cans of salsa.

Soon the meat was sizzling in a cast-iron skillet, the aroma making Kyle's mouth water. It would be even better if he had one of those Strong Blondes to wash it down with. Not to mention an even stronger blonde to curl up with after dinner. He tried not to track her every movement, knowing it made her uncomfortable. But damn, he couldn't help it.

Just like he couldn't help the twinge of jealousy he felt when he saw her talking to one of the other guys. He had to remind himself that she was just doing her job, making sure everyone was settling in. And it was his job to make sure the fajitas would be ready so they could all enjoy a well-earned meal.

With Leia's help, they plated the fajitas and set out tortillas, along with grated cheese, sour cream, and salsa. The two other crews lined up to serve themselves, followed by their guides. A guy named Tyler and a woman named Brooke. Fisher stood back, letting her crew grab dinner before she grabbed a plate for herself.

Kyle found a spot at the picnic table, leaving room for Fisher, but he wasn't too surprised when she chose to eat her meal standing up, keeping an eye on the group she was in charge of.

He had finished his first fajita and was working on the second when Cody showed up.

"How's it going?" Cody asked Fisher. "Looks like everyone made it down the river in one piece."

"Well we had to patch a couple of them back together, but they're all as good as new now." Fisher didn't look at him as she said it, but her posture had stiffened. Yeah, he still had an effect on her. But Cody wasn't the one in her bed.

"Just make sure the glue is dry before they get back on the water tomorrow."

He gave her a pat on the shoulder and Kyle saw her flinch even more.

He pushed his plate aside and walked over to them. "It's going great. Fisher is an excellent instructor. She's informative, entertaining, and inspirational."

"Inspirational?" Cody's eyebrows shot up. "And exactly how did she inspire you?"

Fisher's face turned a dark shade of pink.

"Not just me." Did the fool not know what he was missing? He'd find out soon enough, when he lost her along with the rest of his company. "She helped Leia find her strength and power. And she showed incredible patience with the guys who didn't know what they were doing but would never admit it."

"She is good. The best." Cody's words were a compliment, but he obviously didn't notice that they cut Fisher even more than any insult ever could.

"You're lucky to have her as a guide." Kyle wanted to put his arm around her, to stake his claim, but he didn't know her well enough to know if she'd find the gesture sexy or suffocating. He'd be here a week or maybe more. Plenty of time to learn how to read her reactions and make her feel more comfortable.

Hopefully she'd help him feel more comfortable on the river after he got the hang of reading a current, learning how to make adjustments without overcorrecting, and figure out how to instill confidence in his passengers even when he didn't know what the hell he was doing.

"You're even luckier to have her as your guide." Cody stepped in front of Fisher. Almost as if he was trying to protect her from Kyle. "She has a lot of experience, expertise, and enthusiasm."

"Yes, she does. And I plan on doing whatever it takes to learn the most from her." Kyle edged closer to both Cody and Fisher.

"You know, we don't give grades here." Cody crossed his arms over his chest. "No gold stars for top student."

"I'm not looking for a special award." Kyle put his hands on his hips. "I just want to be the best I can be at everything I do. And I know when to give credit where credit is due. And I have a feeling I'll be giving Fisher a lot of credit before this week is over."

Cody just glared at him. If he had to guess, Kyle would say Cody was wondering what else he'd be giving to Fisher before the week was over. To his credit, he didn't say anything. Maybe out of respect for Fisher, who was standing right behind him.

"Sorry to interrupt such a fascinating conversation." Fisher gave Kyle a serious glare. "If you're done with your dinner, I was just about to show Brett and Nolan how to get the dishes started."

"I can help with that." Kyle dropped his hands and turned toward her.

"You and Leia did most of the cooking. The other two can handle cleanup."

"I don't mind doing extra work."

"Not necessary." Fisher gave her head a small shake. "You already know we don't give gold stars around here."

It pissed him off that she remembered Cody's exact words. He wanted her to forget all about the guy. Well, he would find a way to do just that.

"I'll get my plate." He walked back to the table, finished off his now-cold dinner, and took his plate over to where Fisher was showing the other two guys from their group how to wash dishes along the side of the river.

Kyle didn't say much, but he watched as she made kitchen duty seem like a special treat. It wasn't long before she had Brett and Nolan laughing and joking around. They dumped the solid waste into a bucket lined with a trash bag. Then they washed, rinsed, and sanitized in buckets of river water that had been boiled or treated with bleach.

As soon as the dishes were dried and put away and the kitchen packed up into watertight containers, Fisher gathered the group for a quick pep talk, wrap-up of the day's events, and reading assignment for the night's homework.

Kyle took the booklet she handed out and went reluctantly back to his RV to shower and figure out his next move.

Chapter 6

Fisher didn't know who was more infuriating, Cody or Kyle. Did neither of them realize how insulting it was for them to get into a pissing contest trading compliments about her as if she wasn't standing right there?

The only thing that could have made it worse would have been if Cody had used the word "love" in his praise. It was bad enough with him saying how great she was, what an asset to the team, blah, blah, blah. She just wanted to choke him and tender up her resignation after all.

Yet, there was a reason she couldn't quit. Several, actually. Just being on the river was always calming. It was her happy place. There was something about the movement of the water. It was never the same trip from the first dip of her guide's paddle to the last stroke easing the boat to shore. The current was forever changing, but with her years of experience, she could anticipate what was coming in a given situation.

Life wasn't always so easy to navigate.

And men? She'd rather face Troublemaker, Satan's Cesspool, and Meatgrinder blindfolded in an inner tube than try to figure out what Kyle was up to with his confrontation with Cody. The biggest, most challenging rapids on the South Fork were easy compared to having the man she'd had a brief sexual encounter with defend her to the man she'd loved for years.

Although he wasn't really defending her. They both thought she was great. Which made the whole conversation that much weirder.

She couldn't say anything to Cody, though. If he didn't know how hard it was for her to hear him sing her praises, then maybe, just maybe, she could get past this. This stupid crush that tore at her heart.

Before heading back to the guides' house, she glanced around the campsite. Leia and Dana kicked back with a couple of beers, while they flipped through the guidebook that had been provided for their reference and to supplement what they would learn by doing.

Fisher was proud of how far Leia had come in such a short time. She had been a little timid at first. She wasn't a tiny girl, but she was definitely petite. There was a time when Fisher had envied girls built like her. When she'd been a girl. It was horrible being taller than all the boys through middle school and most of them in high school.

It wasn't until she started her career as a whitewater raft guide that she appreciated her size and strength.

But with experience, she'd learned that size wasn't always necessary for strength. She'd encountered plenty of strong women who weren't very big. And plenty of big men who weren't necessarily strong. And it made her especially pleased when she could help someone like Leia realize she was stronger than she looked.

It didn't matter if it was a potential guide or a passenger. A young girl or a teenage boy or even some guy she'd let see her naked. She always got a thrill out of seeing someone come alive on the river. Watching the often subtle transformation from a somewhat apprehensive newbie to a whitewater warrior in the span of a few hours.

Yes, Fisher loved her job. Once she'd buckled her life jacket, grabbed her paddle, and took command at the back of the raft, she felt in command of her life. She'd been able to leave her troubles upriver and just go with the flow as she guided passengers, students, and potential guides downstream.

Until today.

Having Kyle on her boat upset her balance. She liked him. Maybe too much. But she'd made the mistake of confessing her feelings for Cody. Maybe she thought it would turn him off and he'd wander off, looking for another score. But instead of backing off, he'd seemed more determined to seduce her. It was almost as if he thought he could erase three and a half years of longing with one orgasm.

She laughed and shook her head. Had she somehow met a man even cockier than Cody? Just what she needed. And the two of them combined? It could make for a very long week.

No. She wasn't going to spend the next seven days trying to deal with both of their egos. But she couldn't say anything to Cody. Even if he wasn't busy with his wife and twins, he was her boss. And he was a damn good one. Except for the torment of being in love with him or whatever.

She could, however, have a chat with Kyle. She could convince him that life would be a lot simpler if they pretended like they were not previously acquainted. That they hadn't spent a wonderful, wild night together. And that he didn't need to stand up for her, or whatever he thought he was doing with Cody.

She marched over to his RV and knocked on the door. She tried not to think about how his hands had trembled when he unlocked it last night. How he'd seemed a little nervous once he'd finally got her out of the bar and almost to his bed. But when they actually made it to the bed, well, he had been more than confident.

Let. It. Go.

"Fisher. Hi. Come in." Kyle stood at the door wearing nothing but a towel. His hair was wet and tousled, as if he'd just dried it off before wrapping the towel around his waist. His chest was damp. Damp and glorious. She swallowed so that drool didn't escape her mouth, which was most likely hanging open.

Her gaze traveled down his torso. He had only the tiniest strip of hair leading down from his navel pointing to a part of him that was definitely not tiny.

"You're naked." She finally got her brain to engage enough to speak.

"Yeah. It makes the showering process much more efficient." He ran a hand through his hair, flexing the biceps on his right arm.

Fisher just gaped at him. Her reasons for coming here were suddenly less clear. And she didn't remember stepping up into the trailer.

"What do you want?" A simple question. But she didn't have a simple answer.

"I want…" She took a deep breath, catching a whiff of his shampoo or soap, something clean and masculine. "I want to be able to do my job without distractions."

"And what is causing your distraction?"

"You."

"Me?" He raised his eyebrows, but he couldn't possibly be surprised.

"Yes. You are a distraction." She felt stronger. If she could just keep from staring at his glistening chest, arms, and… "You make it hard for me to focus on my other students."

"I didn't hear anyone complaining." He took a half step forward, making the space seem even smaller. "In fact, I heard plenty of compliments."

"Yeah. About that." She took a half step toward him; they were almost close enough to touch. "You didn't need to say those things about me to Cody. Especially with me standing right there."

"What things?" He looked confused.

"About me being an inspiration. And how lucky he is to have me." She sighed. "It's embarrassing."

"You are an inspiration. You're a great teacher." He looked her right in the eyes. "And Cody damn well should know how valuable you are."

"They gave me a promotion and a raise." Her voice sounded a little shaky. "Both Carson and Cody take care of their loyal employees."

"Good. But I think you go above and beyond loyal."

Damn. Why did she have to let it slip that she had a thing for Cody? It wouldn't have been so bad if Kyle had been just a stranger. Someone she'd never see again. But here he was. And he wasn't going to let her forget that she'd confessed to him.

"Look, I wish I'd never…" She swallowed, hoping it would ease the ache in the back of her throat.

"Do you wish you'd never slept with me?" Disappointment laced his words.

"No. That's not…" She squeezed her eyes shut. "It's hard enough having to pretend like we haven't slept together."

"Then don't pretend." He reached up and brushed her hair off her face. "Fisher, we have something here. There's no denying the chemistry between us. So why even try?"

"Because." She opened her eyes, saw the longing in his gaze. "You're my student."

"It's not like we're in high school. Or even college." He smiled. "You're not going to give me a grade or keep me from passing the course if I fail to satisfy you next time."

"Next time?"

"I hope there's a next time." His hand still lingered by her face, and then he traced a finger across her jaw. "You are the sexiest woman I've ever met."

"Please." She drew back.

"It's true." He dropped his hand and a part of her wanted to protest. "If you truly want me to leave you alone, I will. I don't know how, but I'll do it. For you. But you have to ask yourself why. What's the point of denying yourself something you enjoy?"

She smiled; she couldn't help it.

"Yeah, I know you enjoyed it. You certainly didn't have to fake anything." He moved closer again, taking both her hands in his. "So why would you fake not wanting more?"

"What if I don't want more? What if…" Damn, he was right. She was tired of faking it. Or pretending that she didn't have needs. Physical ones.

"Fisher. Look at me." He brought each of her hands to his mouth. Placed a whisper-soft kiss on her palms. "If you want more, I can give it to you. I want to give you everything you need."

"Everything?" She tried to play it cool, but she was so damn hot for this man.

"Everything you need, sexually." He wrapped her hands around his waist and pressed against her. He was hard and ready and willing. So why was she still standing there, wondering what she should do?

"And what do you need?" As if the answer wasn't pressing against her belly.

"Just you." He dropped a kiss along her neck, making her shiver. "Fisher, I've never wanted a woman as much as I want you."

"Prove it." She yanked the towel away from his hips and looked down at his nakedness.

"Yes, ma'am." He picked her up and carried her the few feet back to the bed. He kissed her before dropping her on the mattress. "Let's get these clothes off you. This is much more efficient when we're both undressed."

Fisher just leaned back and closed her eyes, relishing the feeling of being desired as he pulled off her shorts and bathing suit bottoms. He lifted her shirt over her head and unclasped the top of her bikini.

"Gorgeous." He took in her naked body, looking at her as if she were indeed the most beautiful woman in the world.

"You're not bad to look at yourself." She grinned as he lunged for her. His hands were on her, stroking her skin, caressing her breasts, tracing a line down her belly, moving lower, closer to where she ached for his touch.

He teased at first, his fingers just barely tracing the edges of her. She must have whimpered or something, because he quickly stroked her soft folds.

"You feel so good," he murmured before he covered her lips with his. His tongue thrust into her mouth. Taking. Giving. Loving.

Except this had nothing to do with love. It was lust. Pure. Simple. Hot.

She bucked against his determined fingers. But it wasn't enough. She wanted to feel *him*. All of him. Deep inside her.

She shuddered, unable to hold back the orgasm.

"Condom?" She flailed her arm toward where she thought the nightstand was. "Hurry."

"You got it. Anything you need." He lunged for the drawer next to the bed, grabbed the square packet, and opened it with his teeth.

"You're taking too long." She grabbed the rubber from him, and rolled it down his shaft. Then she pushed him over onto his back and straddled him.

He groaned as she rode him, his eyes rolled back into his head, and it wasn't long before they found a rhythm that worked for both of them.

All too soon, she felt that build up. The waves coming faster, harder. She was going under, and she couldn't fight it anymore. Her body had taken over, and she just had to ride the crest of the wave. Somehow she remembered to breathe.

"Fisher!" Kyle grunted her name as his own orgasm wracked through him. He grabbed her hips and held her firmly in place while he spilled himself into her.

* * * *

Fisher came out of the bathroom and started to gather her clothes.

"You don't need to pick up right now." Kyle had done a quick cleanup and was content to lie back in bed, waiting for her return. "We can take care of that in the morning."

"Actually, I need to get home. I need a shower." She stepped into her bikini bottoms and slipped her shorts up next.

"You can shower here." He sat up. "It's actually quite comfortable. Not like the old ones where you had to step out of the shower if you dropped the soap."

"I should get back." She hesitated. Was she changing her mind about staying or getting dressed?

"I'd like it if you stayed." He moved off the bed, and reached for her. "Please."

"I don't know." He could tell she was torn. At least a part of her did want to stay.

"Take a shower. Then come back to bed." Kyle stroked her arms, pulling her close. "Or better yet, I'll shower with you. Then we can fall asleep."

"Kyle, it's not even dark yet. And I have things to do to get ready for tomorrow. Besides, you have homework. I can't spend the night with you." She continued to dress.

"Sure. I get it. You're busy." He reluctantly slipped on a pair of shorts. "But just know that I'm not going to pretend this thing between us isn't happening."

"What thing? What's happening between us?" A small, uncertain smile teased her lips.

"You find me irresistible." He moved closer, wanting to change her mind. "And I find you fascinating. Sexy as hell…"

He couldn't help it, he had to touch her. Again. He pulled her on top of him. His hands slid down her back, eliciting a small sigh of pleasure.

"You are insatiable." She kissed him, pressing her body against his, stirring his need once again.

"I can't help it." He grabbed her hips, not willing to let her go just yet.

"You're going to get us into trouble, don't you think?"

"With you, it's hard to think."

"That's what I'm afraid of." She scooted off him.

"Is it? Or are you afraid he's going to find out about us?"

"He knows. He was there when I got home this morning. And he saw the way you look at me."

The asshole was married. Cody shouldn't care how he looked at Fisher. Except to realize what he was missing out on.

"Does it bother you? That he knows?"

"I don't know." She shrugged. "I mean, it shouldn't, but this is all new to me. I've never had a completely sexual affair."

"So do you want to stop?" He sure as hell didn't. "Do you want to just walk away from the best sex we've ever had just because it's scary?"

"Well, no..." But she was still afraid.

"Let me ask you this. If one of your students came to you tomorrow and said they weren't sure if they could do this, that the river moves too fast, or they're not used to being in charge or having to rely on their team or they didn't realize the risk. Would you advise them to just walk away?"

"No. Of course not." She shook her head as if she'd just been hit with a splash of cold water. "Not unless it was someone who truly couldn't handle it. If they were putting themselves and everyone else in danger."

"I think you can handle this." Kyle took her hands again. "I think we both can."

Then he pulled her into his arms and kissed her. Kissed her good.

"Are you just trying to get out of doing your homework?" She gave him a playful swat on the ass.

"No, ma'am. Wouldn't think of it."

"Good. Because there is a lot of good information in the handbook." She stepped back, placing her hands in the back pockets of her shorts. "It doesn't replace experience, of course, but reading and then practicing is the best way to learn."

"You're the teacher." He would let her go. For tonight. "And a damn fine one."

"Don't think you're going to get any special treatment because you're sleeping with me."

"I'm not sleeping with you. You're going home, right?" He liked teasing her. Pushing her buttons. Getting her worked up. All of it. "Unless you've changed your mind."

"No. I'm going home. I have homework, too." She shook her head. Maybe she was tempted to stay. Hopefully, she'd be back.

"Good night, strong blonde." He gave her a quick peck on the cheek. He didn't trust himself with anything more.

"Good night." She left and he sank back on the bed. Damn. He was in trouble. He was supposed to be working here. Not flirting. Fucking. Making love. It didn't matter what they called it. It was good. Too good. And he wasn't going to give it up.

He would have to give her up eventually. When the job was done, and he went back to LA. But there was no reason why he couldn't play as hard as he worked. He owed himself that much.

And he owed it to Fisher to keep it going. He wasn't going to hurt her. He'd show her a good time. Help her forget about her boss. Build up her confidence so that when she lost her job, she'd be ready to move on.

Or maybe she'd convince the new owners to keep her on. She was a damn fine guide.

At least he thought she was. He really didn't have enough experience to know for sure. But he liked her. Liked her confidence on the river. She didn't get rattled, even when he screwed up. The only time she seemed nervous was when one or both of them were naked.

Maybe she just needed more experience.

And maybe he needed to hit the books. Not only did he want to be a model student to impress Fisher, he needed to learn as much about the rafting business in general and his brothers' company in particular.

Chapter 7

Today's lessons would be focused on reading the river. Yesterday was about getting a feel for the experience, for her students to try their hand at paddle captaining, and getting from put-in to take-out. They had all gotten their feet wet, so to speak. Now they needed to start learning how to anticipate how the rafts would respond under different conditions.

It would take weeks, if not months, to learn all the nuances of how a river runs through the canyon, but they'd get a basic understanding of the anatomy and behavior of rapids. She would need them to know how to navigate the current, spot obstacles, and use momentum and angles to get the raft to go where they wanted it to go.

They would do the upper stretch of the river this morning, so they would take the van to put-in shortly after breakfast. Tyler's crew would handle kitchen duty this morning. They'd all make lunch on the way, and Brooke's crew would be in charge of tonight's dinner.

Fisher didn't need to be here for dinner. In fact, what she needed was a girls' night. She swung by the office to see if Lily was up for it.

Boy, had things changed in the last year since Lily arrived. Cody's desk had been moved out of the office, and a portable crib had been put in its place. Baby Brandon was playing happily with a few soft toys and balls while Lily worked on the payroll, bookkeeping, and managing of the business office.

"Hey, Fisher, how's your whitewater school going?" Lily looked up from her computer and offered her friend a warm smile.

"Good. It's going really well; I think everyone will be ready to get back on the river today." So how did she explain why she needed a break after only two days? "It seems like it's working out having Brandon here in the office with you."

"Yeah, he does fine until lunchtime, then he gets a little tired of being cooped up. We usually head home for the afternoons and I either finish my work from home, leave him with Carson, or sometimes I'll drop him off with Miranda so he can play with his cousins after naps."

"Sounds like you've got it all figured out."

"For now." Lily laughed. "But I'm sure as he gets older and more mobile, he won't be as happy to stay in the playpen all morning. I have a feeling he's going to be quite the handful."

"But are you loving it? Being a mom?" Fisher leaned against the door, just watching little Brandon chew on one of his toys.

"Yeah. I am." Lily's eyes shone with contentment. "But it's a lot more work than I ever imagined. Even with a job I can bring him to, and a dad who is as involved as Carson is. It's exhausting. Just when I feel like we're settling into a routine, he'll cut a tooth. Or get a growth spurt and want to nurse nonstop."

"Sounds like you could use a break." Fisher was happy for her friend, but she had no idea how she managed. Babies scared her a little. No. A lot. "Maybe a night out? With the girls?"

"Yeah. That would be nice." She looked over at Brandon and sighed. "Okay, so what's going on? I think maybe you're the one who could use a girls' night. Is there something you want to talk about?"

"Yeah. Sorry. I'm not good at this stuff." Fisher had always been one of the guys. She didn't have a lot of girlfriends growing up. Even in college, she hung out with more men than women. Lily was one of the first women she'd felt especially close to, but now Lily was married, and had a baby.

"I think Carson would be more than happy to have Brandon to himself. But, give me a clue here, so I know how long to plan on being out. Is something wrong?"

"Oh, no. It's just that I met someone. The other night after you guys left the Argo."

"Really?" Lily's eyebrows shot up in surprise. "That's great. So tell me more. No, wait. I guess that's what tonight is for, right?"

"Yeah. I guess so. The thing is…" Fisher felt her cheeks warm. "He's one of my students. And he's fun and, okay, hot. I just don't know what I should expect. You know, he's going to be here all week, and he's still interested. Very interested. So…"

She pushed off from the wall.

"Well, that's exciting. Sounds like we could use some backup, though." Lily sounded excited about going out. "You should invite Brooke and Aubrey."

"Sure. That would be fun."

"And, well...how would you feel about me asking Miranda to join us?" Lily had become close to her sister-in-law. They were both new mothers, new wives, and had a lot in common. But Lily knew about Fisher's feelings for Cody.

"That would be fine. I like Miranda." It wasn't a lie. She did like Cody's wife. And excluding her would be even more awkward than having her come along.

"Okay, good. Because if I've got my hands full..."

"She is married to Cody." Fisher meant to be funny. Not mean, but it probably sounded like she was at least a little bitter. "But they are perfect for each other, and those two babies are so sweet."

Time to put down the shovel. She was just digging herself into a deeper and deeper hole.

"So do you want to just all meet up, say seven?" Fisher needed to get back to work. "I'll make a reservation for five of us?"

"Sure. We'll meet you there."

"Great." Fisher now realized that she was both looking forward to and dreading girls' night. Kind of how she was looking forward to and dreading seeing Kyle this morning.

She wasn't sure what his reaction would be. Or hers. Could she continue to pretend that there wasn't this incredible chemistry between them? Could she stay focused on her job when she kept getting distracted by his incredibly wide shoulders and impossibly firm butt? And what if the others thought he was getting special treatment? If Nolan or Brett took dish duty as an insult when Kyle had been charged with slicing and dicing?

This was why she didn't have a sex life. It just complicated things.

No. That wasn't why. It was because she'd turned Cody down that night, years ago, and she'd often wondered what would have happened if she'd gone home with him.

She had learned over the years that the most likely scenario would have been that he would have slipped out early the next morning to head into work while Carson would have made pancakes. Many nights, Carson would have had an overnight guest as well, and she would have shared the breakfast table, passing the butter and maple syrup.

And if Cody had passed her off on his brother for breakfast, how awkward would her first day of work have been? Until Miranda, Cody had been the kind of guy who preferred to keep work and recreation separate. Sure, he'd met a lot of women on the river, but he never got too close until he was sure they would be heading home the next day.

Fisher wondered if Kyle was any different. He'd clearly been looking for a one-night stand. Nothing complicated. But since they were stuck together for the next week, did he just think of their hookup as a one-week stand?

Certainly, neither of them were looking to continue a long-distance relationship. He would go back to LA, or wherever he was from. And she would keep on keeping on. Working hard, doing the best she could to keep her river family thriving. Because this was her family. She had relatives. Her parents were decent people who'd worked hard, sacrificing to put her through college, and helped as much as they could to get her through grad school. They didn't quite understand why she hadn't done more with her degrees. Why she still lived in communal housing, drove an old Jeep, and lived like "some hippie" down by the river.

Maybe they had hoped she'd finish college, get a high-paying job, and never have to worry about making ends meet.

Well, she had two out of the three dreams her parents had for her. She didn't worry about expenses. She didn't have many. And while she might not have a 401(k), she didn't have any debt, either. No mortgage or credit card bills. She didn't even have a car payment.

She did have a roof over her head, money in the bank, and the satisfaction that most days she'd shown her passengers a good time. She'd helped them meet physical challenges, overcome fears, and enjoy themselves on the river. There was nothing wrong with having a good time.

She had learned that long ago in her professional life. Maybe she could accept the idea in her personal life, as well. Surely she could live by the concept of work hard, play hard, don't take life too seriously. You know, like a man.

As soon as she saw Kyle, her heart rate sped up. Her skin flushed and she couldn't help but think about all the ways they fit together. One advantage of being a woman was that her arousal wasn't entirely obvious to anyone who happened to glance her way.

She watched him interact with his fellow guide candidates. Talking, smiling, laughing with the men and women who were basically his peers. Yet there was something that set him apart. Something she couldn't quite determine.

They came from all over the country. Oregon, Texas, Kansas. Some were there just for the experience; others truly wanted to make rafting their career or at least their summer job while putting themselves through school. She wasn't sure what Kyle's goal was. They'd never really talked about it. They never really talked much.

He'd mentioned a change of pace, but she couldn't remember what he did that he needed a change from. Maybe she'd get around to asking him about his job, about his life, his interests, and his family. When they were on the river, there wasn't a lot of time for personal questions. Most of the conversation was about what they were doing, what they needed to do, and what could go wrong.

Maybe she'd stop by and see him after her night out. But who was she kidding? If she stopped by his RV, they wouldn't be talking.

"Hey." Somehow he'd managed to sneak up on her. "Did you sleep well?"

"Fine. I got my notes organized and made sure I have the crews set up for the commercial trips the rest of the week." Fisher could talk to him. Get to know him with his clothes on. Not that he was wearing much this morning. T-shirt, shorts, and sandals. He was holding two cups of coffee.

"I didn't know how you like your coffee so I have one black, one with cream and sugar." Kyle held up both cups.

"Strong and black." She'd already had one cup but could use another.

"Then I guess I'll keep the other. Strong and blond and sweet." He smiled as he handed her a coffee. And grimaced as he took a sip of the sweetened brew.

"A little too sweet?" Fisher figured he took his coffee plain. But she appreciated the fact that he was willing to sacrifice his taste buds for her.

"Yeah. I don't usually put sugar in my coffee."

"I guess there's quite a bit we don't know about each other." She took another appreciative sip.

"Other than your dislike for the designated hitter, and now your coffee preference, I don't know anything about you." He stepped closer and whispered in her ear, "Except that you taste like heaven."

A not-so-small shiver ran down her spine. "I have plans to meet friends for dinner tonight. But if you're a good boy, I could maybe stop by your camper after. So we could, you know, talk."

"I'm a very good boy." He kept his mouth right next to her ear, his breath teasing her skin. "But if you come by later, we won't waste it on conversation. We'll just have to get to know each other better before then."

"Yeah." Fisher found her breath coming at a ragged pace, as if she were just coming off a particularly thrilling rapid. "We should."

* * * *

Kyle almost gagged on the sweetened coffee, but it was worth it to please Fisher. And tease her. He loved how she was so easily riled when it came to the sexual tension between them. They'd had sex twice, but she blushed like a virgin when he mentioned how good she tasted.

"So, tell me what you do for a living." She was making small talk. So they could get to know each other better.

"I'm in sales." He had one of those jobs that wasn't easy to explain. Unlike a teacher or cop or raft guide. "But I'm tired of the rat race."

"So are you looking to become a river rat?" Was that hope he heard in her voice?

"I don't know. Maybe." He thought he wouldn't mind spending the summer up here, living the simple life. "Actually, I wasn't looking for a career change. Just a break, really."

"And you thought guide school would give you a nice break?"

He tried to think about his cover story. The one he'd concocted on the way up. Before he was distracted by his strong blonde. "I had a buddy who posted some pictures on Facebook of a trip he'd taken with his family. But being a single guy, with no one to go with me, I thought it would seem less unusual for me to take the school instead of booking a trip for one. Plus, I wanted to get a feel for what it's like to really live it for a week."

"So you have no interest in staying on as a paid guide?"

"I wouldn't say that." He wasn't going to read too much into her questions. They were just getting to know each other, after all. "A few days ago, I might have, but now... I can see the appeal."

"And what would that be?"

"Besides you?" He loved making her blush. And he could make her flush all over if they were alone. "It's hard to put it into words. But I was reading through the guidebook last night, and there was a lot in there that made sense. About being at peace on the river, and how it can shape you, and change you."

"Yeah." She sighed.

"Did you write that stuff?"

She shook her head, momentarily looking a little sad. "Miranda wrote it. And the website copy. She had input from Cody and the rest of us, but she's the one who has a way with words."

Ah, Miranda. Cody's wife. He hadn't met her yet. But he understood that she probably wasn't Fisher's favorite person.

"So did you always want to be a raft guide when you grew up?"

"No. I wanted to be a mermaid." He thought she was teasing, but maybe not.

"And this was as close as you could get?"

"I just sort of stumbled on it. I had a girlfriend who wanted to do guide school because this guy she was into was teaching it. But she didn't want to go by herself. She even paid for half of it."

"And you were immediately hooked?"

"Yeah, I guess you could say that. I ended up moving here to take environmental studies. Then I went to grad school and got a master's in ecology."

"Planning on saving the world?"

"Something like that."

"What happened with your friend? Did her romance work out?'

Fisher laughed and shook her head. "The guy was gay. Great guy, but definitely not interested in my friend. I made it to his wedding a couple years ago."

"And your friend?"

"Still chasing after guys she can never have."

He wasn't going to point out that Fisher had been doing the same. "So do you have enough work to keep you busy through winter?"

"Last year I helped a lot in the store. With Miranda carrying twins, she couldn't be on her feet too long, but she still would come in for a couple of hours until she was in her last few months." He had a feeling the other woman's pregnancy only added to Fisher's pain. "And before that I was still in school."

"So what about this year? I know the season's just getting started, but what happens when the trips dry up?"

"Well, for a lot of the guides, they travel to the Southern Hemisphere. New Zealand or South America." Fisher must have thought he was asking about the off-season for guides in general. "Others work at the ski resorts in Tahoe, or they travel to other states."

"What will you do once the bookings stop flowing?"

"Well, I'm not sure exactly." Fisher looked a little concerned. "I'm sure I'll do whatever they need. If Miranda is ready to come back to the store, I'm sure she'll get first pick of hours. And the guys have talked about expanding the specialty trips. Maybe pairing up with local wineries to do tastings on the river. Or getting various experts, like having someone from the observatory at the college to do an astronomy trip. Things like that. I suppose there will be a lot of coordination that will need to be done months in advance."

"So this is a real career for you, then?" He was curious about what it could lead to for her, not just how the knowledge could help his employer.

"Are you wondering if it could be a career for anyone? Or are you just trying to get to know me?"

"Both." He wasn't exactly lying. "I mean, this is about as opposite of a lifestyle as I've had the last few years. With sales, it's all about pressure. Getting the next client. Making more money. I know I've only been here a few days, but I have to admit, there's something to be said for just going with the flow. Literally and figuratively. I mean, you can't jump on the river at the crack of dawn, hoping to beat everyone else down."

"For one thing, the water is too low." Fisher laughed. She had explained the first day about how the river was dam controlled, and the water was released to provide hydroelectric power. Even during the leanest water years, they would always release enough water to keep the rafting industry going on the weekends. During dry years, the flow would be reduced to levels necessary to keep the fish population healthy and provide enough energy to sustain the nearby cities and towns. "Besides, it's not a race. There is no finish line. There's take-out, and yeah, sometimes there's a line of trailers, but it's all good. And when we do the upper, take-out is here at the resort, so you're that much closer to a cold beverage at the end of the day."

"Yeah. Totally different." Kyle could almost picture himself living this lifestyle long term. But the seasonal aspect was too iffy. He didn't ski, so he couldn't see himself working at a resort over the winter. Not that he couldn't fake it, like he'd faked many different jobs, but there was all that snow. And New Zealand or South America was too far away from his mother. He still needed to keep an eye on her. He couldn't count on his dad to always be there for her. He had left her more than once. Kyle didn't like the idea of being halfway around the world when she needed him.

"I thought I'd go into teaching," Fisher added. "Not little kids. Maybe junior college, but I don't know."

"You're a good teacher." He wasn't just flattering her. "Really. I've learned a lot already."

"You've been my student less than twenty-four hours." She shook her head. "And I went easy on you yesterday. You might change your mind after today's lesson."

With that, she finished off her coffee and tossed him a devious grin. She handed her empty cup over to the dish crew and made her way to the picnic tables, where many of the students were just milling around after breakfast. Even without hearing a word she said, Kyle knew she was getting the troops rallied for the day's adventure.

He could do this. For as long as it took to close the deal. Was it wrong to hope it took all summer?

Chapter 8

Despite no major injuries or actual disasters, anything that could have gone wrong on the river did. Everyone took a swim, a few more than once. They lost a couple of paddles, almost lost the lunch. And Fisher felt like she'd lost control of her class.

By the time she got everything put away and the dinner crew was busy prepping for the meal, she was more than ready for a hard-earned beer. But maybe she should stick around, make sure her students didn't stage a mutiny.

Before she could consider calling Lily and canceling their plans for the evening, Cody showed up with the twins in a double stroller. Fisher waited for the familiar tightness in her chest, the pang of longing, but all she felt was a strong desire for a shower.

"Looks like you survived day two." Cody offered up his usual relaxed smile.

"Barely." Fisher rolled her stiff neck from side to side. "It was almost as if they'd all forgotten everything they learned yesterday."

"Sounds about right." His grin widened. "So what happened?"

She filled him in on all the little mishaps that had befallen not only her crew, but the other two as well.

"You've given them the gift of failure." Cody bent down to retrieve a toy that one of his daughters had tossed to the ground. "There is no better teacher."

"It was crazy. For some reason, they all went nuts." She was picturing the carnage. Boats bouncing off rocks, bodies knocking in and out of the rafts. Paddles flung into the river. It had been out of control.

"They were starting to feel comfortable. Willing to take risks." Cody couldn't hide the amusement in his voice. "And they were learning what can happen when they make mistakes. I mean, really, would you want them to have a perfect run after perfect run while they're still learning only to have things go wrong for the first time with a group of paying passengers? Kids maybe?"

"No. You're right. Experience is the best teacher." Fisher knew this. She'd just hoped the mistakes would be more spread out over the course of the week.

"But you were hoping to be more in control." Cody rocked the stroller back and forth, to keep the babies from fussing.

"Well, yeah." She laughed at herself. "I know. I have to put my trust in my team. And the river. I guess I thought it would get easier."

"Nah. But that's the beauty of it all." Cody tipped the stroller backward, eliciting giggles from his daughters. "If it were easy, everyone would do it. Then they wouldn't pay us the big bucks."

Fisher laughed. There wasn't a lot of money in being a whitewater guide. The Swift brothers were probably paying her much more than any other company would. For years they'd gotten by, mostly due to the campground and store. Working on the river was a labor of love, for sure.

But she couldn't imagine doing anything else. The thought of working in some office for some corporation or even the government made her break out in hives. She knew enough people who commuted one or two hours a day to a fifty-hour-a-week job so they could pay off their student loans and their car payments and their mortgages. They put money into gym memberships that they never had time to use.

Oh, she supposed some of them were happy. And they could afford to take vacations. Some of them even took vacations on the river. She found it interesting that the people who got off the river with the biggest smiles were often those who'd had the most stressful jobs during the week.

Not that her life was without stress. No. She could use the girls' night out she'd planned.

"So you gonna stick around for a bit? Make sure my charges don't get into any more trouble?"

"What makes you think I won't stir up the trouble?"

"You have two adorable, innocent babies with you."

"Ah, yeah. Miranda told me she wanted to go out with the ladies tonight." Cody grinned that goofy, love-struck grin he often got when he talked about his wife and kids. "Obviously, she's under a lot of pressure if she's leaving the girls with me."

Fisher just smiled. And for once, it was a genuine smile. She was happy for him. He was obviously very happy. Very much in love. He'd become the kind of man she'd always known he could be.

Maybe someday, Fisher would become the woman she could be. Or maybe she already was. She didn't need a man. Sure, one came in handy from time to time. She just needed to be better about seeking one out now and then. Just because she didn't need a man to change her tire didn't mean she couldn't appreciate having a man light her fire.

She just had to be smart about it.

Fisher would never jump on the river without proper equipment—life jacket, commercial-grade raft, paddles, ropes, first aid kit, and knowledge of the river. And she wasn't going to just float along with Kyle without some safety precautions. She was protected against pregnancy even without the condoms they'd both insisted on using.

Neither of them had anticipated more than one night together, so anything beyond that was just a bonus. Kind of like Surprise Rapid. During high water years, the lake backed up and the last stretch of the river was slow as they paddled their way to take-out. But when the water levels dropped, there was one final, fun, and exhilarating rapid that made for one more memory before they parted ways with their crew.

Some companies didn't run the rapid, choosing to go around it since their crews might not have the experience with the hole. Fisher usually went for it, unless her crew was shaken up from falling out on one of the previous rapids. Most recovered, but once or twice, she'd had passengers just want to get off the river as soon as possible after taking an unexpected swim.

So Fisher decided to paddle on through with Kyle. As long as he was up for it, she'd keep on swimming.

She found Kyle sitting at a picnic table. Someone had brought cans of Sierra Nevada, and they would no doubt be reliving the more interesting moments of the day over beers.

"Looks like you are all set for the evening." Fisher stood next to Kyle as she addressed the group. Several of them nodded and invited her to join them.

"Thanks, but I have plans." She gave Kyle a questioning look. Would he wait up for her?

"Have fun. But not too much fun." He gave her a sly grin. "You have to drag us back on the river in the morning."

"Yeah. Don't stay up too late, you guys." She waved and turned to go, but Kyle grabbed her hand before she could slip away. With a gentle squeeze and a smoldering look, he let her know that his bed would be available to her whatever time she knocked on his RV door.

She definitely needed a night—or at least the evening—away from the man.

Fisher stopped by the guides' house to change. She'd invited Brooke along and asked her to mention their plans to Aubrey, but Fisher didn't expect to tear her away from her boyfriend. To her surprise, not only was Aubrey up for a night out, she'd offered to drive.

"Thanks for inviting me," Aubrey said as the three women climbed into Aubrey's Subaru. "I sometimes feel like I'm missing out by not living on-site."

"Missing out on Tyler snoring?" Brooke suggested. "Or the fact that it requires a certain level of estrogen to be able to change the toilet paper roll?"

"Why is that?" Aubrey wondered. "I mean, when I stay over at Rich's, I can't tell you how many times I've found the new roll just sitting there on top of the empty cardboard."

All three women laughed and shook their heads.

"It is a mystery." Brooke leaned in from the backseat.

"I wonder if they can be trained," Aubrey mused.

"Well, we have taught them how to cook." Fisher sometimes felt that was one of the more important lessons of guide school. "And they can wash the dishes, although it seems like they're better at it when they're out on the river. The dishwasher seems to have some mysterious cloaking device."

"Yes!" Aubrey chimed in. "It's like they can't see it unless it's actually running or you specifically ask them to unload it. Then they're like, 'Whoa, how did the magic box clean these dishes?'"

More feminine laughter erupted as they made the short drive to the Argo.

"So, have you found a teaching job for next year?" Brooke asked Aubrey, who had just finished her credential program.

"I thought so, but…" Aubrey put the car in park and glanced through the rearview mirror. "Is that Lily and Miranda?"

Fisher turned around to see the Swift brides get out of Miranda's Prius. "Yeah, I invited them, too."

Brooke gave Fisher a questioning look. "Well, let's go grab a table. I guess Lily might want a heads-up if half our guide school students drop out tomorrow and ask for a refund."

"They're not going to drop out." Aubrey waited for Fisher and Brooke to grab their purses and close the door before she locked up her car. "From what I've heard, they're all having the time of their lives."

"Especially Kyle, right, Fisher?" Brooke wasn't going to let the night go on without getting the scoop.

"Oh, really?" Aubrey asked. "What am I missing?"

"Fisher has a boy toy." Brooke gave Fisher a playful shove. "So, tell me, how is Hollywood?"

"Hollywood?" Fisher asked.

"Yeah, that's what the others are calling him. It's so obvious he's an LA guy."

"Why do you say that?" Fisher was curious about what people were saying about him. About them.

"Well, he takes 'the forty-nine' to put-in." Brooke snorted. "That's after taking 'the fifty' through Placerville."

She had to admit, it sounded weird when people from Southern California referred to highways with the word "the" in front of the number. In this part of the state you took Fifty to Tahoe and Eighty to Reno. Sometimes you'd say "take Highway Forty-Nine or I-Eighty" but no self-respecting Northern Californian ever used "the."

"And I have to ask—but you don't have to answer—does he wax everything?"

"What makes you think he waxes?"

"No one has a chest that smooth. Do you think he's a model or something?" Brooke continued to grill her. And Fisher was too embarrassed to start firing back with questions about Tyler.

"He has body hair where he needs it." Fisher happened to catch Miranda smile as she overheard the conversation.

"This is going to be a fun night. I can tell already." Miranda grabbed the door and held it open for the others. Damn, she looked good for having had twins just a few short months ago. Life was so not fair.

"Oh, we're just getting started," Brooke added as she swept past Cody's wife.

"Yeah. I'm sure we'll be sharing all kinds of stories by the time we head on home." Aubrey blushed as if she had a few tales of her own.

The ladies filed into the bar and grill. They were offered a table on the deck, and since it was a completely smoke-free restaurant, they eagerly accepted. There were umbrellas to offer shade, and since it was midweek, they wouldn't have to worry about talking over the band that played on Friday and Saturday nights all summer long.

Menus were passed around, and the waitress came back to take drink orders. Fisher decided on a Strong Blonde. Brooke ordered a pale ale and Aubrey said she was driving and would just have water. Lily and Miranda each ordered light beers and water all around.

"Is it okay to have a beer when you're still nursing?" Aubrey asked, her cheeks flushed. "I mean, I'm not judging or anything. Just curious."

"I nursed Brandon right before I left. And Carson has a bottle if he needs milk before I get home." Lily was a new mom, but she was quite the expert. Before she married Carson, she'd been married and battled infertility for years. She'd spent a lot of her spare time learning anything and everything about pregnancy, nursing, and motherhood. "But one beer with a meal is seen as safe by most experts."

"Yeah. And I have to supplement with formula, anyway," Miranda admitted reluctantly. "I can usually produce enough milk for both the girls first thing in the morning, and again around dinnertime."

"Oh, that's good to know." Aubrey's blush deepened. "Okay, I guess I should go ahead and spill. Rich and I are getting married."

"Oh, that's wonderful."

"Congratulations!"

"How exciting!"

"And, surprise! We're pregnant." Aubrey squeezed her eyes shut.

This time the congratulations were accompanied by hugs.

The waitress brought their drinks, and once everyone returned to their seats, Lily held up her glass for a toast. "To Aubrey and Rich, may you have a wonderful marriage, a healthy baby, and a beautiful future."

"To Aubrey and Rich!" They lifted their glasses and the celebration was under way.

Conversation centered around wedding plans, due dates, and living arrangements.

"Well, we haven't set a date. But it's going to be soon." Aubrey's hands shook a little as she lifted her water glass to her lips. "Rich has accepted a job in Cupertino. He's going to work for Apple, so that's exciting."

More congratulations were offered all around.

"But, I'm going to have to quit." Aubrey couldn't hold back the tears this time. "I mean, if I wasn't pregnant, I'd wait until the end of the season, but, you know?"

"You know, if you want to have the wedding at Swift River, we could make it amazing." Lily stood and put her arm around Aubrey. "We're getting pretty good at putting together world-class weddings in a matter of weeks."

"Really?" Aubrey was clearly overwhelmed. "I mean, I'm just a summer guide. I don't have a lot of money saved."

"It's not the money that makes a wedding beautiful." Miranda reached out to Aubrey, placing a gentle hand on hers. "It's the love between the bride and groom. And we'll all pitch in to get everything in place. All you need to worry about is the guest list."

"And telling my parents." Aubrey sank back into her chair, relieved, exhausted, and maybe just a little surprised by the support of the women around her. "You guys are so great. Oh God, I'm going to miss all of you."

She burst into tears again. "I feel like I'm letting you down. I mean, the season is just starting and I'm going to have to quit."

"Don't worry about it." Lily was the payroll and office manager. She would know about the personnel situation. But Fisher should be more informed on upcoming reservations, the number of guides needed to fill the trips, and other details like that.

"Yeah, isn't that part of why we do a guide school?" Brooke stated the obvious. "I'd say we have three or four good candidates. Like Kyle."

She stared straight at Fisher with a knowing grin.

"Maybe." Fisher felt her cheeks flush. "We should probably mix the crews up a bit; that way we can all get impressions of the potential guides."

"Yes, but you'll get to make the decisions," Lily reminded her. "You're in charge."

"Sure, but it's also a team effort. I wouldn't want to hire anyone that wasn't going to fit in with the core crew." Fisher wasn't yet comfortable with the added responsibility. She almost felt like her new title was more of a consolation prize.

"I'm sure you'll pick the right people." Miranda was supportive, as always. "You're good with people, and you'll train them well."

"Thanks." Fisher wondered if Kyle would be interested in applying for a summer position. Or would he have to return to his sales job that he seemed to be tired of? Judging by his RV, he liked the finer things in life. That usually required money. A lot more than a first-year guide would make.

She also wondered if it would be weird to work with him all summer. Though Brooke and Tyler seemed to be making it work.

"So, Brooke, how are things with you and Tyler?" Fisher wondered how they would manage if things got serious. Or if they drifted apart.

"Fine." Brooke reached for her beer and took a long drink.

"That's good," Aubrey added. "I always had a feeling about you two."

"It's nothing serious. Just a couple of friends, keeping each other company." Brooke seemed almost too nonchalant, which was unusual for someone who was usually so straightforward.

Lily and Miranda glanced at each other with a knowing smile on their faces.

"Not everyone is looking for lifelong love." Brooke now sounded a little defensive. "No offense, I'm happy for those of you who have found it, but I've still got a lot of living to do before I even think about settling down."

"Yeah. That's cool. I was just curious, that's all." Fisher wondered if things weren't so great after all. Was Tyler pressuring Brooke? Or was Brooke in denial?

"I mean, you're not serious with Kyle, are you?" Brooke asked.

"No, of course not. We're not even friends. Just...you know?" Fisher didn't even know how to describe what was happening between them.

"Yeah. Exactly. Just..." Brooke sighed and dug into her salad.

* * * *

Cody and Carson showed up with their brood. Three babies, just a few months old. Carson had a boy, and Cody two daughters. The girls were content in a double stroller/car seat combination and Carson wore his son in one of those carriers strapped to his chest.

"Hey guys." Cody greeted the male guides and the students who were enjoying a few beers around the campfire. "We just thought we'd stop by to check in and see how everyone was doing."

"And to let everyone know that we're available should anyone need anything," Carson added.

"Yeah. In case you haven't figured it out yet, we're a family here at Swift River." Cody looked around the group, a welcoming smile on his face. Until he got to Kyle. He narrowed his gaze, almost in a warning. Ironic, considering the one person he didn't seem to accept into his river family was actually family.

Someone offered the twins a beer and they joined the newbies in swapping stories. Tales of flips, wraps, broken paddles, and lost lunches—literally, where the cooler full of food wasn't secured and ended up floating down the river—kept them entertained and helped them realize they weren't alone in making mistakes.

Carson and Cody shared each other's worst moments on a raft. But they also told tales of heroics. Like the time they went fishing at Hidden Creek, only to find a woman struggling in the fast-moving current. Carson had been the one to jump in to rescue her, but Cody had assisted in helping his brother reel in the catch of a lifetime—his wife, Lily.

Another time, Cody took out a would-be robber who had held Miranda at gunpoint in the company store. He'd coldcocked the guy and then used his knowledge of tying down a load to keep the perpetrator subdued until the county sheriff's deputies arrived.

"That's right." Cody stood and puffed out his chest. "It doesn't pay to mess with the women of Swift River."

He glared at Kyle once more, adding, "We protect our own around here."

Kyle got up to grab another beer. For the most part, he was enjoying himself, getting to know the guides and potential guides. He was fitting in, but he discovered he'd earned the nickname "Hollywood." With his fancy RV and the fact that he was from Southern California, the name stuck. He didn't mind. And in a way, he was acting a part. There just wasn't a camera in front of him or a big studio behind him.

In the midst of the frivolity, baby Brandon blew out a diaper. Carson just opened his changing bag right there on the picnic table. He cleaned up the baby and was reaching for a clean diaper when the boy let off a huge stream of pee. For someone so little, he could put out a fire with that thing.

Cody doubled over in laughter. "Boy, huh? I'll take two at a time over that."

And as if his daughters accepted the challenge, one of them woke up and started crying, which of course woke up her sister. Cody had his hands full with his two. Carson quickly got his baby diapered and then handed him off to the nearest available person, which happened to be Kyle.

"Here. Can you hold him while I go hose off and pick up a fresh shirt?"

"Sure. No problem." Kyle took the baby, who grinned at him like he knew he had gotten his dad good.

So, you're my nephew.

Brandon stuck his fist into his mouth and gurgled, but it sounded a lot like laughter. The kid was a kick. He had the Swift blue eyes. Something they had all inherited from dear old Dad. Well, he was grandpa to this little one. And his cousins, too.

He supposed the three of them would be close growing up on the river together. He wondered if the two girls would gang up on poor Brandon. Or if they would follow him along, pestering their cousin.

Part of him wished he could be here to witness it. He tried not to wonder too much what it would have been like if his father had brought Kyle and his mother up here when the twins lost their grandparents. Would they have been one big happy family? Or would whatever problems that had sent ol' Joe back home the minute they had turned eighteen have come between all of them?

Didn't matter. The past was the past. And as much as he'd wanted to believe that his brothers were just a couple of world-class assholes, he had to admit they were decent guys.

It wasn't long before Leia and Dana offered to help with the babies. Dana took one of Cody's girls and Leia was making silly faces at Brandon while Kyle bounced him on his knee.

"Oh, hey thanks, man." Carson returned with a clean shirt and some more beer. "I owe you."

"No problem." Kyle made faces at the baby and got a kick out of the little guy's hearty laugh.

"I'll trade you a cold one for a slippery one." Carson offered to take Brandon.

"I'm good. You go ahead."

"I guess I could have one more." Carson popped the top on a can of beer and leaned back against the picnic table. "I kind of miss nights like this. Just kicking back after a day on the river."

"I bet this guy keeps you pretty busy, huh?"

"Yeah. But I wouldn't trade him for anything." Carson got a goofy kind of grin on his face, but then he got more serious. "I just can't imagine how some guys could walk away from it, though."

Kyle didn't feel the need to point out that some guys made a career of leaving kids behind. Including a guy they both knew a little too well.

"I guess I'm luckier than most." Carson seemed to be in a chatty mood. "I have my business and my family and my river. My wife can take Brandon into the office or work from home. And between Cody and me, we're able to keep the resort in good shape. Miranda helped with the store until her doctor put a stop to it. Now she's busy with the twins and her books. Cody has sort of taken over the store now that Fisher's in charge of the rafting side of things."

"So what kind of behind-the-scenes work does she do?" Kyle knew that people were aware of Fisher spending at least last night in his trailer. He hoped that his interest would be seen merely as interest in her. He was interested, and she definitely made this assignment a hell of a lot of fun. "I imagine there was a lot of work putting the guide school together and making sure the commercial trips are staffed."

"Yeah. Among other things." The baby started to fuss and Carson picked him up. "We're actually hoping to expand our offerings."

"Fisher mentioned something about specialty trips. Wine tasting, things like that."

"Yeah. There are a lot of companies that run the one-day trips on the South Fork. Some of them are all about volume, packing the customers in, luring them with coupons and deals." Carson bounced little Brandon on his knee. "But we want to offer something more. The whole experience. Don't get me wrong, we still need to make a profit. And thanks to my wife, we're able to do both."

"Does she take a huge cut in pay or something?"

"She saved our business. Our former bookkeeper set up a secret account. I guess she was planning on taking the money, but Lily found out and was able to stop her before we even lost a dime."

"So it's a family business all the way around?" Kyle felt just a twinge of that old jealousy. Of being on the outside. Maybe if he'd been around, he could have been part of it.

"Yeah. It started out with just me and Cody, a couple of kids trying to work our way through college. And now... Now I hope we can build something for the next generation. Leave a legacy for the future. I want more than anything for this guy to be proud of his father."

Kyle felt a bit of a lump in his throat. He grabbed his beer to wash it away. He knew what it was like to be ashamed of his old man. He would have given anything to have a father he could count on. Not just to show up to his games and school events, but to show up to his job on a regular basis. To come home in time to help with the rent.

"But more importantly, I want him, and any siblings of his, to grow up here. On the river. With good people around him. Hopefully you'll stick around long enough to see what I mean. It's a good place to grow up. It's a good place to grow old with someone. Not that Lily and I are anywhere close to being old, but I can't see moving anywhere else."

"It is pretty here." Kyle had to admit, the scenery was nice, especially when a certain strong blonde appeared on the river. "And you can see the stars at night."

"Careful, my friend. You might just find yourself falling in love." Carson shifted the baby in his arms, snuggling him closer. "With the river, the lifestyle. It's been known to happen. City boy comes up here to get away from the craziness of life, only to find out it doesn't have to be that way. Yet it's still close enough to Sacramento or San Francisco that you can get away to the city for culture or shopping or a ball game."

"Yeah, but how many people can make a living up here? How do you manage to keep your people loyal if they're only seasonal?"

"I guess that's something we're going to have to work on." Carson rubbed his baby's back, and a soft little snore came from the little guy. "The campground and store are open year-round. We have the cabins. But we don't get much rafting business past mid-September. But maybe we'll expand to special events. We have had a couple of weddings here, and they turned out quite nice, if I do say so myself."

"Yeah, but there's a big difference between grilling fajitas over a camp stove and catering a wedding. Or is that tomorrow's lesson?"

"You didn't read the brochure?" Carson teased. "That's actually Thursday's lesson."

"Seriously, though, how could you make this a year-round resort?" Kyle no longer knew if he was asking for his boss or if he had other reasons. Like Fisher. He liked her. Wanted her to succeed. "What about partnering with the ski resorts? Fisher mentioned that a lot of guides work up there in the winter. Why not offer up the cabins here, and take, oh I don't know, the buses you use for rafting up to the resort, drop folks off in the morning, and pick them up in the afternoon. Then offer a catered dinner upon arrival."

"You know, that's not a bad idea. I wonder how many of our guides would be interested in offering guided ski tours. You know, take the guests on a few runs, just to get them comfortable with the ski resort, offer a personalized go-to person, and then send them off on their own while our people skied at their own pace. I think you're onto something. You ski?"

"Not really." Kyle had always been good at coming up with ideas for others. Must be why his boss let him have free rein on the last few projects. That and the fact that he was still making him money. "I suppose if I had the right guide, I'd be more into it."

"Like Fisher?"

"Yeah." He wasn't going to deny the attraction. What fool would? Maybe the guy coming up to them, now that his twins were settled back into their stroller thingies.

"I see you dried off." Cody ribbed his brother. The brother he knew about. "Dude, don't you know boys are nothing but trouble?"

"Yeah. But I'll take the trouble now compared to what you'll face in about fifteen years. Times two." These two teased each other, but there was no mistaking the affection they had for one another. They were close. Would Kyle have been included in that, if he'd been around? Or would they have seen him as the other brother?

"They're not going to be any trouble at all." Cody found an empty camp chair and lowered himself into it, keeping his sleeping babies nearby. "Not in the convent."

"We're not Catholic," Carson pointed out. "And I'm pretty sure it wouldn't work that way even if we were."

"I'll just hire their cousin to pee on any boys who even try to get close to my girls."

"Oh, I'm sure they'll love that." Carson chuckled. "Besides, you'll need to save every penny you have. Prom, times two. College, times two. Weddings…"

"Oh shut up." Cody threw an empty beer can at his twin. "Just you wait, Lily's going to want more kids. I hope you end up with triplets next time."

Kyle listened to their ribbing, more than a little envious of their bond. He wondered what would happen if he just told them the truth. That they were half brothers. But he kept the knowledge to himself. It wouldn't do him any good in negotiations. He could be friendly, but getting too close would backfire. Better to send them a postcard after the fact. From wherever he chose to celebrate his big commission. Maybe he could even convince Fisher to come along. Someplace tropical and luxurious, perhaps with a private beach. He leaned back, satisfied with the idea.

Chapter 9

"You know what? I like you. I like you a lot." Kyle had just blown Fisher's mind with a series of orgasms that made her collapse against his chest.

He rolled them over onto their sides, grinning like a fool.

"You like me because I just rode you like a class-four rapid at high water." Fisher laughed—exhausted, exhilarated, and a little elated.

"Class four, that's good, right?" He propped himself up on one elbow. "Not like on an airplane, where first class is the best?"

"Right." She had to remember he was still learning. "Most of the big rapids we run are a three, three-plus. A class five is pretty much crazy, a six unrunnable, so I guess you could say a class four is pretty fucking spectacular."

"That was pretty fucking spectacular." He chuckled, the sound warm and deep. "But I like you even when you're not spectacularly fucking me."

"Oh really?" Something warm bloomed in her chest. Warm and scary. "You like me?"

"Yeah. I do. And I know you like me too." He brushed a lock of hair off her forehead. Yeah, she must be a hot mess.

"Maybe." She didn't want to talk about feelings. Not when she was so unsure of what all this meant. Hadn't she and Brooke spent part of their evening convincing each other and their friends that it was perfectly reasonable for a woman to have a relationship with a man that was purely physical?

"Maybe?" He wasn't buying it. "Is that why you keep coming back for more?"

"More sex? I think it's obvious why I keep coming back for sex." She was so full of shit. It wasn't just about sex. As much as she wanted to believe that it was. She liked Kyle. Liked the way he made her feel. And not just in bed. He challenged her. In ways she couldn't quite explain. Nor did she want to spend too much time talking or even thinking about it.

"You're amazing." He looked at her in a way that she'd never seen before. At least not in a man who was looking at her.

"I need to go to the bathroom." She scooted away from him and made a dash for his surprisingly comfortable facilities.

She cleaned up and splashed cold water on her face. She ran damp fingers through her hair and then opened the door that led to the bedroom area of the RV.

"Your turn." She tried to sound casual, but her heart was beating way too fast.

He jumped up, pulled her into his arms, and whispered in her ear, "Don't you dare go anywhere. You're spending the night. And we can talk. Or not."

"What if I choose 'not'?"

"I'm sure I'll think of something." He brushed a soft kiss on her forehead and then moved past her into the bathroom.

She fell onto the bed as waves of conflicting emotions washed over her. Satisfaction, fear, contentment, nervousness, hope, panic.

Kyle slipped back into bed with her and pulled the light blanket over them. "So what's got you all worked up? And I don't mean sexually. I think I've got that covered pretty well. But something's bothering you."

"Nothing's bothering me. Really." Except for the fact that she couldn't just enjoy the moment.

"How was your night out with the ladies?"

"Good. I hope you weren't bored all alone without me." She snuggled against his broad, comforting chest.

"No. Not bored. We fellas had a little party of our own. With Leia and Dana to keep us company." He held her, and it felt too good. "Your bosses came by, with their herd in tow."

"Really?"

"Yeah. They hung out with us for a while, kicking back, drinking beer, changing diapers."

"Diapers?"

"Oh yeah. It was quite entertaining." He chuckled, as if there was something that went on that would be kept between the guys.

"I guess it's weird to think of there being babies around here." Fisher hoped he wouldn't think that she was interested in babies. "And girls' night out ended up being a preplanning session for Aubrey's wedding. And baby shower."

"Who's Aubrey?"

"One of our core crew. Or at least she was until she announced her engagement, pregnancy, and upcoming move to follow her soon-to-be husband for his new job."

"Well, I guess that's exciting for her." He was being far too supportive.

"Yeah. But now we'll have to fill her spot. And I still don't know who's here looking for a job or who's just looking for an adventure. I don't even know what you're looking for." Great, now he was going to think she was trying to find out what he was looking for in a relationship.

"Sometimes you don't know what you're looking for until you find it." He dropped a little kiss on her neck, ran his hand down her arm, and pressed against her. "When I signed up for this, I just knew I needed a change. I took a sabbatical hoping to get a fresh perspective. I didn't think I'd spend more than a week up here, figuring I'd quickly tire of the slow pace, the woods with all the dirt and bugs and wildness. But the lifestyle is growing on me. If I was offered a job for the summer, I'd be a fool not to take it."

"Who said anything about offering you a job?"

"No one. But if you need to fill Aubrey's position, I'd like to be considered."

"Then you'll understand why I'm going to mix up the crews tomorrow." Fisher turned around to face him. "I can't have this getting in the way of what's best for the company. I want to get a look at the other potential guides. And have my crew get a really good look at you. I'm going to hire the best man or woman for the job. No one gets any special favors."

"I wouldn't dream of it." He kissed her forehead. "Did I tell you how amazing you are?"

"No." She closed her eyes, feeling the weight of everything. "You just told me you like me."

"I do. I like you a lot." Kyle chuckled softly. "And I know you'll do the right thing. You don't know any different."

"What's that supposed to mean?"

"You're not like any other woman I've ever known."

"I know my shortcomings."

"No. It's a good thing, Fisher. Really."

"I think I need to sleep now." She closed her eyes. "I promised Brooke I wouldn't be home before six."

"Six a.m.?" He groaned. "I thought the breakfast crew didn't start until seven thirty."

"Yeah, but I have to do my hair and makeup and iron my clothes." She couldn't help but laugh at the idea.

"Or you could sleep in. And do me." His suggestion was not without merit. Although, the way he pressed up against her, she had a feeling the order would be reversed.

* * * *

Kyle felt the bed move, but it seemed like they'd just fallen asleep minutes ago. He cracked one eye open and glanced at the clock. 6:02. He opened the other eye and watched Fisher get dressed.

"Sorry to wake you." She slipped a T-shirt over her practical yet damn-sexy-anyway bra. "I was trying to be quiet."

"What is it about you and early morning escapes?" He sat up even though he wasn't even close to being ready to get up. Well, part of him was up. The part that wanted to entice her back to bed.

"What can I say, I'm a morning person." She shimmied into her shorts.

"I can think of a much better use of your energy than to hurry on home." He crawled across the bed to where she was standing. "Come back to bed. I promise to make it worth your while."

"Didn't you get enough last night?" Her cheeks turned a sexy scarlet.

"Nope." He grabbed her hips and pulled her down on top of him. "I don't think I can ever get enough of my strong blonde."

"Oh please." Her blush deepened.

"If you're begging, I can't say no." He started to slip her shorts down her hips.

"Don't." She grabbed his hands. Her grip was powerful. "I can't. Please understand."

"Okay." He let go. "So are you no longer satisfied?" She would have to be the greatest actress on the planet if that were the case.

"What?" She turned to face him, a puzzled look on her face.

"I don't think you're faking it, but if there's something that's not working for you, let me know. I'll do what I can to take care of your needs. Sexually."

"Everything's fine. Really." She shrugged her shoulders, rolled her neck.

"Yet you can't wait to rush out the door." He joined her in sitting up, the sheet just covering his naked body.

"I'm just busy. That's all." She glanced toward the door.

"You have plenty of people who can help you out." He ran a hand through his hair. "I know I've only been here a few days, but it's long enough to know the kind of people you work with. They've all got your back."

"Yeah, but they're busy. They've got a lot on their plates. And their high chair trays." Was that longing he heard in her voice? And if it was, why wasn't he pushing her out the door as fast as he could? Besides the fact that he still hadn't had his fill of her.

"You're scared." He just wasn't sure of what.

"Don't be ridiculous." Yeah. She was scared.

"Are you afraid I'm going to leave?" He reached for her, grabbing her wrist and pulling her toward him with a playful grin.

"I know you're going to leave." She tossed her long blond hair over her shoulder. "It's just a matter of when. I don't see what the big deal is. Why can't I just come over, have sex, and then go home to get ready for work? Why do we have to talk about it?"

"We don't."

"And why do I have to figure out every step of my future? I'm not even thirty." Ah, the girls' night out that morphed into wedding planning. And all those babies. That's what was eating at her. "I mean a little more than a year ago, Lily was sure she was going to have to use artificial insemination to get a baby. And Miranda was busy traveling the world, writing about her adventures for a magazine that no longer exists. They didn't have everything figured out."

"I still don't have everything figured out." Kyle would have to ask for permission to apply for the guide's job. He was pretty sure his boss would grant it, since it would give him more of an edge in buying out the company. "Hell, I'm seriously considering becoming a river rat. I might even grow my hair out—on my head, my face, and my chest."

"I knew it. You do wax?" A grin escaped those perfect lips.

"Doesn't everyone?"

"No. Not around here." She laughed and shook her head. "But really, I need to get home. I need a shower and a cup of coffee before I can face the day."

"You could shower here. I'll make coffee."

"I have my shampoo and conditioner and stuff back home." She did give him an encouraging smile. "Thanks for the offer, but I also need a little bit of space. Time to paint my nails, read a magazine, or goof off on the Internet."

"That's fair. If you need space, why don't you just say so?"

"Because I didn't want to hurt your feelings." She got up and finished dressing. "And because, well, I like you too."

"That's good enough for me." He rolled out of bed and helped her to stand. Kyle gave Fisher a good-bye kiss. A long, slow, deep, and meaningful kiss. He would let her go for now, but he didn't want her to forget just how good it was between them.

As soon as she shut the door to his RV, he reluctantly headed for the shower. He made it quick and then dressed and made coffee. He opened his laptop and sent a quick e-mail to the boss. Before he had to head to the main camp to start working on breakfast he was given the all clear to do whatever it took to get the job.

And if he got to spend a little more time with Fisher, even better.

Chapter 10

Fisher didn't paint her nails, read a magazine, or goof off on the Internet. Instead she took a long shower. Long for her, anyway. She didn't waste water if she could help it, but she may have shampooed her hair twice. She was a little distracted. In all the years she'd been hung up on Cody, she hadn't been this mixed up.

She turned off the shower, toweled off, and slathered on the sunscreen. Teeth brushed, hair combed and braided, Fisher slipped into her swimsuit, board shorts, and T-shirt, ready for another day at the office.

Grabbing a notepad and pen, she headed downstairs to grab a cup of coffee and draw up a list of how she would redistribute the student crews. She would move Kyle and Nolan to Tyler's crew, Leia and Brett to Brooke's, while she took on Dana and Chad. Then she divvied up the rest of the twelve total students.

With her notebook still in hand, she started a different sort of list. She needed to get a handle on this thing with Kyle. She started with the facts.

Fact: Kyle was in Prospector Springs temporarily.

Fact: He was a skilled and generous lover.

Fact: Although not as skilled on the river, he was willing to work hard and learn from his mistakes.

Next, she listed the unknowns.

Unknown: How long would he stay? She supposed part of that was up to her. If she hired him on for the season, he'd be here until August or September.

Unknown: What was he looking for from their time together?

And the biggest question of them all: What was she looking for from their time together?

She wasn't sure. The only thing she knew was that she didn't want to say good-bye at the end of the week. Regular orgasms were quickly becoming her favorite way to end the day. And she thought he had the potential to be a pretty good guide. He had people skills. Even with their clothes on, he had a way of making her feel comfortable. Everyone else seemed to like him as well.

Tyler was the first one down. He had a satisfied grin on his face and his hair was sticking up in every direction. "I guess you weren't kidding about being home by six."

"What time did Brooke kick you out of bed?"

"Quarter till." He headed straight for the coffee.

"I didn't mean you had to get up so early." Fisher felt bad for disturbing their sleep. "I only warned her so there would be no surprises."

"It's okay. We're all good." Tyler flopped into the kitchen chair opposite Fisher.

"So, is it weird at all? Working together after, you know?" So much for being a modern woman. She couldn't even use euphemisms for sex when talking with someone she'd known for years.

"Nah. When we're on the river, there isn't time for weirdness." Tyler didn't seem to be bothered at all. "And as for the rest of it, I think it was inevitable, you know?"

"No, I don't know." Fisher sipped what was left of her coffee. "For a while there, you were working on giving Cody a run for his money at being the biggest player in Prospector Springs."

"Yeah, right." Tyler chuckled. "Not even Cody could live up to his reputation."

"And now he's as settled and committed as a man can be." Again, Fisher expected a tightness in her chest at the thought of Cody happily married, but it didn't come.

"Look, I'm not going to do anything to mess things up for Brooke or me." Tyler's tone took on a seriousness Fisher hadn't heard from him. "We both know we've got a good thing, and not just with our jobs."

"Good. That's good." And Fisher hoped she could be as easygoing and pragmatic as her friends. "Well, I'm switching up the crews today. I thought you could take a few students down in an oar boat, and Brooke and I could do an oar/paddle combo."

"Sure. Sounds like a good plan." Tyler would agree, even if she wasn't his boss now.

Fisher tore off two pages from her notebook. She wrote a list of the students she wanted Tyler to take with him—including Kyle—and handed it to him. Then she wrote up the new crew for Brooke and folded it up to give to her still-sleeping roommate.

"I'll get the breakfast crew started. You can give this list to Brooke when she gets up." Fisher started for the door but then remembered one more thing. "Oh, I don't know if you heard, but Aubrey's getting married and moving away. We're going to need to fill her spot. And probably one or two more. Be sure to keep an eye out for any potential candidates."

"Will do." Tyler took his coffee cup and headed upstairs.

Fisher refilled her travel mug with the Swift River logo on it. She made her way to the campsite to get her original crew started on breakfast.

Just a few steps away from the temporary camp kitchen, she stopped short. There was Kyle, cracking eggs into a stainless steel bowl, whisking them up, and then pouring them into two hot skillets. He added diced veggies to one, and ham and cheese to the other. Scromelets—a riverside special.

Fisher felt a tightening in her chest. A shortness of breath. The man was gorgeous. She stood rooted in place, watching him cook. Was there anything sexier than a man who knew his way around a kitchen? Well, yeah. When that same man knew his way around a woman's body. Her body.

He said something that made Leia laugh, and Fisher could no longer just stand there watching. She had to touch him. "Something smells good." She placed her hand on his left shoulder, the one without the spatula.

"Yeah, you." He turned and placed a quick kiss on her cheek. "The eggs are almost ready. Do you want ham and cheese or veggie?"

"I'll probably have a little bit of both." Her stomach rumbled in anticipation. "Maybe wrap it in a tortilla."

"Go find us a seat and I'll bring it to you." He smiled and Fisher's legs went weak. She'd only run a class-five rapid once. The kind where she'd had to get out of the boat and look over the edge to find the river churning, wild and dangerous. Her heart raced in fear and anticipation. As part of her wondered if she was crazy for even thinking about going over it, an even bigger part of her knew she had to do it. She had to dive in and take on the challenge.

Being with Kyle made her feel the same way. Excited. Scared. Unable to turn back.

Not long after she found a spot at the table, Kyle appeared with her breakfast. He set a plate down in front of her and grazed her neck with his lips.

"Mmmm." Her first reaction was pure pleasure. Then she realized they weren't alone. "Kyle. You shouldn't do that."

"Why not?" He sat down next to her. "You taste good."

"Because. People can see." She glanced around, expecting to find everyone staring at her, judging her. But they were all busy with their breakfasts, their conversations. No one even noticed. Or else they didn't care.

"So what?" He shrugged his shoulders and dug into his breakfast. After swallowing the first bite, he leaned over and whispered, "I'll wait until we're alone to kiss you where I really want."

"Please. Don't say things like that." Her whole body felt on fire, but especially her cheeks. "It makes me regret not coming back to bed."

"So why didn't you?"

"These people would starve, because we'd still be there."

He laughed. A loud, hearty, sinfully sexy laugh, and this time everyone did look up. But she was met with smiles before they returned to their meals.

They spent the next few minutes eating. Kyle would occasionally brush her arm or press his thigh against hers, sending warmth throughout her body. His touch was easy, comfortable yet incredibly sexy.

Just before they finished their breakfast, Carson pulled into camp, followed by Cody. They walked over together, and Fisher felt Kyle's hand snake around her waist.

"Morning." Carson stood in the middle of the group, where everyone could see him speak. "I hope you're all ready for another day of adventure."

Most people nodded and murmured in the affirmative.

"I know it's only your third day out, but I wanted to give everyone a heads-up." Carson looked around and made eye contact with his current guides. "We're going to be hiring in the next few weeks. I think most of you saw last night why Cody and I aren't going to be available to guide very many trips this summer."

That got a few chuckles from the crowd.

"We are also hoping to expand the number of trips we do each week," he continued. "So, we're looking to hire four to six new guides. And, I hope at least some of you will consider joining us for the summer."

Cody stepped forward. "Let Fisher know if you're interested. She'll give us a list of names by the end of the week, and we'll see how things shake out."

He nodded toward Fisher, his usual cheerful smile fading a bit when he saw how close Kyle was to her. Cody quickly looked away, and she got the feeling that there was at least one person who was bothered by her sleeping with Kyle.

Kyle felt it too, as evidenced by his stroking her back.

"You already know I'm interested." He leaned close to her ear but didn't take his eyes off Cody. "I'd like to apply for the job, as well."

"Thanks for the update." Fisher stood, smiling at Carson and Cody before turning to face the crowd. "That is exciting news. I'm sure we'll end up with an amazing crew. Now I know some of you are here just to push your limits, and that's fine, too. Some of you might even change your mind. Either way, we're going to mix things up a bit. Step outside of our comfort zones a little.

"If you'll meet me at the boat barn by nine, I'll go over further instructions and our plan for today."

She picked up her plate and dumped it in the washtub. She gave Kyle a small wave and headed toward the barn. Kyle was on kitchen crew and would need to stay behind to help clean up.

Fisher needed to get the gear together. Three oar frames, nine oars, eight paddles, and enough water for a long day on the river.

"Hey, Fisher, wait up." It was Cody. Great.

"You sure you have time to help get the gear out?" She didn't mean to sound irritated, but she was.

"Yeah, I can help." He practically had to jog to keep up with her. "So, what is the plan for today?"

"They're going to learn all about rowing." She didn't slow her steps, just kept marching up the slight incline toward where the rafts and equipment were housed. "I thought we'd take one oar boat and two combos down today. And we're going to mix up the crews a bit. That way Brooke and Tyler and I can all get a look at any potential guides."

"Sounds like a good plan." Cody stopped when they reached the large overhead door. He punched in the code, even though she was perfectly capable of doing it herself.

"Hey, listen," he said once they stepped inside. "I don't know what it is, but I kind of have a feeling about that Kyle guy. I don't think he'd be a good fit."

"Really? And why is that?" A year ago, she would have taken a statement like that as encouragement. But that was before Miranda.

"I don't know." He leaned against the workbench near the door. "I just don't like the guy."

"Well, everyone else does." Fisher wasn't going to think about why he didn't. "And I think he'll be a good guide."

"Are you still sleeping with him?" he asked.

"Not at the moment. But that's none of your concern." Not when he'd slept with more than a few passengers in his day. And he'd been sleeping with Miranda when he'd hired her to work in the store last year.

"You're right. It's just that I don't want him to use you."

"Really? You think he's just using me to get the job? That no man in his right mind would want to have sex with me unless he got something out of it?" She knew she was a little too defensive, but that's what years of near celibacy would do to a woman.

"No, of course not. It's just that…you're my friend, Fisher." He let out a frustrated sigh.

"Yes. And I'm also your river operations manager, which you and Carson led me to believe meant that I am the one managing the operation of the river activities. That includes personnel decisions, correct?"

"Yes."

"Okay then." She started pulling an oar frame down off the rack. "If you'll excuse me, I have a river operation to manage."

He took a step back. Perhaps it was sinking in that she didn't have time for his bullshit.

"Look, Fisher, if you were my sister—"

"I'm not. And if you keep being such an ass, you're not going to be my friend much longer."

"You think I'm being an ass?" He stood there, his mouth hanging open. It wasn't like it was the first time she'd told him off for being an insensitive jerk. And she wouldn't be surprised if he called her out for being a bitch, but he didn't.

"Yes." She took a step toward him, poking him in the chest. "Go home, Cody. Your wife needs you. Your daughters need you. I don't need you to be in my face. I have a river operation to manage, unless you want to fire me."

She stuck her hands on her hips and dared him to say anything more.

"Sure." He shook his head. "Just don't come crying to me when the guy breaks your heart."

"Believe me, Cody, you'd be the last person I'd go crying to over some guy." With that, she marched over and started taking down oars, piling them up to get ready for her day's work.

* * * *

Kyle got the water ready for cleanup and gathered all the dishes, but he was more than happy to let the others take over finishing the task. He wasn't shirking his responsibility. Cody had followed Fisher to the barn, and Kyle didn't want to leave him alone with her. He also wanted to make sure if she needed help, he'd be the one to offer her a hand. Or anything else she needed. And if Cody didn't like it, well, that was too bad.

Speak of the devil. Cody was heading this way. He looked a little frustrated, so Kyle just smiled his biggest full-of-shit smile. "Hey, how's it going? Beautiful morning, isn't it?"

"Yeah." Cody looked like he wanted to punch somebody. Probably Kyle. "It sure is."

"I hope Fisher doesn't have everything loaded already." Kyle continued his fake smile. "I got here as soon as I could to help."

"She's working on it."

"That woman is too efficient sometimes." Kyle smiled, this time for real. "She's something special."

"Yeah. She is." Cody looked Kyle up and down, as if he was hoping to find him lacking in some way. "You keep that in mind."

"Oh, I will. I most certainly will." Kyle gave a nod, indicating the conversation was over, and he hustled on up to join Fisher. He couldn't help it; he started whistling.

Chapter 11

At first, when Kyle found out that Fisher had assigned him to work with Tyler, he was a little disappointed. But he quickly realized her strategy. She mixed up all the groups, so that each of the guides would have the opportunity to work together. Fisher was one smart cookie. A tasty one, too.

It took a little getting used to using the heavy wooden oars instead of the lightweight paddles. But once he got the hang of it, he felt good about his ability to take the raft in the direction he wanted to go.

He was getting better at reading the currents, too. Starting to notice subtle changes in the pattern of the water as it moved over obstacles just below the surface. Yesterday, he and the others had learned the hard way that there was more to the river than the obvious. The giant boulders were easy to spot and sometimes easier to avoid. The smaller, submerged rocks were trickier. He couldn't see them until he was almost—or in some cases already—stuck on top of them.

Today, he noticed the way the river curled around hidden objects. He was beginning to recognize eddies, and even when it wasn't his turn to row he kept his eye on the river, soaking in every opportunity to learn.

The river wasn't as crowded as it had been on the weekend, but there were still plenty of people enjoying the beauty and excitement of the river. Many people just set up their lawn chairs right on the edge, with their feet and their beer coolers in the water. There were several companies that ran commercial trips, and a few private boaters using ancient but still serviceable rafts.

And then there were the people using pool inflatables, which seemed like a really bad idea. Most of them put in on the river at the state park and they took out at the Bureau of Land Management access point just above the bigger rapids. The commercial rafts were made out of heavy-duty rubber with reinforced bottoms. The toys from the discount sporting goods stores didn't seem like they'd hold up against submerged hazards.

Sure enough, just past one of the smaller yet still exhilarating rapids was a young woman standing on a small spit of land in the middle of the river. She wore a tie-dyed bikini and nothing else. No shoes, no life jacket. She was holding the shredded remains of some plastic sea creature. A penguin, maybe? No. It was probably an orca. She waved and shouted when they got closer.

"Hey there! Any chance I could catch a ride?" She didn't seem to be too distressed, just stranded. "My friends made it downstream, but I had a little problem."

She held up the deflated orca. On closer inspection, the markings were pretty clear.

With two quick strokes, they pulled up alongside her and she jumped into the front of the raft.

Tyler looked at him with an amused grin.

"Thanks a bunch." She perched on the bow, her long legs stretched out, her back arched. She looked like she was ready to shoot the next issue of *Sports Illustrated Swimsuit Edition.* "Beautiful day, isn't it? The perfect day to be out in nature, right?"

"Absolutely," Tyler agreed.

"Beautiful," Nolan added.

"Gorgeous." Wyatt didn't even hide the fact that he was checking her out.

"Yeah. Sure." Kyle was trying to figure out where he'd find a safe spot to drop her off. But he'd been busy concentrating on learning the landmarks of the river itself, not access points where he could unload hitchhiking mermaids.

There was a time when he would have been much more interested in finding out where she was from or the significance of the tattoo on her ankle than figuring out how to get her to safety. Maybe she would have been better off staying on the island. Not that it was much of an island. If the water came up any higher, her pedicure would be underwater.

Damn, he should have paid closer attention to the fluctuation of the water flow. He'd quickly scanned the section in the handbook about when and how much water was released each day. He'd only read enough to familiarize himself with the vocabulary, so he could fake his way through a conversation. But he really couldn't judge the difference between 1400 cfs and 1800 cfs. He just knew that it had something to do with cubic feet per second.

"Hey, there they are." Bikini girl turned to wave at a group on the right bank of the river. Nemo, Dory, and a great white shark were beached alongside a couple of beer coolers and dogs running in and out of the water.

"Thanks for the ride. You guys wanna join me for a beer?" She seemed to be focused more on Kyle than any of the other guys. Maybe it was because he had command of the raft, or maybe she was just interested in him. Didn't matter. His interest was in the boat behind him.

"No thanks. I'm working." He angled the raft so they could slide onto the sandy riverbank just upstream of her group.

"Some other time, then." She turned, sliding her feet over the side of the raft to hop out. "Maybe I'll see you at the Argo?"

"If you do, I'll be there with my girlfriend. Take care." Kyle didn't want to lead her on. Besides, he liked what he had going with Fisher. He had nothing to hide.

"You too. All of you." She waved to the other guys in the raft who had been quietly watching her. Maybe they'd engaged her in conversation and Kyle was too busy trying to keep from flipping the raft or bumping a rock and ejecting her to notice.

Kyle backed the boat into the current and felt about a thousand pounds lighter.

"That was interesting," Tyler finally said when they had gotten under way. "Man, I don't think I've ever picked up a hitchhiker before. Especially not a hot bikini-clad one."

He chuckled and the rest of the guys joined in.

"She was pretty fine, wasn't she?" Nolan let out a low whistle.

The others murmured in agreement.

"I thought maybe it was part of the test." Kyle's shoulders loosened. "And that I failed by not offering her a life jacket or at least suggesting she book a trip with Swift River Adventures next time. You know, for her safety."

That brought howls of laughter from the rest of the crew.

"You're all right, dude," Tyler said. "Take this next rapid and then we'll switch off."

"Oh man, I should have offered her my life jacket." Nolan shook his head at the missed opportunity.

"Are you kidding?" Wyatt joined in. "And cover up that view?"

They were all still laughing when Fisher's crew came up alongside them.

"Who was that girl?" Fisher asked.

"What girl?" Nolan feigned innocence.

"The nearly naked one you guys just picked up in the middle of the river." There was an edge to her voice. Was she jealous?

"Oh, that girl!" Wyatt nearly doubled over, laughing.

"She was stranded. And needed a lift to safety," Tyler informed her.

"Is that what happened?" She turned her gaze on Kyle. He could feel the heat in her eyes even behind her dark sunglasses.

"Yeah. That's what happened." He noticed she'd left her busted inflatable orca in the bottom of their raft. "She was riding this discount-store raft and it popped or something. We couldn't just leave her there in the middle of the river."

"Sure." She turned to Dana, who was at the oars. "Let's put some distance between us and the other boats."

Dana dug in her oars and rowed away from them.

"Whoa." Tyler looked over his shoulder at Kyle. "You are in some serious trouble, mister. I've never seen her like that."

"Oh shit. Is it against company policy to rescue someone stranded on the river? Did I make a major etiquette breach?"

"Nah. It's no big deal." Tyler chuckled. "But your *girlfriend* isn't too happy about you picking up other women."

Kyle started to say that Fisher wasn't his girlfriend, but he'd been the one to label her as such just minutes before. Besides, he kind of liked the idea of her being his girlfriend. Even if he was in trouble.

"What?" He tried to keep the smile from his face. "I was just being a Good Samaritan."

"Yeah, right." Nolan joined in the ribbing. "Did you see the rack on that girl?"

"Not really, no."

"Yeah, right, Hollywood. You are some kind of actor." Wyatt laughed along at his expense.

In fact, they teased him mercilessly the rest of the ride. Nolan took a turn at rowing and then Wyatt. Tyler was a pretty laid-back instructor, only giving direction when needed. Once or twice he was almost too late, but they managed to make it to take-out in one piece. And Kyle felt a little like he was part of the fraternity. He didn't feel like he needed to work as hard to impress them as he had when he was in Fisher's raft.

Now he'd have to work even harder to impress her. He was looking forward to it. Maybe a little too much. But he'd already figured out that his strong blonde was a little too much. And that was why she still held his interest.

The sex was good. No. It was great. That wasn't it. There was something about her that really got him going. She was so real. So what-you-see-is-what-you-get. And now she was pissed at him. For saving a woman's life. Okay, so he hadn't saved her life. Just her party time.

And Fisher was jealous. Normally that was the kind of shit that sent him running. But for some reason, in this case, it got him hot. Real hot.

When he got on the bus, she was already sitting up front. And there was no room for him to sit next to her. He made his way toward the back, where Wyatt and Nolan were sitting, telling the other guys about the hottie they'd saved. The way they were telling it, Kyle was surprised they hadn't included the need for mouth-to-mouth resuscitation.

He leaned back against the seat and closed his eyes just briefly. He wondered if this was what summer camp was like. The fresh air, activity, and comradery. It felt good to be a part of this. For a moment, he thought he could get used to this lifestyle. Spending his days on the river, his nights with his woman.

* * * *

Chocolate. That's what she needed. A nice, sweet, nutty, creamy bar of chocolate. Fisher was the first one off the bus, and she told Brooke she'd be right back. Brooke could rally the troops, get them started at putting the gear away. They knew what to do by now. Maybe with the exception of the oar frames, but they'd figure it out.

And Fisher would figure out why she'd been so upset by Kyle's hitchhiking bikini girl. After she had some chocolate.

She marched up to the store and pushed open the door a little too hard. The bell clanged against the door and Miranda looked up from behind the register.

"Oh. I didn't expect to see you here this late in the day." The last person she wanted to see her upset.

"I needed to get out of the house." Miranda offered a warm smile. "Between the book and the babies, I needed a break."

"Most women would go shopping, get a pedicure or something." Fisher had given up the idea that she could hate Miranda. And she was close to accepting the idea that Miranda didn't hate her.

"Yeah, well, we're not like most women, are we?"

"I don't know. In some ways, I think I am." She headed straight for the Snickers bar.

"Rough day?"

"No. Yeah. I don't know." Fisher placed the candy bar on the counter.

"You want me to put this on your tab?"

"Yes, please."

"Hey, before you go"—Miranda leaned on the counter—"I wanted to tell you how much I appreciate all you do around here."

"Me?"

"Yeah. Cody's under a lot of pressure these days." Miranda laughed.

"Hard not to be with twins. But I know that the only reason he's able to sleep at night is because he knows you've got the rafting and the guides under control."

"I hope that's not the only reason he's sleeping." Did she just say that out loud?

"Well, actually, at night, we take turns sleeping. But there is naptime." Miranda grinned wickedly. "You know, a lot of women might feel threatened by...well, by anyone who shared her husband's loyalties. His brother, friends, some might even be jealous of the time spent with his children."

"But we've already determined we're not like most women."

"Maybe we're just not like the women we see on TV." Miranda came around the front of the counter. "Since I've been here, the women I've met have been pretty great. Lily's become a sister to me. And I hope you will too."

"Me?"

"You are planning on sticking around, right?"

"I'm not going anywhere."

"Good. Then we should become friends. Family, even." Miranda gave her a tentative hug. "I know Cody thinks of you as a sister, so I should, too."

"That would be great." Fisher didn't know what to think. She waved good-bye to Miranda and headed up to the boat barn to make sure the equipment was all put away.

She wondered how Miranda could be so trusting. Here Fisher was flipping out over a stranger Kyle had met on the river. He would meet dozens, no, hundreds of women if he continued on as a guide. And many of them would be beautiful. Dressed in little more than a swimsuit. And they would laugh at his jokes, admire his skills, and even recommend him to their friends. Wasn't that part of the training? Making people feel at home on the river?

Maybe it wasn't training as much as natural friendliness. He'd certainly hooked her immediately. Kyle had a charisma that rivaled even Cody. In fact, the only person who hadn't been drawn to him was Cody.

She wasn't going to let herself think too long and hard on why. *Little sister*. That had to be her only relationship with Cody.

Because she didn't love him. No. She did. But it really was more like a brother than a lover. She had a lover. And now she understood the difference.

Cody had been nothing more than a crush. A useful one, especially when she was still in school. She'd seen too many of her classmates get caught up in relationships that sometimes derailed their plans. The roommate who'd dropped out to get married with one semester left to go. The classmate who finished her degree and took a job, supporting her boyfriend through grad school, only to have him dump her for his study partner because they had more in common.

In a way, Cody had protected her from a broken heart. She never got too close to any of the guys she met in school, because in some small way she'd compared them to Cody. And of course, she only compared those ways that they would come up short.

So what was the deal with Kyle?

That's right. She was mad at him. For picking up a gorgeous girl in a bikini. The woman was stunning. All curves and femininity.

Maybe she wasn't mad. Not really. But she'd had some kind of primal reaction. A lifetime of insecurities brought to the surface by a stray hitchhiker.

She remembered the chocolate bar in her hand and tore open the wrapper. One bite. Then another. Soon, she'd eaten half of the Snickers bar, and the edge seemed to soften, just like in the commercials. Folding the wrapper over the unfinished candy, she sighed before shoving it into her back pocket for later.

Still. She couldn't let Kyle completely off the hook. There was a liability issue, for one thing. Yeah. She'd lead with that. Fisher wouldn't want him to think she was one of those irrational females, jealous of him even looking at another woman. She'd make him squirm for a little bit, though.

Most of the gear was put away by the time she got there. And only a few guides and students lingered. Kyle was, of course, one of them.

She kept her smile to herself, though. He didn't need to know she was pleased that he was usually the last to quit for the day.

Nolan was the first to spot her. He cast a nervous glance at Tyler, who nodded and somehow communicated to everyone but Kyle that worktime was over. They vacated the barn, leaving her alone with Kyle.

He finished the task he was working on and then he looked up. "Am I still in trouble?"

"That depends. Just what did you think you were doing?" Fisher tried to sound stern, like her fifth-grade teacher. But a smile kept teasing her lips.

"Just helping a fellow human." Kyle kept his tone cool.

"Are you sure she was human?" She had to glance away, to keep that pesky grin at bay.

"Well, she wasn't a mermaid. She had legs." He went back to checking in the last few pieces of gear, sliding an empty cooler onto a shelf.

"I knew it. You were checking out her legs. Her body." She had to bite her lower lip to keep from giggling. So much for being the tough boss.

"No. I wasn't checking her out. I just happened to notice she didn't have fins or a tail."

"She also didn't have a life jacket." There. That was something she could be serious about.

"That was a bit of a concern, but I couldn't just leave her stranded in the middle of the river."

"Why not?" If he looked at her, he'd see she wasn't really mad.

"Ah, come on, sweetheart. What's really bothering you? That I picked up a non-paying passenger or the fact that it was a woman?" Finally he looked up, confusion showing in his eyes.

"In a bikini." Fisher stood with her hands on her hips, not quite sure how to end this charade. "Without a life jacket."

"Yeah, well, we didn't get far enough that I had to worry about her safety. She was only in our raft for maybe ten minutes before we caught up with her friends."

"What if you hadn't caught up with her friends? What if she'd stayed in your boat down the more challenging rapids?"

"I don't know. I guess I would have pulled over somewhere before it got to that point." He took two steps toward her, and she really wanted to call a time-out. "Believe me, I wasn't going to take her down a class three or three-plus without shoes or a life jacket. Besides, I'm sure Tyler would have taken over if she'd been in any real danger."

"Yeah. I guess he would have. But…" And that's where her argument finally ran out of steam.

"Are you upset that I picked her up because of liability issues, or is there some other reason?" His tone started to soften.

"Like what?" And she knew he was onto her.

"Oh, I don't know? You tell me." He stepped even closer, just a heartbeat away. Getting her riled up, but not with pretend anger. Or even real jealousy. "Why are you so worked up about this?"

"Because…" She couldn't help but laugh. "You get me *worked up*."

"I've never wanted any woman as much as I want you." He pulled her against him, breathing her in, burying his face in her hair. "I want you and I'll do whatever it takes to have you. For as long as you'll have me."

Fisher sucked in a breath and he came down on her mouth with his own. He'd kissed her before, but not like this. This was hunger, possession, raw desire.

He backed her up against the workbench, kissing her deeper with every step. Her body went limp, and he lifted her up onto the flat surface. He tugged at her shorts, shimmying them down her hips.

"Kyle." She pulled her mouth away from his long enough to gasp his name. "The door. Close it."

"Yes, ma'am." He stepped away from her and reached up to pull down the overhead door, letting it hit the cement floor with a loud thud. "Now.

Where were we?"

Kyle returned to her, yanking her shorts off completely; then he buried his face between her thighs. "So sweet. You taste so damn sweet."

He plunged his tongue deep into her folds, working his magic, bringing her closer to the edge of insanity. She draped her legs over his shoulders and threw her head back in complete surrender. Finally, she went limp and Kyle gently pulled her to her feet.

"Turn around." His voice was a harsh whisper. "Bend over the table. Hang on tight."

Fisher did as he commanded. One hand snaked around her waist and dipped between her legs. The other guided his hard, pulsing cock deep inside her. She wasn't sure if her feet lifted off the ground or it just felt like it, but he plunged deeper. Harder. Faster.

She reached for the edge of the bench but only succeeded in knocking things over. What, she had no idea, nor did she care. This. Felt. So. Good.

Then it happened. She plunged over the edge, falling, drowning in pleasure. Wave after wave after wave crashed over her.

Chapter 12

As soon as he felt Fisher shatter, Kyle gave one last hard thrust. He emptied himself inside her with a primal yell. Then he stilled. With his hands still on her hips, he held himself inside her, not yet wanting to separate. Maybe he wasn't able to pull away. Not yet. Not while dozens of aftershocks shook her body.

His legs started to shake, and he knew if he didn't let go, he was in danger of dropping her. Reluctantly he pulled out. He reached down to take care of the condom, but in his haste, there hadn't been one.

"Fisher. Baby." His voice was steadier than he anticipated. "I don't know how to say this, but I forgot something. Something important."

She turned around, looking at him with trust in her heavily lidded eyes. "What was that?"

Now she wrapped her arms around him, nuzzling up against his chest. The woman was clearly satisfied.

"I, uh, forgot the condom." Seriously, where was the panic in his voice? This had long been his worst nightmare.

"That's okay. I'm covered." She lifted her head briefly. "I mean, for birth control. Is there anything else I should worry about?"

"No. I've never forgotten before." He held back a curse. "I swear. Not ever."

"Well, I guess there's a first time for everything." She let out a nervous laugh. "But seriously, we don't have to worry about an accidental pregnancy. There are more than enough babies around here. I'm not taking any chances."

"That's good." He wrapped his arms around her and held her close, wondering why he felt the tiniest bit of disappointment crowding his overwhelming feeling of relief.

"Let's go back to my place. Get cleaned up and go to bed."

"What about dinner?"

"Oh, food would probably be good." He brushed her hair off her forehead; it had come loose from her braid. "But we should definitely get cleaned up first."

"Why don't you come to the guides' house? The shower should be available by now." Fisher tried to smooth the rest of her hair back but quickly gave up. "You could get a feel for the place. In case, you know…"

"I have my RV. I like it. I have some pretty great memories."

"Yeah, but you might want a real shower once in a while. A full-sized kitchen."

"I like the privacy of the RV. But how big is this shower?"

"Big enough." She grabbed his hand and started for the side door.

"Uh, Fisher. I guess I'm not the only forgetful one." He stared at her bare lower half. "Maybe you should put your shorts on."

Her cheeks flamed a deep shade of red. "Yeah. I guess so."

Kyle helped her get dressed and then he took her hand and followed her back to the house she shared with Brooke, Tyler, Ross, and a few others. Mostly guys.

"So tell me about the sleeping arrangements here."

"Well, Brooke and I share a room. There's a loft, and plenty of space for tents or just sleeping bags out back. You could probably park your RV back there."

"Sounds good."

"There's a nice-size kitchen with a big farmhouse table." Fisher sounded like she was giving a tour on one of those home and garden shows. "And there's a living room where there's a TV. We have satellite and an old PlayStation, but mostly we hang out on the deck or down at the Argo."

"Nice place. The Argo. I met a girl there once. She was pretty hot."

"Oh yeah. What happened with her?" Fisher led him up the porch steps.

"She just keeps getting hotter and hotter." He kissed her, pressing her against the front door.

"Maybe instead of a shower, you should go cool off in the river."

"Aren't you afraid I'll pick up some girl in a bikini?"

She looked at him, almost in disbelief. Then she slugged him in the shoulder, before turning the doorknob and leading him inside.

"I guess I deserved that."

"Yeah. You'd better watch it, mister." But she took his hand anyway and led him to the back of the house and into the bathroom.

Fisher turned on the shower and got undressed. She ducked behind the shower curtain and he quickly stripped and stepped inside with her. He took the shampoo bottle from her and poured a generous handful into his palm. Then he lathered her long, gorgeous hair, massaging her scalp and making her moan with pleasure.

She returned the favor by soaping him up. Up and down. She dropped down to her knees and lowered her mouth over his shaft. Oh yeah. He leaned his head back, waiting for the exquisite pleasure of her mouth on his cock.

But that little fantasy was interrupted by a gagging sound. She coughed, sputtered, and then dashed out of the shower and held her head over the toilet. More coughing, heaving, and finally she collapsed on the floor and burst into tears.

He turned off the water and went to her, kneeling next to her on the soft bath mat. "Hey, are you okay?"

"No. I'm mortified." She looked up at him; her hair was plastered against her face, which was pale, her lips quivering.

"Here." He stood up, grabbing a fluffy white towel from a rack above the toilet. "Dry off, honey. It's going to be okay."

Kyle wrapped the towel around her and helped her to stand. He still had shampoo in his hair, but he could always rinse it out later, once he knew she was going to be all right.

"I'm so embarrassed." Fisher shivered as he rubbed her skin with the terry cloth. "I've never done that before. I mean, I tried, once. But the guy said it was the worst he'd ever had. I guess he was right."

"No. The guy was an asshole." He lifted damp strands of hair off her face. "You're incredible, Fisher. Like no woman I've ever known. And while your technique is a little unorthodox, I love your enthusiasm."

She laughed. The kind of laugh that was 70 percent tears, but there was enough laughter to make him think that she was going to recover.

"Look, I need to get the soap out of my hair, but then let's grab something to eat and take it to my RV."

"Yeah. Sure. Just as long as it's not hot dogs." Fisher gave him a wry smile.

"If it is, I'll be sure to cut it into tiny pieces." He ducked back under the shower before he could say anything else.

"I'm going to brush my teeth. Then I'll change and meet you outside." She avoided eye contact. She was embarrassed but she didn't need to be. He was the one who'd made her gag.

He rinsed off quickly, hoping to catch her before she could get too far away, but she was quicker than he was. He practically had to jog to catch up to her at the campsite.

"Hey. It looks like tacos. You want beef or chicken?" He kept the conversation light.

"I'm not really hungry." She shrugged, still avoiding his gaze.

"Tell you what. I'll make you one of each. Grab something cold to drink and we could head to my RV. If it gets cold, you can always reheat it in my microwave."

"You don't have to go to all that trouble for me." She looked up at him then, with a soft resignation in her eyes.

"It's no trouble." He kept his voice down, so that the conversation was private. "Maybe we can just chill for the rest of the night. Unless you want to hang out with everyone?"

"No. Not really." She sighed. "Your place sounds fine."

"Great." He made his way over to the buffet line where he grabbed a plate and made up six tacos, three of each kind. Then he grabbed two beers and, balancing them on his plate, motioned for Fisher to follow him.

"You sure you're okay?" he asked when they got to his RV.

"Fine."

"Fisher. Look at me." He smiled, hoping to encourage her. "You have nothing to be embarrassed about."

"Please don't say that." She took the plate from him so he could open the door. "It makes me not believe anything you've ever said to me."

"So you want me to tell you it was horrible? That I don't want to see you again because you tried something new and it didn't work out?" He unlocked the door and held it open for her.

"No." She stepped up into the RV and set the plate and two beers on the table just inside. "Just don't act like it was nothing."

"Hey. It wasn't nothing." He reached for her, twisting a strand of her long blond hair between his fingers. "It was actually kind of hot."

"You can't be serious." She backed away, as if she thought he was nuts.

"Yeah. I kind of am." He took both her hands in his. "You were trying to do something for me. Obviously it isn't something you are into, but the fact you wanted to try. To please me. That's hot."

"But me rushing for the toilet, choking and gagging?"

"Still, kind of hot." He pulled her closer, wrapped his arms around her waist, without letting go of her hands. "I must be incredibly well endowed."

She laughed. And he chose to take it as a sign that she wasn't as embarrassed anymore.

"Let's eat." He let go of her and reached for the beers. He popped open both cans and offered her one. Then he sat down and grabbed a taco.

Fisher sat opposite him in the cozy kitchenette of the RV. She devoured two and a half tacos before declaring herself full.

"You want another beer?" He ate his three tacos and polished off the rest of hers. "I have some in the little fridge."

"Sure. I'll get it." She slid out from behind the table and crossed to the small refrigerator. She pulled two cold ones out and opened them. "It's a nice night. You want to step outside?"

"Sure." He grabbed the empty plate and set it in the sink. "Do you want to head back to the campsite?"

"No." Fisher shook her head. No longer rattled, she was still somewhat subdued. "I was thinking of taking a walk down to the river."

"Sounds perfect." He picked up his beer, ready to follow her just about anywhere.

With a relieved sigh, she led the way out of the RV and down a small path to the river. The water level had gone down quite a bit, and the moonlight shone down on the smooth, dark river.

The river not only looked different at night, it smelled different, too. Maybe it was the lack of sunscreen, sweat, and bodies. Or maybe the plant life gave off different scents in the evening. It smelled reedy. Or willowy. He didn't know all the plants that grew around here. Maybe Fisher did, and she could teach him.

But she'd taught him a lot so far. Some of it had nothing at all to do with the river or rafting or guiding.

He followed her, neither of them saying much, but he liked that he could just be with her. No talking. No touching. No sex. Yet he felt connected to her just the same. Maybe even more so than when they were naked and rubbing up against each other.

* * * *

Fisher trotted down to the river, where she usually felt the most grounded. She had a semisecret path that she took when she needed quiet contemplation. Only this time she had a companion. A sexy, too-good-to-be-true companion. Even after the most humiliating sexual experience of her life—no, the most humiliating experience of any kind—he stuck by her.

And she wasn't going to spend too much time worrying about why.

Making her way to her special spot, Fisher glanced upstream. The lights were on at Cody's house. Cody and Miranda's house. Were they busy putting the twins to bed? Or were they already enjoying a glass of wine together out on the deck? For the first time in a long time, she couldn't picture him.

How many nights had she looked up at the house, knowing he'd taken a woman home? She'd sit out here, wondering what it was like. Had he been a skilled lover? Adventurous? Generous? Dirty?

She shuddered, thinking about how much time she had wasted pining for a man who had clearly lost interest in her as a woman about five seconds after she'd stammered an uncertain "I'm not that kind of girl."

Almost instantly, Kyle's arms were around her shoulders. "You cold?"

"No." Should she tell him? That she was over Cody? That no matter how things ended up between her and Kyle, she no longer longed for another man? "It's just... There's something about the river that soothes me. Makes everything else seem to wash away."

"I'm starting to see what you mean." He leaned into her, simply holding her. There was no lustful intention behind his touch. But it felt good just the same. "I may not be able to return to Southern California."

The thought filled her with joy. Until she realized that it probably wouldn't last. Eventually the season would end. And the work would dry up. Unless the man was independently wealthy, he'd leave. Well, when she'd met him, she'd only expected one night. So anything more was a bonus, right?

"So, I was thinking." Kyle sat with his left arm around her, sipping his beer with his right. "Maybe we should carry an extra life jacket, in case of emergencies."

"Like girls stranded in their bikinis?" She loved that he was thinking not about the girl but what he could do next time.

"Or kids, or old men." She could hear the amusement in his voice. "And if liability is an issue, we could always tuck extra forms in the dry bag with the first aid kit."

"That's not a bad idea." She looked up at Cody's house, wondering why he'd never thought of something like that.

Kyle must have followed her gaze, because he glanced over just in time to see two figures appear on the deck.

"Ah. Is that his house? I wondered why you kept looking up there." His arm slid from her shoulders.

"Yeah, it's his place." She took a long swallow of her beer. "Look, I know I told you had feelings for my boss. But you don't have anything to worry about."

"Who's worried?" He stared straight ahead, his voice distant.

"I shouldn't have said anything, that first night." She leaned forward, wrapping her arms around her knees. "I guess I was protecting myself."

"What were you protecting yourself from? A good time?"

"I didn't think I stood a chance with someone like you."

"Why, because Cody rejected you?"

"Actually, I rejected him. At least at first. But then he moved on. And on and on and on." She sighed, realizing for the first time that it wasn't Cody's rejection that she'd clung to all these years: it was her own fear.

"My brother's an idiot." He stiffened the minute the words passed his lips.

"I'm sorry, did you say your *brother*?" She must have misunderstood. "As in related to each other?"

"Shit." He stood up and started pacing. "Part of the reason I came here was to get to know them. My big brothers."

"Your brothers?" She still couldn't believe it.

"Yeah. But I don't want them to know who I am yet."

"Why?" She rose to her feet, dusted her backside off, and approached him cautiously. "I mean… Why wouldn't you want them to know about you?"

"It's complicated."

"Complicated?" She was having a hard time processing why he would hide something like that.

"Look, my dad…" She heard a lot of pain in his voice. From what she'd learned from Cody, and to some extent Carson, they never had much of a relationship with their father. The man had abandoned them at birth. He came back briefly, when their grandparents died, but as far as she knew, they hadn't kept in touch with the man.

Apparently, he had another child. She searched his face, and now that she knew, she did see some resemblance. The eyes, mostly.

Yeah. He was definitely related. And she didn't quite know how to feel about that. Was she only attracted to him because he reminded her of Cody? No. That wasn't it. He wasn't just a replacement for her crush. Kyle was a great guy. A great guy who was struggling with family issues.

"I didn't even know they existed until I was ten years old. One day, my dad just left. Said he had to go take care of his sons. It didn't even occur to him to take us with him."

"I'm so sorry." She placed her hand on his shoulder, and he tensed up.

"We got by, though. Me and my mom." Kyle moved just enough for her hand to slip. "And then five years later, the son of a bitch shows up. Like he was just on vacation."

"That's terrible." Her heart wedged in her throat. He'd lied. To her, and to Carson and Cody. Yet, a part of her understood why he'd kept his connection hidden. She knew how much resentment Cody had toward his father, and she imagined how much worse it would have been to be abandoned at ten. Old enough to know the man.

"I hated him. And for a long time, I hated them, too." He shook his head. "I guess I thought if I met them on my own terms, got to know them, let them get to know me, it would be better than just showing up."

"Oh, Kyle." She couldn't just stand there and watch him suffer. All she could do was wrap her arms around him. Lean on his chest and wait.

"I had this image of them in my mind. Two spoiled guys who had everything. I worked from the time I was thirteen, just trying to keep food on the table. And these two guys had a house and a college fund and our dad." He didn't push her away this time, but he also didn't accept her comfort.

"Then I found out they have their own business." His voice was tense, full of hurt. "And I thought I'd check it out. See if these rich assholes were really as bad as I thought."

"They're hardly rich." She bit back a laugh. "And they're not really assholes."

"What about Cody?" He stepped back. "He's not exactly been friendly toward me. And I know it has something to do with you."

"He's protective, that's all. He seems to think of himself as my big brother."

"Well, it's a good thing he's not."

She couldn't help it. A laugh escaped her lips. "It's a very good thing. But at some point, you might want to let him know who you are. And Carson, too. You're family."

"Yeah, but I want people to know me for me. You know? If I get the job, I don't want people to think it's because I'm related to the bosses."

"You'd rather them think you got the job because you're sleeping with the supervisor?"

"Yeah." He smiled, and that made her melt. "That's exactly what I want people to think."

"You're not just sleeping with me to get the job?" She was at least halfway joking.

"No, sweetheart. I can't resist you. I don't know what I'd do if there wasn't a job available. I guess I'd have had to apply as a bartender at the Argo just to keep seeing you."

"So you're not independently wealthy?"

"No. I do have some money in the bank, but that's where it's going to stay."

"For a rainy day?"

"Yeah, I've had enough of them to know they come up whether you're prepared or not."

Chapter 13

Damn. He'd blown it. Fisher now knew that Carson and Cody were his brothers. Would she keep his secret? Did it matter?

His rainy day would come sooner or later. Right now, at the beginning of summer, being out on the river, life seemed full of possibilities. He'd even found himself a woman he'd love to spend more time with. But summer would come to an end. He would have to return to LA. And somehow, he'd need to close this deal.

"Look, Fisher, I think I should take you home." He reached down and picked up the two beer cans; both were empty. "Neither of us has had much sleep the last few nights. I have a feeling there will be plenty of surprises on the river tomorrow."

"Yeah. And you'll have to earn your spot on the team." Fisher was too good for him anyway.

They walked back through the campground, near each other but not touching. He knew if he touched her, he wouldn't be able to stop. And he needed space right now. He needed to get his head on straight and finish the job he'd come up here to do.

They got to the porch.

"Well, good night." Fisher turned to walk away from him.

"Fisher, wait." He pulled her into his arms and kissed her. Kissed her with everything he had. He couldn't let her think he didn't want her.

"I didn't expect you." He pulled away reluctantly.

"I didn't expect you either." Her lips were swollen, her hair tousled, and her eyes sparkled in the moonlight. "And I know you have a lot on your mind. Sleep tight."

With that, she turned and walked into the house.

Kyle did have a lot on his mind. The last few jobs had been so much easier. The surf shop, bar and grill, and even the automotive shop and gas station had been easy to take over. Mostly because they all were struggling when he showed up. By the time he'd come in with an offer to buy the businesses, they'd been relieved more than anything.

But this time it was different. For one thing, the company was in good shape. He didn't have a chance to look at the financials yet, but it seemed like they were in a position to grow. If they were looking to hire several new guides, they weren't ready to dump and run.

He'd need a really good incentive. Of course, he hadn't counted on both the partners being recently married and new parents. That would make it harder to convince them to sell. Take the money and travel the world. Or maybe it would be the best time to pack up the babies while they were still portable.

Then he remembered how much work it had been for them to bring the three infants down to the campsite.

He'd never failed an assignment before. But he'd never worked with anyone he was related to, either. He had to admit, he liked them. And the company they'd created.

And then there was Fisher. She complicated the hell out his life. If he was able to pull off this deal, he'd need to make sure she was taken care of, too.

Although, with the money he'd make, he could take care of her himself. He could whisk her away and they could travel all the rivers of the world. New Zealand, Costa Rica, wherever she wanted to go.

Surely she had dreams that took her beyond the South Fork of the American. He needed to find out what they were. And somehow make them come true.

But he was a realist. He also needed a backup plan.

Instead of getting extra sleep, he spent the next few hours researching the other rafting outfitters in the area. Maybe one of them would be better suited for his bosses' plans. A cash deal, quick transition, and everybody would go home happy.

At least, that was the idea.

The next morning was painful. Once he had fallen into bed, he hadn't slept well. Something was missing. Or rather, someone. Normally, if things progressed this far in a relationship, he'd start pulling back. Claim to be slammed with work. Or family commitments. He tended to use the family excuse only in dire emergencies, as women often wanted to help. To meet his mother, take her shopping, stuff like that.

He couldn't use the work excuse with Fisher. He worked with her. Or for her. Well, he hoped he would. And now she knew about his family. His brothers who were her bosses, and potentially his as well.

The weird thing was that he didn't want to make excuses to see less of her. He thought he wanted space, but it had come at a price. He missed her. Missed her naked body pressed up against him. Missed her scent. And most of all, he missed the way she tasted. The way she moved and took pleasure in his touch.

Instead of wanting to run as far and as fast as he could, he wanted to run to her.

After he made some coffee. He'd need caffeine to face the day. The river. And his brothers.

A soft tap on the door of the RV startled him. But when he opened the door and found Fisher standing there with two steaming mugs of coffee, he couldn't help but think he might be able to pull this off.

"Good morning. I brought you some coffee. I hope you slept well." Fisher had a smile on her face and her eyes shone brightly.

"Not at all." He reached for the caffeine, took a long, heavenly sip, and sighed. "Did you sleep well?"

"Not really, but I make sure we have good, strong coffee for those times when I need a pick-me-up."

"Why didn't you sleep well last night?"

"I guess I was lonely." She didn't even try to play it cool. He liked that about her. She was so genuine. "And I kept thinking about what it must have been like when you were just a boy. Your dad driving off one day and leaving you behind. I don't know, for some reason, I picture an old beat-up station wagon and you standing in the street wanting to chase after him, but being more afraid of what would happen if you caught up with him."

The coffee sank like a stone to the bottom of his stomach. Had she read his mind? Had she been there that day? "It was a Tercel hatchback. But yeah, I wanted to run after him. But I was afraid. Afraid he'd take off with me hanging on to the door handle until I couldn't keep up anymore. Like that dog in that Chevy Chase movie. The one with the girl in the Ferrari."

"That is my dad's favorite movie. You have no idea how many vacations I went on, driving a hundred miles out of the way to see the world's largest potato chip."

"Really? And where would one find that?"

"In Blackfoot, Idaho, of course. At the Idaho Potato Museum. Free taters for out-of-staters."

He laughed, but she wasn't kidding.

"Tell me more about your family. Do you have brothers or sisters?"

"Nope. An only child." She sighed. "Always wanted a brother, though." Then she laughed.

"What's so funny?"

"Well, I guess I should be careful what I wish for." She sipped her coffee and slid into the booth.

"Why is that?" Although he knew. At least, he knew who she was referring to. Cody.

"Well, I always thought it would be cool to have someone look out for me. You know, stick up for me when people made fun of me for being too tall or too strong or too smart."

"Who made fun of you?" His jaw clenched just thinking of her former bullies. Even though they'd all had some.

"The popular kids. You know, the guys who thought they were such athletes, and then when I'd beat them in something, they'd get their panties in a wad. Or the girls who played dumb because they thought the boys would like them more."

"And you thought having a brother would fix that?"

"Yeah. I mean, if someone was bigger and stronger and smarter than me"—she wrapped her hands around the coffee mug—"then no one would mess with me."

"So have you discovered you can take care of yourself?"

"Yeah." She smiled, seemingly pleased that he had noticed. "But now I've got this brother figure who thinks he needs to protect me. From you."

She laughed again, shaking her head.

"Do you think you need protection? From me?"

"No." But her eyes took on a cautious look. "I'm pretty sure I can handle you. I even managed to survive a night without you."

"Not exactly." He couldn't help but remember the encounter in the boat barn. "We didn't sleep together last night, but we still haven't gone twenty-four hours without making love."

"You're not issuing a challenge, are you?"

"Oh, hell no." He downed his coffee and slid closer to her. "I didn't sleep last night. I think you might be even more addictive than coffee."

"Speaking of coffee." Fisher held up her cup. "I'm going to need more. We're doing a full river today. You want a refill?"

"How 'bout a quickie?" He nuzzled her neck.

"I don't think you could be quick. You're very thorough." She slid out of the booth, stood up, and held out her hand.

"Coffee will have to do." Kyle followed her to the door.

Fisher hesitated. She turned around and laughed. "You know, I just thought of something."

"What's that?"

"Your big brother might want to protect you from me." She grinned wickedly.

Then she bounded out the door and across the campground to the house she shared with the other guides.

* * * *

Fisher hadn't slept well last night. She kept picturing Kyle as a boy who'd been abandoned when he was old enough to understand that his father hadn't wanted him enough to make it work blending two families.

Now Kyle was here, trying to make his father's other family accept him. But not because they shared half their DNA, but because of the man he'd become in spite of it.

She'd lain awake wondering if Cody would have accepted him if it weren't for her. If he didn't have some misguided need to look out for her, even when she was doing just fine on her own. Kyle was a good man. And Cody was a good man. So was Carson. It seemed like the only Swift man who wasn't was their father. She didn't even know his name. Only that he'd abandoned two families for whatever reason, and all three of his sons resented the hell out of him.

She got a small tingle up her spine as she thought about somehow helping them find comfort in each other.

"You okay?" Kyle must have noticed her reaction.

"Yeah." She stopped, letting him catch up and take her hand. "Just thinking about how you're going to owe me for keeping your secret."

"Oh really?" He squeezed, sending even more shivers up her spine. How could one man make her feel so tingly in so many places? "What if you're the one who owes me?"

"And what do I owe you for?" She pulled him closer to her. "I can buy my own beer."

"I'm sure you could probably give yourself an orgasm, too, but it's not as much fun as the ones we share." He closed the remaining distance and brought his mouth down on hers, brushing her lips softly before whispering, "Everything is more fun when we do it together."

She couldn't help but laugh, but it didn't last long, as he kissed her again. Thoroughly. His tongue claiming hers. His body pressed against hers. His heart beating in time with hers.

Fisher could feel his arousal growing as the kiss grew deeper. She was drowning in him. It was as if her sexuality had been dammed, and Kyle had come along, opening the floodgates of her desire.

They were four feet from the guides' house. Yet she wasn't sure if she could resist him long enough to make it inside.

"Get a room!" Cody's voice broke through to her. Kyle started to pull away, but she just grabbed his hips and kissed him even harder. She wasn't going to let Cody ruin this for her. She would stop kissing her man when she was good and ready.

"Seriously, guys, this is a family establishment." Cody's voice was laced with amusement, though.

Finally, Fisher let go of Kyle. Well, not completely. She still held his hand. "Was there something I could help you with?" she asked innocently.

"No, I was just going to grab some coffee." He looked over toward the house. "You do still make the coffee around here?"

"Yeah. In fact, we were just on our way over for a refill." Fisher led Kyle up the steps to the kitchen. "Then we're doing a full river trip. So that means pizza at Mario's tonight. You should bring the wife and kids and join us."

"I might just do that." Cody followed them inside. "I'll see if Carson and Lily want to come. Make it a party."

"One big, happy family." Fisher squeezed Kyle's hand gently. "I was telling Kyle—well, all the potential guides, actually—about how we really are like a family around here. Brooke and Aubrey are like my sisters, and I have all these pesky brothers."

Kyle gave her a return squeeze. "Well, I don't see you as a sister."

"No. But we are close." She gave him a quick kiss on the cheek. Her choice in a lover was her choice. Both men would just have to deal with that.

Chapter 14

After an exhilarating run on the upper stretch of the river, Fisher led her crew to the sandy beach where they held their wilderness camps. They would camp there Thursday night, and she wanted the newbies to get a feel for the place before they took a loaded gear boat and all the necessary gear for an overnight trip.

Plus, it was a great place to stop for lunch that wasn't crawling with tourists.

She wandered around, checking in with her guides and with her students. She wanted to make sure everyone was still good. There were a few who had made it clear that they weren't interested in staying on for the summer. Wyatt and Samantha were actually a couple; it was the only way they could go away together without their families realizing they were together. Grant had recently accepted a corporate job; he'd start a week after getting home from his last little adventure.

Fisher had talked to Tyler and Brooke. They agreed that Leia and Dana would make good candidates. Neither had committed to applying for a job, but both were considering it. There was a good chance Chad would look for a job in his home state of Idaho.

So that left Nolan and Brett to compete for the last position, unless one of the women turned the job down. Fisher was pretty sure the others agreed with her decision to offer a job to Kyle. Only Cody wasn't on board, but she could always work on convincing Miranda that it would be a good idea. No way Cody would go against his wife's wishes.

Hopefully, Miranda would come to pizza tonight. Then Kyle could work some of his charm on her. He was entirely too charming for his own good. Must be a family trait. Both Cody and Carson were very personable. Carson's charisma was a little under the radar. He'd always been a little uptight, until Lily came along and softened him up. And Cody had been over the top until his wife had tamed him.

Kyle didn't need softening or taming. He was just right already. Friendly, enthusiastic, and generally personable. He seemed to get along with everyone in the group, and he even attracted strangers in bikinis. She'd passed along his idea for carrying extra liability forms and a spare life jacket, and the trip checklists had been updated accordingly. He'd make a great addition to the team. To the "family."

But Fisher wondered what she could offer him, beyond a job. Maybe that would be enough. The job would give him the opportunity to stick around a little longer. Actually get to know his brothers. She was sure that Cody would come around and accept their relationship as a good thing. And once he did that, he'd accept Kyle.

She had visions of them truly becoming one big, happy family.

But would she be a part of it? Would she continue to be part of Kyle's life?

With lunch over for the most part, it was time to start thinking about getting back on the river. She looked for Kyle, who she hoped to grab a quick kiss from before they headed back into their separate boats.

He was kicking back, reclining against a beached raft. He looked like he was taking a nap. She almost didn't want to disturb him.

Almost.

* * * *

Kyle couldn't remember the last time he'd been so relaxed, other than after sex. He'd had a good morning. His runs were getting, if not easier, at least more manageable. With each rapid, he was able to anticipate the current and the movement of the raft and react less.

Daily rowing and paddling was increasing his strength in a way he never would achieve at the gym. Not that he was one of those guys who worked out to achieve a certain look or results. He went to keep himself in shape, that was all.

He was getting used to the lifestyle. The long, hot days on the river. The hotter nights with his woman. Fisher was his woman. She'd made that clear when she kept kissing him in front of Cody. And it hadn't felt like she was putting on a show. She liked kissing him. She was enjoying their mutual sexual exploration at least as much as he was.

The woman couldn't get enough. And he was perfectly fine with that. Even if she was feeling him up on the side of the river. Her arm snaked up his left thigh, the weight of it heavy yet smooth.

"Kyle. Don't. Move." Fisher sounded too far away to be touching him.

He started to sit up, but there was something in her voice that kept him still. "Just freeze."

He opened his eyes and saw Fisher standing a few feet away. It wasn't seduction in her voice, more like panic. And if she was over there, who or what was crawling up his leg?

He glanced down.

Oh shit. A snake. Wasn't there a kind of snake that looked just like a rattlesnake? But wasn't poisonous? He closed his eyes again, his heart hammering, his muscles frozen in fear. Slowly he opened one eye. Yeah. There was the unmistakable diamond pattern. The heavy triangular-shaped head. If he looked at the tail, he was sure he'd see the rattles.

His shorts gaped open, making a nice safe place for the snake to hide. Safe, from the snake's point of view. But that was the last place Kyle wanted to get bit.

He tried to think of a scenario where that wouldn't happen. He knew any sudden movements would startle the snake and make it strike. But he couldn't just sit there and watch it continue to slither up his leg toward his crotch.

After what felt like an eternity but was probably less than a minute, Fisher stepped forward. She had a paddle in one hand, and a determined look on her face. Was she going to try to stun the snake by hitting it with the paddle?

No. She had a different plan. Somehow she managed to hook the T-shaped grip of the handle under the snake, several inches from its head, and grabbed the tail end at the same time. With one quick movement, she lifted the snake in the air and away from him. Then, with a jerk, she tossed the snake and the paddle into the river.

"Thanks." Kyle's voice sounded small. Weak. But at least he hadn't pissed himself.

"No problem." Fisher's voice didn't sound much stronger, but damn. What a woman.

"You didn't have to drown the poor thing." He tried to lighten the mood, but he was still shaking.

"Oh, they can swim." She dropped to her knees right next to him.

"They can?" He found the strength to crawl toward her. "Just when I was becoming comfortable on the river, now I have to watch for snakes swimming by."

"Yeah." She fell into his arms, trembling. "Did I forget to mention that in the orientation?"

Kyle wrapped his arms around her, holding her tight, helping them both relax.

"You saved my life."

"We would have made it to Prospector General, where they keep rattlesnake anti-venom on hand." She sounded nonchalant, but he could hear the fear in her voice. Feel it in her body.

"Well, you saved me from a lot of pain, especially where the damn thing was headed."

By then the others had gathered around.

"Was that a rattlesnake?" someone asked.

"Yeah. Big sucker, too," someone else answered.

"Damn, Fisher! You've got a set of stones!" one of the guys shouted. "I mean… That was pretty fucking brave!"

They were all talking about it. Kyle would bet that by the time they got off the river, the size of the snake would double in the stories. "You are pretty amazing," he whispered to her as he helped her to stand.

"Dude." It was Tyler. "What was going through your head when that snake was crawling up your leg?'

"No worries. Fisher's got this." He wasn't about to admit that he was praying for bladder control, among other things.

Laughter rang out.

"And Fisher? How did you manage to keep so calm?" Leia asked. "I mean, I would have been freaking out if I saw a snake on my boyfriend. Or even near him."

"I only freak out over hitchhiking girls in bikinis." Fisher laughed with them.

"I'm never going to live that down, am I?" He joined in the levity. "If I didn't know better, I'd think you planted that snake to teach me a lesson."

She glared at him, hands on her hips, but a smile cracked her lips. They both knew she'd forgiven him yesterday. Forgiven him right there on the repair table of the boat barn.

The group started to break up. There was still some cleanup left over from lunch. No one expected him or Fisher to help. Not this time.

"You okay?" He wrapped his arms back around her and could feel her trembling had mostly subsided.

"I was so scared," she admitted. "I just reacted."

"I'm glad you did. You have great instincts, by the way."

"Well, I'm not going to let anyone, human or reptile, get into my man's pants." Her laugh sounded a little more genuine.

"I am your man." He breathed her in. Her hair smelled like sunshine, the river, and everything he now held dear.

"Were you afraid?" She looked up at him with concern in her blue eyes.

"Terrified. But you're my hero. You know that?"

"I was terrified, too."

"Yeah. But that didn't stop you." He kissed her gently. "You're the bravest woman I know. The bravest person."

She was brave on and around the river. He'd seen her become more confident in the bedroom as well. Her inhibitions were shed as quickly as her clothes.

But Kyle wondered if she would be as fearless when it came to trusting him. Especially when she found out the other reason he was here.

Chapter 15

By the time they had finished the lower stretch of the river, word had spread about the snake. Fisher had become a legend. She had a feeling she'd never have to buy another beer in this town again.

Everyone was calling her brave. Quick thinking. Heroic.

She felt like the biggest coward around.

And if her legs hadn't been weakened by the adrenaline letdown, she would have run. Diving into the river after the snake.

They'd only known each other a few days. Nights, really. But just because the sex was so incredible, amazing, and otherworldly, it didn't mean she was in love with him. She couldn't be.

Besides, she just got a taste of sowing her wild oats. She wasn't ready for a trip downtown to Beverly's Bridal. She shuddered just to think about it.

After a quick shower and change of clothes, she met Kyle and the others in the parking lot. They piled in the van and Aubrey offered to drive them all into town for pizza at Mario's.

The back room had been reserved for their large group. The twelve students, three instructors, plus most of the guides on staff and Cody, Carson, and their families would fill up the party room. The big-screen TVs were tuned to the Giants game, and salad plates, pitchers of water, and extra shakers of parmesan and red pepper were placed on all the tables. Soon pitchers of beer were passed around, and breadsticks were brought out.

Kyle poured her a Strong Blonde, and her heart did a funny little flip. If she felt this way in a month, or three months, would she call it love?

"To my hero. My strong blonde." He raised a glass, admiration shining in his eyes. He looked like he wanted to say more, but held back.

She took a long, well-earned sip of her beer. It felt good going down. Some of the shakiness in her legs finally started to ease. Kyle's hand rested on her thigh. It felt good to have him there. Especially not in the emergency room.

Did the fact that her stomach clenched just thinking about how different the day could have turned out mean that her feelings were deeper than she wanted to admit?

Just as she was starting to relax, she felt Kyle's hand stiffen. She looked up to see Cody, Miranda, and the babies come through the door. Carson and Lily followed with baby Brandon.

Fisher wished she'd never disclosed her crush on Cody, especially now that she knew he was Kyle's brother. But that was water under the bridge. Along with her paddle and hopefully the long-gone snake.

She leaned over and kissed his neck. He shivered, almost purring. It was on the tip of her tongue to whisper her feelings. Just to reassure him that the only thing he needed to worry about Cody was what to get his brother for Christmas.

Cody's face lit up and he led his family over to their table.

"Fisher, I heard about what you did today." He beamed at her. "I can't say I'm surprised."

She couldn't keep from blushing at the attention, but it wasn't because it was from Cody.

"You're one lucky man." Cody gave Kyle a nod in that way guys do.

"I know." Kyle put his arm around Fisher, claiming her. She'd never understood how a guy being possessive with his woman was considered sexy or even desirable. And a part of her wanted to stand up and tell these two to just go outside, throw a few punches, shake hands, and call it a day.

Yet, there was a part of her, somewhere deep and primal, that made her feel protected. Connected in a way she'd never felt before. She found herself leaning into Kyle's embrace. Accepting his claim on her, publicly.

Miranda stood on her tiptoes and whispered something in Cody's ear. "I guess I'd better go buy the next round."

He set the double stroller at the end of the table and went off toward the bar. Miranda slid into the chair across the table from Fisher and dug through the diaper bag for a couple of toys to distract the babies with.

Within seconds, one of the toys went flying across the table and landed in Kyle's beer, splashing the contents onto the table.

"Oh, I'm so sorry." Miranda stood up, grabbing a handful of napkins to mop up the mess. While her sister laughed, the baby without the toy burst into tears.

"Here, let me." Kyle reached for the little one, picking her up and instantly stopping the tears. "Which one is this?"

"That would be Ava. She's got a little too much of her father in her."

Miranda let out an exasperated sigh. "Here, I'll take her."

"I've got her." Kyle bounced the child up and down and she curled up against him, contentedly shoving her chubby little fist into her mouth.

"You two are quite the couple." Miranda sat down, pouring half a beer into an empty glass. "A snake charmer and a baby whisperer."

Fisher looked over at Kyle and his…his niece. She felt a slight sting in her eyes and she quickly grabbed her beer to soothe the accompanying ache in her throat. She was simply noticing what a good uncle he would become. Uncle. Nothing more.

Miranda caught her eye and smiled. Of course, she would be happy that Fisher had found someone to distract her from Cody. But there was something more. A genuine warmth that made Fisher feel like the worst person ever for every moment she'd spent longing for the other woman's husband. And that included the years before they'd even met.

Leaning over the table, Miranda mouthed, "You've got yourself a good one." And her smile widened.

The pizza arrived, several varieties set on each table. Extra plates were brought out, and the hungry guides and students reached for their favorite slices.

"Uh, I think she's asleep." Kyle stood with Ava on his shoulder, gently swaying and rubbing her back. "What should I do?"

"I'll get her." Miranda stood and went over to collect her offspring. "Wow, she looks so peaceful."

"Is this unusual?" He looked like he was afraid to move, afraid to break the spell.

"Usually, she's only happy when her daddy has her." Miranda laughed. "Or when she's eating."

Fisher couldn't watch any longer. It was all too much. She didn't want to start picturing Kyle holding their baby, but the image tried to push its way into her imagination. Air. She needed air.

"Excuse me." She shoved back from the table. And marched into the main area of the restaurant. Running directly into Cody, who held a pitcher in each hand.

"Whoa, slow down. Someone need help with snake removal?"

"Shut up." She was so not in the mood. Or maybe she was. She kind of missed her friend. And yeah, it was the sparring and the razzing and the giving each other shit that she'd had to give up when Miranda came along.

He really was like the brother she never had.

"There's my girl."

"I've never been your girl." But it didn't bother her the way it used to.

"You've always been my friend."

"Yeah. Friends."

"You seem different." He set the pitchers on a nearby table. "Happy. I'm glad."

"Really?" She wasn't going to let him off so easily.

"Look, I admit, I didn't think the guy was good enough for you. Maybe he isn't, but he does make you glow."

"Glow?"

"Yeah. You glow. And I'm glad."

"I thought you didn't like Kyle."

Cody dropped his head. "You know no one will be good enough for you."

"Just stop. Right there." Before her knee connected with his groin. She had no idea if his wife was interested in more children or not.

"Sorry. It's just that it's been hard to lose my best friend. Simply because I fell in love." He sounded so sincere. "Seriously, Fisher, I've missed you. I've missed my buddy."

"You have Miranda."

"Yes. And she's the best thing that's ever happened to me." The love he felt for his wife shone in his eyes. In his voice. "Her and my daughters. But you're still important. I want to make sure you're okay."

"I'm good." Fisher picked up one of the beer pitchers and nodded toward the back room. "I'm real good."

"I'm very happy to hear that." He grabbed the other pitcher and indicated that she should go first. "So are you in love?"

Fisher stopped short, barely avoiding to spill her full pitcher. "We just met. It's way too soon to even ponder that question."

"I fell in love with Miranda almost instantly," Cody reminded her. "And I was stupid enough to let her walk away the first time. I mean, who falls in love with someone in a week? And if it weren't for the babies, she might not have given me a second chance."

"I'm glad everything worked out for you." What else could she say?

"I just hope things work out for you, too." He sounded like he truly meant it. "I hope Kyle's smarter than I was. That he realizes what he has with you."

"You should try to get to know him." Fisher wanted them to become close. They were brothers.

"I guess. It just seems like he's hiding something."

"Says the guy who pretended to be his twin when he met his wife."

"Yeah, I'm lucky she forgave me."

"You're very lucky." Cody had fought with Carson; then he took his place on the Yampa River, where he'd met Miranda. When she showed up more than a month later, to tell Carson he was going to be a father, Cody had had to convince her that he'd been the man she'd encountered. The man who would make her fall in love with him.

"I was a dog."

"No, you were a snake."

"Speaking of snakes, I can't believe you caught a rattler. With your bare hands."

"I didn't catch it. It's more like I threw it in the river with my paddle. Which we'll need to order a replacement for."

"I'd take it out of your pay, but you're probably going to ask for a raise for adding snake removal to your job description, aren't you?"

"Hey, I was just trying to save on workers' comp costs."

"That's my girl."

"No, Cody, I'm not your girl." She sighed. There was a time when that was what she wanted most. "I'm your river operations manager."

"Yes. But you were my friend first," he reminded her. "You'll always be my friend."

"As long as our friendship doesn't get in the way of the job." Or his relationship with Miranda. She'd rather take a corporate job than threaten their marriage.

"That's what makes Swift River Adventures so special. We're not just a company…"

"We're family."

Yeah. And she had to help Kyle become included in that family.

* * * *

Kyle reached for his second slice of pizza, but he noticed Miranda had barely touched her first. One of the babies was sleeping, but the other was fussy. And her father was still getting beer.

"Let me try." Kyle offered to take Addy from Miranda. "So you can eat."

"Thanks. I don't know what's taking Cody so long."

He was bouncing the baby happily when Fisher walked in followed closely by Cody. The tension in his posture must have shown because Miranda slid over two seats to talk to him.

"I know it looks like they have a special bond." She kept her voice low, so that only he could hear. "They do, but it's not the kind you think."

"So, you're saying they're like brother and sister?" He tried not to get too agitated and disturb the baby.

"Not exactly." She put her hand gently on his shoulder, and he just hoped it wouldn't give Cody another reason to be suspicious of him. "I worried when I first saw the two of them together. But I completely trust my husband."

"Great."

"And I trust Fisher, too." Must be nice to be blissfully ignorant. "She doesn't look at him the way she used to."

Okay, so maybe she wasn't totally naïve.

"But she never looked at him the way she looks at you."

He wanted to believe her, but he'd heard from Fisher's own mouth that she was in love with Cody. Sure, she'd been sleeping with him, but her heart belonged to someone else. It didn't matter as much when they were just having sex. When all he wanted was her body. But now?

He was a fool to think he could change her mind. Change her heart.

The baby let out a loud giggle and both Fisher and Cody turned to the sound.

Cody looked suspicious, but Fisher… No one had ever looked at him the way Fisher looked at him right now.

He barely even noticed when Miranda lifted the baby from his arms. Because Fisher was walking toward him. The woman had taken on a snake. For him.

Could he trust her? Her words, just minutes after meeting him, told him she was emotionally unavailable. But her actions had told a completely different story.

His whole life, he'd been told lies.

Dear old Dad had made so many promises. And his mother had told Kyle time and again that this time she believed in him. That this time would be different.

Women had said what they'd thought he'd wanted to hear. Told him he was the only man in the world for them. Until he wasn't.

Fisher had told him she wanted someone else. Yet she'd given her body to him. And in those moments behind closed doors, when it was just the two of them, with no words to exchange, he'd swear she was his, 100 percent.

Then there was her reaction to his picking up the girl in the bikini. If she didn't care about him, she wouldn't have been bothered by it.

"Hey." She set the pitcher on the table and wrapped her arms around him. "Having a good time?"

"Yeah. You?"

"Sure, but you really should talk to Cody. And Carson. Get to know them."

"I've been hanging with some pretty ladies." He smiled at his nieces, who were both sleeping now.

"Really?" She glanced over at Miranda, who was flirting with her husband, popping a slice of pepperoni into his mouth and laughing at something he said.

"I don't think he's interested in any male bonding right now." Kyle leaned back in the chair. He reached for his beer, hoping he'd look relaxed. Like a guy who wasn't once again jealous of the brother he barely knew.

Cody's relationship with Fisher was only part of it. Cody had it all. A thriving business, wife, kids. Except for the business, Kyle had never even considered those other things.

All he'd ever wanted was to make money. Enough to support himself, his mother, and keep her from ever having to rely on Joe Swift. He had enough, more than enough. Bought her a nice little house and set aside enough for property taxes and upkeep on the place. But Joe still came around far too often.

Kyle had his own condo, not on, but near the beach. He'd bought it at the bottom of the market and the equity was steadily climbing. He had enough investments that he didn't have to hustle for each new job. Yet the hustle was all he'd ever known. Going back to when he had to mow just another lawn in order to keep the electricity on, there had always been this deep-seated fear that he'd never make enough money. The wolf would always be at his door.

The funny thing was, he had enough set aside that he could buy Swift River Adventure Company and Resort without using his boss's cash. Yet, he wasn't as happy as his brothers. He wasn't even as happy as the part-time guides who would need to supplement their incomes in the winter, as a lift operator, waitstaff, or a Christmas tree cutter.

Kyle gave Fisher's hand a squeeze. Was she happy? At the moment, she was the talk of the town. Everyone was telling the story of her heroics with the snake. Even people he'd never met, from other rafting outfitters, had come up and congratulated her. They'd stayed and shared stories. He overheard other tales of Fisher's bravery and skill. She was well liked, and well respected on the river.

It seemed like the only one who didn't know how great Fisher was, was Fisher.

He blamed Cody for that. Even if he hadn't meant to, his rejection had hurt her, undermined her confidence, and made her feel like she wasn't quite good enough.

Kyle had spent his whole life feeling that way. And he'd give anything he had to show Fisher that she was more than worthy. That she was the best person he knew. The best person any of them knew.

Chapter 16

After the snake incident, the rest of guide school was uneventful for Fisher. Nolan, Leia, and Dana had all accepted her job offers. Dana was local, but the other two had gone home to get their gear and make arrangements to be gone for the summer. They would return in time for Aubrey's wedding.

And of course, Kyle had taken the job. He'd moved his RV from the paid spot down by the river to the large parking lot behind the guides' house. He didn't have hookups, but then he didn't need them, since he mostly just slept there with Fisher. Slept and made love. They showered at the house, had breakfast and coffee with the other guides.

Life was good. Work picked up with more kids getting out of school, more people taking vacations and making weekend plans. Sometimes Kyle worked the same trip as her; sometimes he worked with Tyler or Ross or Brooke or Jake.

Neither of them had talked about their feelings. But he'd treated her with tenderness, respect, and passion. The man obviously cared about her, but the whole idea of falling in love just seemed so out of reach. Something that happened to other women, not her. Women who were petite and curvy and feminine.

Yet Kyle made her feel like she was beautiful. From that first night, he'd made her feel like someone worthy of being worshipped for her body. He looked at her with smoldering eyes, and a hunger she'd only dreamed of.

Before she met Kyle, she'd longed to be simply desired. Wanted as a woman, and not just a cool chick who was fun to hang around with.

Fisher had just gotten out of the shower after a long run on the lower stretch. There'd been a group ahead of them who had nearly flipped at Satan's Cesspool. They'd lost all their passengers, their guide, and their paddles. Fisher had come up behind them and with her passengers, she'd been able to help them round everyone back into the raft, and they'd even managed to collect most of their gear.

At least her passengers had been cool about the delay. They were from the Bay Area and were staying in Prospector Springs for the weekend.

Kyle must have been stuck behind them, because he was coming in as she was heading downstairs.

"Hey, looks like you already had your shower. I was hoping we could save water and shower together." His sexy smile made her feel like she did need another shower. A cold one. "But maybe we could order some takeout, take it back to my RV."

"That sounds nice, but I'm heading out for Aubrey's bachelorette party."

"Oh, right. That's tonight." His voice dripped with disappointment.

"I shouldn't be too late." Since Aubrey was pregnant, it wasn't going to be too wild.

She'd suggest he hang out with Cody or Carson, but they would have the babies.

"Maybe I'll see if Tyler wants to go grab a beer or something." He shrugged, even though he seemed to get along with Tyler pretty well. He got along with most people. Especially the customers. They'd already had e-mail reviews just raving about him. Enough that Cody didn't dare question her decision to hire him.

"Well, have fun, then." She gave him a quick kiss on the cheek.

"You, too." He leaned in for a full-on kiss. Fisher melted into him. Reluctantly, she pulled away.

"I've gotta go." She smoothed her hair and realized she'd forgotten to dry it. They were just going to Lily's house. They'd swap stories, have some wine or virgin mojitos. They would each bring something naughty and something nice for a gift. Fisher knew Beverly's sold lingerie, but she couldn't bring herself to step inside the bridal shop, so she'd made the trek to Roseville to the Victoria's Secret in the mall. She got a see-through nightie and a cute little cotton robe that was feminine yet comfortable. She also found the cutest little pair of Teva sandals that she couldn't resist buying for the baby.

"Let me know if you need to sleep over."

"I'm sure that won't be necessary." She couldn't help but feel loved by his concern. "You're the one who needs to watch out for those strong blondes. I know how much you like them."

"There's only one blonde I'm crazy about."

"I'm talking about the beer."

"I like the beer, and I'll pace myself." He ran his hand up and down her arm, making her tingle all over. "But you know I can't get enough of the woman."

"Careful, we might need to put you into a program," she teased, but he didn't seem to find it funny. He stiffened immediately. "Are you okay?"

"Yeah." He shook his head, as if whatever thought he had could be easily dismissed. "It's just that my parents met in a program. Not booze, but drugs."

"Oh, Kyle, I'm sorry. I shouldn't have joked about it."

"It's okay. You didn't know." He ran a hand through his hair. "Hell, I didn't even know until I was an adult. My mom was able to stay clean, just the occasional drink."

"And your dad?"

"Yeah, and my dad. She can't seem to shake that addiction." The bitterness in his voice was heart wrenching.

"No, I mean, was your dad able to get clean?"

"He had a couple of relapses over the years." He let out a heavy sigh. "But I think he's hanging in there lately."

"Do they have any idea?" She didn't really have to ask. Cody and Carson had very little contact with their father. None, since she'd known them.

"Who?"

"Your brothers." She was still frustrated that, although they had all gotten along, they hadn't become close. And Kyle still hadn't told them who he was.

"They don't give a damn."

"How would you know? Have you asked them? I'm pretty sure they don't even know about you. So how can they care about family they don't even know they have?"

"They know they have a father." He couldn't hide the bitterness. Was it for his brothers, father, or all of the above?

"Yeah, but I'm pretty sure they have no idea he had issues with drugs. And they have no idea that he remarried."

"He never married my mother." Kyle's voice was tight. Tense.

"Well, I'm sorry to hear that." She fisted her hands on her hips. She'd held her tongue because she didn't want to cause problems. She didn't want him to decide she wasn't worth the trouble.

"Look, I don't really want to talk about this right now."

"Yeah, well, I have to go anyway." She didn't want to fight with him, but damn it. She cared about him. About all of them. And they were family.

"Drive safe." He offered up his sexy, sweet smile, probably hoping she'd drop the issue. And she would. For now. Because if he went to the Argo, there would be plenty of women who would have a hard time resisting that smile. Women who wouldn't care about his issues with his family.

"You too." She headed out to her Jeep, hoping Brooke wouldn't be too long. Fisher had almost forgotten that she'd offered to drive. Well, at least it would take her mind off her frustration with Kyle and his inability to connect with his brothers. She'd thought for sure they'd be as close as the twins were with each other by now, or at least acknowledge their kinship.

As mad as she was at Kyle for not coming clean, she was even more angry at herself for not speaking up before now. She'd known for almost two weeks, and while it wasn't her secret to tell, she hated keeping it.

* * * *

Kyle was ready for a beer. Tyler had jumped on the chance to go out without the women. They'd invited the other guys and most were game. It was Friday night, after all. The Argo would be hopping. It had been three weeks since he'd met Fisher at that very bar.

Three weeks since she'd cast some sort of spell on him.

He'd been avoiding his boss's e-mails. Sure, he'd given the excuse of poor cell coverage, but they had wireless at the guides' house. He could get on the Internet if he wanted to. He just hadn't wanted to.

The deal that seemed like a dream come true—a way to make a ton of money and get back at his brothers at the same time—was no longer so attractive. For one thing, he had quickly discovered that the company was solid. The only reason they would have to give it up would be for the ridiculous amount of money he'd been prepared to offer. But he'd since learned that they weren't as motivated by money as he'd anticipated. Sure, they needed security, to support their family and pay their employees. They weren't into making money just for the sake of money.

He'd learned that some companies were more interested in making a profit, but at Swift River Adventures, they were also about the experience. About taking in all that the river had to offer. He'd taken it in. And been able to share it with his guests. He no longer thought of them as customers, or even passengers. He made sure to include them as much as possible in making sure their trip was memorable and exciting.

And the tips had been pretty damn good.

He could get used to this life. Working his muscles on the river all day, and snuggling up to his woman at night.

Oh, he knew she wouldn't be satisfied to sleep in a camper forever. Even if it was nicer than most of the homes he'd lived in growing up. But Fisher deserved more.

She definitely deserved better than to have the company she worked for bought out from under her. Oh, part of the negotiations would include a promise to keep the existing staff, but when the business was resold, that promise wouldn't be transferred.

He'd have to figure out how to block the sale.

The Argo was packed. They ordered a couple of pitchers and settled against the bar to wait for a couple of tables to clear.

"Well, look who walked in with a girl on each arm," the bartender called out to a newcomer. Cody. "They're a little younger than you used to bring in."

"Hey, these are my daughters." Cody did indeed have one girl in each hand. They were in those car seat carrier things. He set them each on a bar stool and ordered a beer for himself and one for Carson, who followed closely with his own infant.

"I never would have thought I'd see the day. The Swift brothers all settled down." He shook his head as he poured a couple of pints.

"We're not that settled." Cody acted cool, but when he looked down at his daughters, it was obvious that he was pretty much domesticated. "We are out on the town without our women."

"I heard about Aubrey getting married. Tell her congratulations from all of us here." He offered a sincere smile and then reached behind the bar. "And when you see Fisher, I think these are her sunglasses. She left them here a few weeks back."

"Sure. But I'm sure Kyle will see her before I do." Cody nodded in Kyle's direction.

The bartender looked over at him, smiled as if he recognized him from the other night, and handed over the sunglasses.

"Thanks." Kyle pocketed the mirrored aviators. "I'll make sure she gets these back."

Cody eyed him, not as suspiciously as he used to. Maybe the other man had finally accepted him as Fisher's lover. But as much as Fisher would wish it, they would never be friends.

Kyle couldn't stand how Cody had hurt Fisher. Yeah, he cared about her, but that didn't keep him from hurting her with his ambiguous affection. While Cody might not realize it, he was still sending her mixed signals. So Kyle could never truly trust the guy.

Then again, Cody did have reason not to trust Kyle. He might attribute it to Fisher, but Kyle was here to take something from him. It wasn't his manager, though. It was the whole damn company. Or it had been. And maybe if it was just Cody who would be screwed over if the deal went through...

No. Because it was never that simple. There was always collateral damage to any business acquisition. Kyle had just chosen to ignore it. To convince himself that if the prior owners had done a better job, if they hadn't let themselves get into trouble in the first place, then they wouldn't have lost.

But if he truly believed that, then that would mean that he'd deserved to have been abandoned by his father. That if his mother had somehow made better choices, then she would have deserved something better than his worthless piece of shit of a father.

One of the babies started to fuss. Kyle was closest, so he made a funny face, and the little girl broke into a precious giggle.

"Hey, thanks." Cody put a hand on his shoulder. "She likes you."

Cody leaned over and lifted his daughter out of the baby seat. He made goofy sounds and dropped kisses on the child, and Kyle had to look away.

She didn't deserve anything other than a loving family. Shit might happen to her and her sister along the way, but the only thing she deserved was to be loved.

It was all any of them deserved.

So why was it so damned hard to accept?

Kyle grabbed his beer and leaned against the bar where he'd met Fisher. Even then, she had told him that she didn't believe she deserved to be loved. But why?

Because she'd been rejected by a guy who saw her as nothing more than a friend? Because she was different than the girls she grew up with? So she was taller than most women, and quite a few men. She was stronger and smarter than most people. That didn't make her any less desirable to him.

And still she refused to acknowledge that they had something more than just sex. Maybe the upcoming wedding would change her mind. Maybe sharing in her friend's happiness, surrounded by love, she might start thinking about the possibilities.

She might even catch the bouquet.

Cody got the baby settled and turned to Kyle.

"Hey man, maybe I was too quick to judge you." Whoa, where did that come from?

Kyle just shrugged.

"I mean, if all the women in my life have taken to you, you must be a pretty good guy."

"All the women in your life?"

"Fisher, of course." Cody leaned against the bar next to him. "But Miranda likes you, Ava—well, Ava has never met a stranger—and she adores you. But now Addy has given her stamp of approval."

"More like a drool of approval." Kyle pointed to the wet spot on his shoulder.

Cody extended his right hand. "What do you say we start over?"

"Sure." Kyle shook his hand, mostly because he knew it would please Fisher.

"Great." Cody grinned like all was right with his world now. "You know, I'm glad Fisher stuck with her guns and insisted on bringing you on board."

"Really?"

"Apparently you're a big hit with your passengers." Cody sounded reluctantly pleased. "Miranda can't keep up with the rave reviews."

"Miranda?"

"Yeah, she's taken over our website." He beamed with pride. "She's a writer, you know. Her first book comes out in a couple of months."

"I think Fisher may have mentioned something about that." Had she? Didn't matter. Fisher didn't say much about Cody's wife, other than admit she liked the woman.

"I'm real proud of her." Cody continued to puff up with pride. But why not, the guy did have everything. "And I'm proud of Fisher, too."

Kyle's jaw twitched, but he didn't say anything.

"She's a good manager." Cody didn't seem to notice that Kyle was only tolerating him for Fisher's sake. "A good manager, and a damn fine woman."

"Yes. She is." Too bad it took her finding someone else for Cody to realize it.

"I don't want to see her get hurt." Cody leaned a little too close into his space.

"I don't want to see her get hurt, either." Apparently Cody had been blind. Because he'd been the one to hurt her the most.

"Just as long as we're clear."

"You're not her brother, you know. You're not her protector. And you know what? She doesn't need one. Fisher is a damn fine manager. She's smart, tough, and fair. She doesn't need anyone looking out for her." Kyle had had enough. He pounded the rest of his beer. "Believe me, if I screw things up with Fisher, the only person I'd have to worry about would be Fisher."

The hostess came in and announced that their tables were ready. Kyle made sure to sit as far away from Cody as he could. He was supposed to be out having a good time tonight. Tomorrow would be another long day, and then the wedding was Sunday evening.

He'd need to have something for his boss on Monday. Even if it was a report on why he couldn't come through for the first time since he'd been fifteen.

Chapter 17

Most weekends were busy on the South Fork in the summer. Fridays, Saturdays, and Sundays were when they did the majority of their business. Mondays, Tuesdays, and Wednesdays were usually slow days, where the guides would get a day or two off. Thursdays were hit or miss. Sometimes they'd have big crowds, usually some kind of corporate event—leadership retreat, team-building excursions, or entertaining clients in hopes of gaining their trust and their business.

This weekend was busier than usual. Sunday, especially, when they had to get off the river by four so they could get everything put away and ready in time for Aubrey's six o'clock wedding.

This would be the third wedding held at Swift River Resort. First Carson and Lily, then Cody and Miranda. Now they were rolling out the aisle runner so that Aubrey could say good-bye to her old life and celebrate her new one.

Fisher tried to think of a life anywhere else. She couldn't do it. Oh, she knew this wasn't what her parents had wanted. But then again, her parents had wanted so much more than they were given.

She brushed the thought away. No time to dwell on things that couldn't be helped. Not when she had to rush back upstairs to get a quick shower and put on that party dress. She wasn't a bridesmaid, so there was no satin or lace to contend with. Aubrey's sister was the only bridesmaid and her fiancé's fraternity brother was the best man.

Fisher showered, dressed, and put on makeup. Well, she put on lip gloss and a little eyeliner. She even blew her hair dry and instead of one big, thick braid, she twisted two tiny braids that joined together in the back, like a princess or something.

Brooke was a little more dressed up. She'd actually curled her hair and added mascara and blush. Once again, Fisher felt like she was failing at this being female thing.

Then she descended into the living room. Kyle had been sitting on one of the sofas but when he saw her he rose to his feet, a look of sheer wonder on his face.

"You look amazing." He smiled and took a step toward her. Fisher had to force herself not to turn around to see if he was speaking to Brooke, only a few steps behind her.

Kyle was the one who looked amazing. He wore black dress slacks, a silk tie, and a blue button-up shirt that wasn't quick drying, packable, with an SPF of fifty. He looked like a movie star. That one guy, in that one movie, whom all the girls were swooning over. His hair was combed and he'd shaved. The man was sexy as hell.

And he was walking toward her.

Fisher's heart raced, her legs felt weak, and she couldn't breathe. This would be the first wedding she'd ever attended with a date. She'd spent Carson and Lily's wedding flirting with Cody, wondering how she could let him know she'd wanted more than friendship. She'd endured Cody and Miranda's wedding, trying to keep her heart from breaking wide open. Now she would sit next to a man who had come into her life at a time when she'd needed him most.

"Are you ready?" He extended his hand and she took it. Hopefully he wouldn't notice that she was trembling.

"Yeah." She wasn't sure why she was so nervous. It was just a date. It wasn't like everyone didn't already know they were together. It was just that they'd never been on a *date* date. Where there would be dancing. Champagne. Flowers. All things romantic.

She wasn't ready for this. She wasn't ready to put their relationship in the spotlight. To have people watching while he whispered in her ear or pulled her close while they danced. And she certainly wasn't ready to have him hold her hand while the minister spoke of love and marriage and commitment.

Fisher was glad she wore flat sandals. Heels would put her as tall as Kyle, but they would also make her feel even more unsteady.

Then he placed a soft, sweet kiss on her neck, just below her ear, and she knew she was in good hands. She could relax and enjoy herself.

They waited until everyone was gathered in the living room. Twenty minutes until the wedding would begin. Someone stepped into the kitchen and returned with a bottle of champagne. The cork was popped and the bottle passed around. Each of them raised the bottle and offered a toast to their friend and now former guide. After taking a sip straight from the bottle, they each passed it on.

By the time it got to Fisher, the bottle was half-empty.

"To Aubrey. May she live happily ever after." She took a swig and then handed it to Kyle.

"Cheers." He kept his toast simple before pressing the champagne to his lips.

There was still enough champagne left that it took a second pass through everyone. With a bubbly, giddy feeling, they marched toward the meadow where the ceremony would take place.

Kyle put his arm around her waist, guiding her and claiming her at the same time. She melted into his touch, deciding she would relax and enjoy the moment. Enjoy the evening with her man at her side. She would celebrate with her friends. Send one of their own off on the next adventure. And try not to think about anything beyond tonight.

Soft guitar music welcomed guests to find their seats. Kyle chose a spot near the middle. Not too close, but not all the way in the back. She sat, smoothing the skirt of her sundress over her knees.

After sitting next to her, Kyle reached over and twined his fingers in hers.

Fisher didn't want to get too emotional, but by the time they got to the exchanging of the rings, the reciting of vows, and the kiss, her eyes were damp. She couldn't look at Kyle. Didn't want him to think she was getting any ideas.

As the happy couple walked past them, with looks of sheer joy on their faces, Kyle gave her hand a reassuring squeeze.

When the music ended, the bride and groom kept walking toward the river, where they would take some pictures. The guides started moving chairs and setting up tables. By the time the couple returned, the caterers had set up the dinner buffet and the bar was already doing a brisk business.

Kyle brought Fisher a beer and they looked for a table. Carson and Lily, Cody and Miranda, and all the babies had a table nearby. The diaper bags, strollers, and baby paraphernalia took up a lot of space, so there wasn't much room for others to join them. As much as she would like to have Kyle spend more time with his brothers and sisters-in-law, she didn't want him to think she wanted to be close to Cody.

They ended up sitting with Brooke and Tyler, Ross, Gavin, Jake, Dana, Leia, and Nolan.

The food was fabulous. Once again, the Argo had been convinced to serve as caterers. Fisher wondered if they would be interested in partnering with Swift River to do some special events. Maybe a craft beer and food pairing trip, or package deals for bachelor and bachelorette parties.

She wondered if they would start renting out the resort for weddings.

So far, they'd all been for their own. They'd also been put together fairly quickly. And each of the brides had been pregnant.

Maybe they wouldn't want to put that in the brochure.

Fisher caught Kyle staring at her. Damn, that was one sexy man. Who was hers for the summer. She wouldn't think about anything beyond that. She'd just appreciate what she had for the moment.

And she'd just have to trust that her birth control method was as reliable as her doctor had promised.

* * * *

The wedding had gone off without a hitch. Or rather, the couple had gotten hitched and the reception was under way. They had just finished dinner and it was time for the toast and cake cutting.

The bride and groom had their first dance, and then all the guests were invited to join in.

Kyle took Fisher into his arms and whisked her onto the dance floor.

"Are you having a good time?" He pulled her against him, loving the feel of her body next to his.

"Yes." She leaned her head against his chest. "Are you?"

"Absolutely." She fit just right in his arms. He wasn't going to worry about how he would fit into her life. Not tonight.

Tonight they would dance. They would dance until she begged him to make love to her.

Or he begged her.

The band picked up the pace, and Kyle spun Fisher around the dance floor. But he never went too long without pulling her close. Pressing his body against hers. Reminding her how their bodies fit together. How they fit together.

They worked up quite a thirst, and finally the band took a quick break. Kyle wandered over to the bar to grab a couple of beers.

"Thanks." Fisher took the plastic cup from him and downed about a third before letting out a breath. "What a night."

She kicked off her shoes and leaned back against the white plastic chair.

He just sat there, admiring her. Wanting her. And he'd was man enough to admit—at least to himself—loving her.

The band picked up their instruments, but he was content to sit out a song or two. Let them catch their breath a bit.

"Hey, Fisher." Lily approached with baby Brandon. "Would you mind holding him while I dance with my husband?"

Fisher's face drained of color. She gulped the rest of her beer.

"I…um…" She gave Kyle a desperate look. "I have to go to the bathroom."

She jumped up, knocking her chair over, and she made a mad dash toward the campground restrooms.

"I'll take him." Kyle held his hands up. "We're old friends."

"Thanks." Lily handed over her son and dragged her husband out on the dance floor.

Carson and Lily danced three or four songs; then Carson took Brandon while Lily wandered off to powder her nose or grab a drink or whatever.

"He give you any trouble?" Carson grinned at his baby boy.

"Nah." Kyle was more troubled by Fisher's reaction. And by the realization that in the time he'd known her, she hadn't held any of the babies. Her reluctance to pick up Cody's kids was somewhat understandable, considering her feelings for their daddy. But why would she freak out about picking up Carson's little boy? "Would you excuse me?"

He went to find her. Something didn't feel right about her reaction.

She wasn't by the bathrooms. He waited, but when no one else came out, he wandered on down toward the river. A few couples had stolen away, looking for privacy and romance beneath the rising moonlight.

A path twisted upriver, away from the crowd, and on a hunch, he followed it.

Sure enough, Fisher stood barefoot, skipping rocks into the water.

"Hey, there you are." He wasn't sure why, but he knew he had to be gentle with her.

She shivered, despite it being around eighty degrees out, and he pulled her into his arms.

"Mmmm," she purred, sliding her hand up his chest. "Let's get out of here. I'm ready for bed."

"Not yet." He took her hands in his and held them out to her side. "Talk to me first."

"What's to talk about?" She dropped his hands and turned away.

"I don't know, but I get the feeling it's important." Frustration welled inside him. He knew she was hurting. And he realized that it wasn't about Cody this time. Maybe it hadn't ever really been about him.

"I'm fine. Just, I don't know…" She turned and offered a weak smile. "I guess I sometimes feel weird in certain situations. You know, like when I'm wearing a dress."

She held her skirt out and shrugged her shoulders, but he knew there was more to it than that.

"You were fine until Lily asked you to hold the baby."

"So, I'm not a big baby person." Her shoulders stiffened. "I know women are supposed to have this instinct...."

No. There was something deeper than that.

"Look. I tried to tell you. I'm not like other girls. Women. I guess there's something wrong with me."

"There's nothing wrong with you." He reached up and brushed her hair off her face. She wasn't crying, but he thought maybe she wanted to.

"I've always been, you know, different. Odd."

"What? Because you're tall? Strong? Amazing? You think that makes you less of a woman?"

"I'm not feminine." She crossed her arms over her chest. Protecting herself.

"What the hell is that supposed to mean? Because you don't wear makeup or paint your nails, you don't think you're a real woman?"

She turned away from him.

A part of him wanted to pick her up, throw her over his shoulder, and carry her back to his RV and show her just how feminine and sexy and desirable he found her.

But another part, a part he never knew existed before her, wanted to get to the bottom of whatever pain she was suffering.

"Fisher. Why do you feel like you're not woman enough? I know I've never said anything or done anything to suggest that I see you as anything but the sexiest, loveliest, most desirable woman I've ever known. So it must come from somewhere else."

"My parents always wanted a boy. I knew that. My whole life, I knew that they missed out on having a son."

His heart ached for her.

"And they had a son. But something happened to him."

His heart froze. There was something in her voice. Something haunting. Tragic.

"I remember, but I don't." She took a step closer to the water's edge. He stood back, not knowing what would help. "I remember the excitement of a new baby coming. And I had to be careful when they brought him home. But..."

"But what happened?"

"I don't know." She stepped farther away from him. "They never talked about it. Sometimes I feel like I only dreamed I had a brother. And other times..."

Another step. He felt like he was losing her.

"I think maybe I did something." She turned, and for a minute he feared she would throw herself into the water. "Like, maybe I hurt the baby somehow. I remember wanting desperately to hold him."

She stepped into the water, and her shoulders relaxed a little. Right. The river was her happy place. The current was low, just barely swirling around her ankles.

"What if I dropped him? Or put a pillow over his face to stop him from crying?"

"What if it was just one of those things? You know, how sometimes babies just die and no one knows why?" Kyle stepped into the water. He didn't care if his dress shoes were ruined. He reached for her hand and she accepted.

"But why would they keep it from me?" She turned toward him now, with so much pain in her eyes.

"Maybe it's too painful. Maybe they didn't want to burden you with something they think you were too young to remember." He took her other hand in his. "Have you ever asked them about it?"

"Once. A long time ago." She withdrew, dropping his hands and looking away. "They denied it. I asked my mom what happened to my brother and she said I didn't have a brother. Then she said she had a headache and went to her room."

"Look, Fisher, sometimes people go through stuff, stuff that makes it hard for them to be good parents...." He was thinking of his mother and father. More so his father.

"That's why I'm never having kids." She crossed her arms, closing herself off even more. "I can't be trusted around babies."

"How old were you?"

"Four. I think. I know it was before I started school."

"Look, even if you did somehow hurt your baby brother, you were too little to know better."

She gave him a look of horror.

"Fisher. You would never hurt someone on purpose. Especially not a child. You're great with kids. Great with teenagers. Retirees. And everyone in between."

Why was he so determined to change her mind about ever having kids? He never really gave it much thought himself. But he figured if he ever did, he'd do it a lot differently than his dad.

"Not babies."

"You don't know that." He couldn't let this go. Couldn't let her think that she wasn't good enough. "Maybe if you tried, you know, with Brandon or the twins?"

"Like how you've tried with your brothers?"

He stepped back as if she'd slapped him, and he almost tripped over his own feet.

"Okay. You're right. I haven't tried to get too close to them. I guess I'm afraid. Worried I'm not good enough." He reached for her hands again. "My dad made sure I've never felt good enough."

"Oh, Kyle." Suddenly, her problem seemed to float away. She was the one comforting him, now. "You're the best man I know."

"What about Cody?" He didn't want the jealousy to surface, but there it was. Bubbling up.

"Maybe if he had a chance to know you better, he'd agree." She fisted her hands on her hips.

"You're right. I should give him a chance." Something loosened in his chest. "But it's damn hard when…you know?"

"What?" She sounded genuinely puzzled.

"Are you or are you not in love with him?"

"No." A small smile twisted her lips and he wanted to believe her. Wanted it more than almost anything.

"No?"

"I told you, he's like my brother."

"First you told me you were going to quit because of how you felt about him."

"I was, well, not exactly drunk, but just…frustrated." She looked down as if she was just now noticing that they were standing in the river. "I never should have said anything."

"I won't hold it against you." He led her toward the sandy bank. His shoes were ruined, but at least his girl seemed to be feeling better.

"I hope you'll hold something against me." She looked at him with heat. With hunger. The look she had on her face while they were dancing.

"What's that?" He tried to play innocent.

"You." She pressed against him, running her hands up his chest. He knew what she wanted. He just wondered if she'd ever want anything more.

Or was she like him? Convinced that she didn't deserve more. Were her childhood wounds so deep that she didn't think she could love and be loved? That shit about her brother—well, it made his problems seem so minor.

"Tell you what." He placed a kiss on her forehead. "I'll make love to you. You know I can't resist the sexiest woman on the planet."

"Oh, please!" She shoved him, obviously still not believing her worth.

"Keep begging, but I want you to do something for me."

"Okay." She eyed his zipper. "I know it was a disaster last time, but I'm willing to give it another shot."

"Good. I'd like you to be able to hold my nephew and nieces."

She jerked back. "What? I thought we were talking about…" She made a circle with her thumb and fingers and brought it toward her mouth, curving her lips into a wide O.

"You've convinced me that I need to put my issues behind me. I need to come clean with my brothers." He put his arm around her. "I guess I never realized how lucky I am to have brothers. And they're pretty decent guys. I mean, they were smart enough to hire you."

She leaned against him and sighed.

"So, what do you say we arrange a dinner? Maybe we could bring takeout to Cody's house or something. And I can come clean with them about how we're related. But I can't do it without you."

"Okay." She seemed to pick up on the fact that he wanted more than just her presence when he told them. "What else?"

"Maybe you could try to hold one of the babies?" He hoped he wasn't asking too much, too soon.

"Maybe." She sounded scared, yet willing to try. "But you'll have to work really hard tonight to convince me."

"How hard?"

"Well, if there are three babies..." She got a wicked look in her eyes. "I'm gonna need at least three, well, you know?"

Oh, he knew. He knew what she wanted from him. And he knew he'd give it to her. But he didn't know how to get her to want more.

Chapter 18

Since they both had the day off after the wedding, Kyle was hoping to sleep in. He'd done his best to satisfy his woman last night. And he'd more than risen to the challenge. Yet here it was, the sun barely up, and Fisher was snuggling up against him. Rubbing her hands up his back, over his chest. Down.

"Damn, woman, you're insatiable." He wasn't complaining, though. Far from it, as she now ran her tongue across his skin.

"Mmmm. I guess I'm just making up for lost time." Her lips were soft and warm on his skin. Her hands glided over his muscles, and her heated breath sent shivers up and down his spine.

"Do you think anyone noticed we didn't stay for the bouquet toss?" He groaned as she wrapped her hand around his throbbing erection.

"I don't care. This is more fun than some stupid tradition."

"Can't argue with you there." He stretched out on his back as she kicked off the sheets and climbed on top of him. His body was fully awake as she straddled his thighs. She was absolutely in charge and he loved every minute of it.

"I think this is even better than coffee." She moved ever so slowly, inching closer and closer. And he was powerless to stop her. Not that he wanted to. He never wanted to stop her from loving him with her body.

"You're so beautiful." He couldn't take his eyes off her. Every inch of her glorious body. "So strong and sexy and—"

She slid down on top of him, drawing him in and cutting off his words. His eyes rolled into the back of his head as she started to move. Slowly. Deliberately. Powerfully.

Primal sounds escaped his throat as she rode him. Higher and higher. Deeper and deeper. He could drown in this. This bliss. This ecstasy. This powerful emotion that he dare not name.

Fisher threw her head back with wild abandon. With her eyes closed, she let out a cry that shook him, almost into oblivion.

Kyle grabbed her hips, holding her as he thrust deeper, higher, closer. God, he couldn't get close enough. Not until she shattered around him. And shattered. And finally collapsed against him, breathless.

He could feel the aftershocks coursing through her. Still he held back. Was it possible to give her more?

Slowly, he began to move. Together, they rolled onto their sides. He reached down and stroked the place where they were joined. She shuddered. Oh, yeah. She wasn't finished. He withdrew and she whimpered.

"Remember, good things come in threes. That was one." He stroked her sensitive spot, slowly, wanting to build her back up. "That was just the first one."

"Are you trying to kill me?" She moaned, lifting her hips.

"No." He brought her closer yet again. "Just trying to love you."

She made a sound, a cross between a moan and a purr and something he'd never heard before. But she didn't move away from him, so he kept going.

"Please." She shuddered once again. "I need you."

He kept going.

"Inside me." The tension in her voice rose.

Still, he teased.

"NOW." Her demand shook the RV. He hoped it didn't wake the whole campground, but he couldn't worry about that at the moment. He had to fulfill her request. He was pretty sure his life depended on it.

Swiftly, he positioned himself over her. In one smooth motion, he entered her. He pumped. Once. Twice.

Oh sweet, sweet heaven.

The sounds that came out of her were unlike any he'd ever heard. And he'd done a damn fine job of pleasuring her over the last few weeks.

She shook beneath him. He trembled on top of her. Both of them lay there, utterly spent. Breathless. Shivering.

"I owe you one." He flailed his left arm out, reaching for the blanket. Grasping the edge, he pulled it over them. "And I'm good for it. Or I will be, if I can ever walk again."

She mumbled something unintelligible.

"Exactly." He pulled her limp, boneless body against his.

He liked to think it was her way of acknowledging the feelings growing between them. It wasn't just about sex. Sex had never been like this.

And he knew it would never be like this with anyone else.

He wanted to tell her he loved her. But she'd only begun to trust him. Last night's confession had been a huge step in their relationship. He knew he couldn't push her.

Besides, he had all summer.

He started to close his eyes. Maybe they'd fall back asleep. Then they could enjoy their day off any way they wanted. They wouldn't even have to get out of bed. He still had some energy bars and bottled water in the RV.

Life was indeed good. It was very good.

A loud banging on his door startled him.

"Kyle, I know you're in there." *Shit.* He knew that voice. "Since you won't answer your damn phone I had to come up here and drag your ass out of bed."

"Who in the world?" Fisher asked, the sleepy satisfaction gone from her voice.

"My boss." Kyle bolted upright. He reached over to the bedside drawer. He grabbed a pair of shorts.

"I thought I was your boss now." Fisher sat up, the sheet sliding off her.

"He's my former boss." He tossed her a T-shirt. "And he doesn't sound happy I'm not going back to work for him."

"Oh." Fisher slipped the shirt over her head.

"I'll get rid of him. And come back to bed." He yanked on the shorts and went to answer the door, closing the partition to the bedroom and bath behind him.

"Mr. Wilson, what a surprise." Kyle opened the door. "Would you like some coffee? It'll just take a few minutes to brew."

"I had my coffee hours ago." He did not sound pleased. "And how many times have I told you to call me JP? I'm not your high school principal."

"Yes, sir. Sorry, we were all up kind of late. There was a wedding here last night and this was my first day off in weeks." Kyle motioned for him to come inside.

"So you did forget you were sent here to do a job?" JP stepped into the RV, making the space seem too small. "I still expect you to make the deal."

"About that." Kyle wished he had a big strong mug of coffee. Hopefully he could get this over with soon and he could grab a cup for Fisher, too. "I don't think this is the deal you're looking for."

"I'm sorry, did you presume to tell me what it is that I want?" JP sat, leaning his elbows on the kitchen table. "Because I'm pretty sure I know what I want. I want this company."

"It won't work." Kyle continued to stand. "The owners won't sell. Trust me on that."

"They'll sell. You'll make sure of it." JP glared at him, his steely gray eyes boring into him. Waiting for Kyle to flinch.

"Look, I know I've never let you down before." Kyle had always closed the deal. "But this time, I'm absolutely certain they won't sell."

"You'll just have to find a way." JP's voice rose with impatience. "Sleep with someone. Do whatever it takes."

The door to the bedroom opened. Fisher appeared with a shocked and hurt look on her face. She didn't say a word as she slipped past him and out the door.

"I didn't realize you had company." JP watched her leave. Watched her a little too closely. "I can see now why you're so distracted from your job."

"She's not a distraction." Kyle felt like he'd been kicked in the chest. "And I think you should leave. We're done. With this job. With all of it."

"Oh no. We're not done here." JP blocked the door so Kyle couldn't run after Fisher. "Not by a long shot."

* * * *

Fisher knew she shouldn't have listened to Kyle's conversation with his boss. Not former, but current boss. And his job? Apparently it was to somehow buy Swift River Adventures. To make a deal by any means possible.

Including sleeping with her.

Damn. The man deserved an Oscar for his performance. She'd really believed that he cared about her. Maybe even loved her.

But no. It was all a lie.

He was here to screw over his brothers.

And her.

She ran toward her Jeep, needing to get as far away as possible from Kyle and the horrible man who sent him into her life. Into her heart.

"Whoa, where's the fire?" Cody tried to get out of her way, but he wasn't quick enough. She plowed right into him.

"Sorry. I just…" She looked down at her bare feet. She'd put on her dress from the night before, but she didn't have her shoes. Just her purse. And, thankfully, her keys.

"What did he do?" Cody placed a hand on her shoulder. "I'll kill him."

"No. He's not worth it." Fisher felt hollow.

"Hey, look. I know men can be stupid sometimes. But I can see that he cares for you. It's been obvious from the minute he got here."

"It's a lie." She somehow kept her voice from breaking. Too bad she couldn't say the same thing about her heart. "He's just trying to get on the inside so he can somehow buy you out."

"Like we'd ever sell." Cody laughed, but she didn't find anything about this situation amusing. "Especially not when things are going so well."

"His boss seems pretty determined." And rich. She could tell just by the clothes he wore. And the attitude. He had that attitude of someone who was used to getting what he wanted. Because he could buy anyone.

He'd obviously bought Kyle.

"You are determined. That's one of the reasons we gave you this promotion." Cody wasn't listening.

"Not me. His real boss. The guy in the suit." Fisher couldn't compete with that. "I'd bet he flew a Lear jet up from LA."

"Yeah, so?" Cody wouldn't be swayed by a lot of money or flash. "When we started this business, we still rode the rapids in old bucket boats. Some of them were more patches than raft. But we worked our way up. Eventually we bought a couple of self-bailers. And just this last year we were able to purchase more state-of-the-art equipment."

"Yeah. I know how hard you and Carson worked to get where you are." Her heart broke, mostly because Kyle was missing out on a relationship with two really great guys. "But he resents everything you have. It's personal."

"Whoa." Cody seemed shocked and maybe a little offended. "Just because he heard rumors that you used to have a little crush on me, that's no reason for him to resent me."

Fisher let out a heavy sigh. "First of all, it wasn't a rumor. I did have a crush on you. A big one. And I told Kyle all about it. The first night we met. But that doesn't have anything to do with why he wants to destroy you."

"What are you talking about?" Cody finally dropped his it's-all-good attitude.

"He's your brother." She still felt like she was betraying Kyle, but she couldn't keep his secret any longer.

"My brother?" Cody just stood there, looking at her like she was nuts. "You're joking, right?"

She shook her head. "He's your brother. And he's never forgiven you and Carson for taking his father away from him."

"What?" He turned away from her, as if trying to come to grips with the news. "Wait, he thinks we took his father away from him? It was the other way around."

"What I don't understand is why your father didn't bring him here when your grandparents died." It was one of many questions she'd had.

"You don't know my father." Cody's resentment bubbled to the surface. "He's by far the most selfish man on the planet."

"Yeah, well, like father, like son." She saw the deflated look on Cody's face and backtracked. "I mean Kyle. Not you."

"Oh, Fisher. I'm so sorry. I know you really care about him." Cody put a gentle hand on her shoulder. A gesture of brotherly affection. "And I really thought he cared about you, too."

"It doesn't matter." She shook him off. "I should have listened to you. I never should have hired him."

"He's a good guide. But then he was well trained." Cody shoved his hands in his pockets. "It's too bad I'm going to have to kick his ass."

"You don't have to do that." Fisher knew Cody had her back, but even he couldn't fix her broken heart. "But you could let him know that he can pick up his final paycheck whenever Lily can get it processed."

"Damn. I really hoped this would work out for you." He gave her a quick pat on the back. "I want to see you happy."

"Hey, it was just supposed to be one night. So I still came out ahead, right?" She couldn't let on how much she was truly hurting. Especially not with Cody. She was over him. At least she got that out of this whole mess.

She just wished she'd be able to get over Kyle as easily.

Chapter 19

Kyle stood in his RV, stunned that Fisher had walked out on him. He stared at JP, the man who had helped him get everything he'd thought he wanted. But with a few careless words, he may have lost him what he truly wanted.

Fisher.

He shook his head. "I've gotta go. You can let yourself out."

"You're really going to walk away from me for some piece of ass?" JP shook his head in disbelief. Or maybe it was disappointment. But Kyle was more disappointed in himself than his former boss could ever be.

"Fisher isn't some piece of ass." She never had been. "She's the best thing that's ever happened to me."

"No. I'm the best thing that's ever happened to you." JP was starting to sound like a petulant child. Kyle almost expected him to start stomping his feet. "Without me, you'd be no better than your old man."

"Look, I appreciate all you've done for me." Kyle was grateful, but he didn't owe the man his life. "And I think you appreciate all I've done for you, too. I've made you a ton of money. And for the first time, I've failed to make the deal. But that doesn't make me a failure. Surely there will be other opportunities for you. But I'm out."

With that, Kyle pushed past him and slipped out the door. He headed toward the guides' house but stopped short when he saw Cody coming toward him. His big brother didn't look too happy, so he guessed he'd run into Fisher already this morning.

Kyle braced himself for a punch, but Cody simply stared at him, shaking his head.

"I told you not to hurt her." Cody tensed as if he did indeed want to punch him.

"I know. I know you care about her, but I love her, man. I do. And I'll fix this. I swear."

"I don't know, she's pretty pissed. She said you're only here to ruin my business." Cody relaxed his fists, but he still seemed on edge. "Said you're pissed at me and Carson for taking your daddy away from you."

"Our dad." Kyle knew he should have come clean days ago. "But everything changed the minute I met her. I swear."

"Really?"

"Yeah. Really. I'd love to stay and chat. Catch up on family history, but I've got a woman to grovel with."

Kyle turned once again toward the house. But his path was blocked by the appearance of his father. The man looked like he'd been out all night. His hair stuck up in all directions. Dark circles bagged below his eyes.

"Kyle. Son, I need to talk to you." Joe Swift took a tentative step toward him.

"Not now. I've got a situation."

"Look, son, I've driven all night to get here. I really need you to listen to me." Another step, this time with his hand outstretched.

"It's a little late for you to play the devoted father."

"Please. I know I've let you down in the past." He stopped shuffling toward him, his shoulders slumped in defeat.

"In the past?" A lifetime of bitterness threatened to drown him.

"Okay, so your whole life. But I wouldn't have come if it wasn't important. And your mother—"

"What about Mom? Is she sick? Hurt?" Or worse, using again.

"No. Just worried." Joe Swift shuffled toward him, barely steady on his feet. Was he high? Or just worn out? "We're both worried. You were supposed to be gone a week."

"I like it here." He turned toward Cody and couldn't help but notice the look on his brother's face. He recognized that look. A familiar mix of disappointment, resentment, and reluctant affection for the man who'd given them life. "I feel like I belong here. It's too bad I had to wait so long to discover this place."

"Look, Kyle. That was a long time ago." Joe closed his eyes, regret showing in the creases on his face. "I wanted to bring you, but your mother..."

"Don't you put this on her." Kyle's jaw clenched, along with his fists.

"We both made mistakes, too many to count, but, son"—Joe shook his head—"I don't want you to make the same mistakes I made."

"Don't worry. I won't. I've managed to stay away from drugs, for one thing." And he'd managed to make a good living so far.

"Maybe you have, but that man you look up to? The one you've worked for for so many years? He's bad news. He's involved in all kinds of bad stuff." His father lifted his head, staring Kyle straight in the eye. "Including drugs."

"No. His business is legitimate." Kyle looked away, not wanting to believe it. "He deals in companies. Not drugs."

The door to the RV opened, and JP Wilson stepped out. Kyle got a bad feeling creeping up his spine. He wasn't sure what to think. He'd never trusted his father, yet, somehow, maybe he'd always known something wasn't right about Wilson's business dealings.

"Tell him." Still, Kyle hoped that he was wrong. That his father was just making things up to…what? Regain his son's affection? It was too late for that.

"You didn't get very far." JP had a smug look on his face. As if he was above everyone else. "Did you change your mind? Are you going to have a deal for me soon?"

"No. There is no deal. I'm done." Kyle shook his head. "And it doesn't matter what your business dealings are. Not anymore."

"You think you can just walk away from me?" JP's voice boomed.

Both Cody and Joe took steps toward them. Joe looked desperate, but determined to protect his son. And Cody? He looked like a man itching for a fight. But instead of Kyle, he was glaring at JP.

"Yes. I can just walk away." Kyle had never stood up to the man before. He'd never had to. "So maybe you did take me on when I was desperate. When I needed a job. But I don't need you anymore. And you don't need me."

"I might not need you, but that doesn't mean you're going to just get away so easily." The threat was subtle.

"What? Do we have a contract? No. Just a verbal agreement." Kyle hoped to hell he wasn't making things worse. "I would look into this company, with an eye toward buying it. Then, if and when a deal was made, you'd pay me a commission. My standard finder's fee."

"Is that what you call it?" JP was referring to the fifty grand or so Kyle had stood to make off the deal.

"I believe my yearly 1099s call it a 'nonemployee compensation,' but I'd have to double-check my last tax return." They'd been very careful to keep his status legitimate but vague. "As an independent contractor, I'm the one who decides when and where I work. And I've decided I don't want to work for you. Not here. And definitely not in LA."

"Oh, is that so?" JP's face reddened, his jaw twitching. "I don't think you understand who you're dealing with."

"I think you should leave." Cody stepped forward. "The man has made it clear that he doesn't want to work for you. And as this is my property, I'm making it clear that you're not welcome here."

"Oh really? And who the hell do you think you are?" JP bellowed.

"I'm his brother. And I'm also a close, personal friend of the county sheriff. I have his direct number." Cody pulled his phone out of his pocket. "So unless you want to be arrested for trespassing and harassment, I suggest you head on back to your limo or jet or whatever it is that will take you away from here as fast as possible."

"Is that a threat?" JP glared at him.

"No. Just a fact. And while you're making your phone calls to your big LA lawyers, my local sheriff's department will do a thorough background check on you. If you so much as have a parking violation or late tax payment, I'd worry. And speaking of taxes, I'm sure you wouldn't want to deal with the IRS. They tend to crack down on those employers who try to get out of paying their employment taxes by calling them independent contractors yet treating them like employees. My sister-in-law has a contact down at the Sacramento office. I'm sure she'd be happy to make a few phone calls on Kyle's behalf."

JP looked ready to explode. But he took a step back. "This rinky-dink operation isn't worth it. I'd probably lose money, but not enough to make a decent write-off."

He stormed off toward the limo that was indeed parked out front.

"Thanks, man." Kyle heaved a relieved sigh when the car pulled away. "I owe you. And Lily, too. Does she really have a contact at the IRS?"

"Yeah, the guy she calls when our quarterly tax payments are due and the online system goes down." Cody laughed and patted him on the back. "So why didn't you tell me we're brothers?"

Then Cody turned to their father. "Why didn't you tell me? Did you not know about him?"

"I knew." Joe Swift hung his head. "I knew I didn't deserve any of you boys."

"So why didn't you bring him with you when Granny died?" Cody asked. Such a simple question, but one Kyle had been afraid to ask his whole life.

"I figured the boy needed his mother." Joe looked at Kyle with such regret in his eyes.

"You could have brought us both." Kyle didn't even try to hide the bitterness in his voice.

"Yeah, we could have used a stepmother." Cody sounded like a disappointed little kid.

"Too many ghosts." Joe shook his head.

"So you left him and his mom behind." Cody pointed to Kyle. "Because my mom died?"

"It's more than that." Joe couldn't quite make eye contact with either son.

"Enlighten us. Please." Cody obviously had a lot of resentment bottled up, and it was pouring out now. "Because I sure as hell would like to know how you could walk out on us and then walk out on him and still manage to think you're the only one haunted by ghosts."

"You see her too?" Joe lifted his head, a look of desperate hope on his face.

"I'm not talking about real ghosts. Shit." Cody shook his head. He turned away, stomping his feet and flexing his fists. He let out a few heavy breaths before turning back around. "Just go. You've done enough damage. I don't need you here. He doesn't need you. We'll take care of each other. Like Carson and I always did."

"I'll go." Joe turned back toward his beat-up old Toyota. "But Kyle? Call your mother. She worries."

"Yeah. I'll call her." Damn if tears didn't prick his eyes. He wanted to go after the old man. But since he wasn't sure if he wanted to hug him or slug him, he let him walk away.

"Do you think he really sees her ghost?" Cody asked after what felt like a lifetime. "I mean, is that why he stayed away?"

"It's possible, I guess." Kyle rubbed the back of his neck, which was as tight as an overinflated raft. "Maybe he only thought he saw ghosts when he was high. Or maybe he got high to get away from the ghosts?"

"He has a drug problem?" Cody sounded disillusioned. "Shit, I had no idea. Of course, I had no idea he had another family."

"Surprise." Kyle's head was pounding. His neck and shoulders ached, and his stomach was growling. But most of all, his heart was breaking. He needed to get to Fisher. "Look, man, I'd love to play catch-up with you and Carson. We could share notes about our shitty childhoods, but I need to find Fisher. I've got to fix things with her before it's too late."

"She took off in her Jeep. She was pretty upset. About you only being here to screw us out of our business."

"Yeah, that asshole said I should sleep with her to make the deal happen." He wanted to go kick the shit out of the man for that. "But I swear, she's the reason I gave up on the deal. Well, the main reason. That, and you guys have a good thing going here. No need to mess with success."

"What about Fisher? What are you going to do about her?"

"Whatever it takes. I love her, man. I really do. I know it sounds crazy, since I've only known her a few weeks, but…"

"I know what you mean. When it hits you, it hits you hard." Cody had a shitty little grin on his face. "But there's something you should know about Fisher."

Shit, was his brother going to give him some advice that would ensure she never spoke to him again?

"What's that?"

"She's one of the most loyal and giving people I know."

"I figured that out on my own, but thanks."

"What I mean is, she doesn't give her heart easily, but when she does, she's all in." Maybe Cody was aware of any feelings she'd had for him? "But by loving so deeply, that means she can be hurt just as deeply."

"Yeah, I also figured that out on my own. What I need to know is how to make it up to her." His frustration level was rising. "I mean, what do I have to offer her?"

"How big would the commission on this place have been?"

"About fifty grand. That's just about two and a half percent of the selling price." Kyle didn't want to crunch numbers here. "I would have made another fifty or sixty on the subsequent sale."

"Wait. Two percent? I'm not a big numbers guy, but that would mean a selling price of like two million dollars."

"Yeah. I know it was a lowball offer. But most of the companies I dealt with were in financial trouble, so they often took what they could get."

"You were going to offer two million dollars?" Cody didn't seem to be able to wrap his head around the number.

"Yeah, I know, the land itself is probably worth that. With the business and the resort, I would have screwed you good." He would have felt bad about it until he'd cashed his check.

"Thanks."

"But you don't have to worry. Fisher taught me that what you have here is worth more than money."

"Yeah, but two million dollars is a lot of money." Once again, Cody didn't seem to realize what he had.

"And he would have turned around and sold it for twice that."

"No shit?" Cody let out a low whistle.

"Cool it, or I might just buy it from you myself." Kyle was joking. Kind of.

"You've got that kind of money?" Cody looked at him with skepticism, but also a small dose of respect—or maybe it was just envy.

"Not in cash. I'd have to sell my condo and some stocks. But that's not the point." Kyle really wanted to end this conversation so he could go after Fisher. "The point is, I couldn't do that to Fisher. I know how much this life means to her. Her job, her friends, her river family."

"You could always buy her her own company." Cody tossed it out as a joke. But maybe…

"You mean steal her away from you?"

"Okay, yeah, that would suck." Cody grinned and rubbed his short beard.

"But there's some property not too far from here. It's been on the market forever. With your cash and her expertise, you could make it work."

"Wouldn't we be competing with you?" The idea was starting to grow on him.

"Look, it's not as big as our place, about half the size, so you wouldn't be able to do as much with the resort. But you could set up a nice little rafting operation." Cody's smile widened. "Yeah, there'd be some competition, and you'd be taking our best guide. But it would take you a year to get it up and running."

"You think?"

"But if you think Fisher is worth it, I'd be willing to lose some business if it meant she was taken care of." *Cody must really care about her.*

"Of course she's worth it." Kyle's respect for his brother began to grow. "But I still need to get her to forgive me."

"Why don't you put a shirt on and some shoes." Cody gave him a brotherly pat on the back. "We'll go take a look at the property. Maybe something will come to you while we walk the acreage."

* * * *

Fisher got in her Jeep and drove. She didn't care where she was going. She just needed to get away. But she didn't have anything other than her keys and some lip gloss in her purse. No cash. No debit card. She didn't even have shoes on.

Still, she couldn't just turn around. Not when she needed a friend. A shoulder to cry on. But since she'd lost her best friend a year ago, she hoped her next best friend would have time for her.

Fisher found herself turning up the highway toward Hidden Creek. Lily had a cabin on the banks of the small tributary that eventually connected with the American. Carson had moved in with her shortly before their wedding. And if she wasn't mistaken, he'd just passed her on his way into town.

At least she wouldn't have to worry about disturbing their happy little family. Hopefully the baby would be napping or something.

Lily must have heard her pull up, or else she was already on the deck, because she met her at the top of the steps leading to the front door.

"Hey, Fisher. I'm surprised to see you this morning. I thought you'd be enjoying your day off with Kyle." Lily had a big smile on her face and a steaming mug of coffee or tea in her hand. "Wasn't that a beautiful wedding?"

Fisher tried to make the expected small talk, but the lump in her throat rose as big as the full moon.

Lily must have noticed the look on her face because she set her cup down and rushed down the steps to fold Fisher into a hug.

"What happened? I thought you two were…" Lily stepped back, with a look of sadness on her face.

"Yeah, me too. But I guess I was wrong." The words barely escaped her quivering lips.

"Come in. Carson made coffee, and I've got some muffins still warm from the oven."

Suddenly, Fisher's stomach grumbled. She hadn't eaten yet and she was so overdue for a strong cup of coffee.

"Thanks." She managed a pathetic squeak.

"Anytime." Lily placed a comforting hand on her shoulder. "You've been there for me. Remember when Carson and Cody had their big fight? And Cody left, not telling anyone where he was?"

"How could I forget?" She still had nightmares about the blood from the fight. Well, not recently, but it had been horrible.

"And Carson was so torn up he wouldn't even look at me, let alone…" Lily looked away, probably thinking about how she'd already conceived little Brandon. "I don't know how I would have gotten through those days without you."

"Carson would have come around; he's always been the most reasonable of all the Swift brothers."

"Oh, he has his moments." Lily led Fisher into her warm and sunny kitchen. The smell of coffee nearly brought Fisher to her knees.

"Coffee smells good." Fisher tried to be gracious and appreciate her friend's hospitality.

"Yeah, I let myself have a half a cup after I nurse Brandon. But he's sleeping in this morning. I guess the wedding was a big night for him, too."

"And I'm intruding on your quiet time." Fisher felt like she had nowhere to turn.

"No. Not at all. Carson just left to make sure everything got cleaned up from the party. He didn't want to leave it all on you guys. He really wanted you to have the day off."

"I guess you were expecting to have a day off, too. But I'm going to ask you a favor. Could you cut one final check?" Her voice cracked. She couldn't say it.

"Oh honey." Lily evidently knew who she was referring to without having to say it. She wrapped her arms around her and let her cry on her shoulder. "You need a muffin. And some chocolate. Then you can tell me what happened."

After two cups of coffee, three muffins, and dozens of tears, Fisher had told Lily everything, from Kyle knowing he was the half brother of Carson and Cody to his boss's arrival and the deal he'd come up here to make.

Lily had been great. She just listened, without judging, without defending Kyle or making Fisher feel like even more of a fool than she was.

The phone rang. Lily looked at it as if it was an intrusion.

"Go ahead. I'm fine." Fisher picked at the crumbs on her plate.

Lily grabbed the phone. "Hello. Yes. Uh-huh. Sure."

She gave Fisher a small shrug and a smile before stepping out onto the deck.

All that coffee went right through her, so Fisher took the opportunity to hit the ladies' room. She was splashing cool water on her face when she heard Brandon's cries from his room.

After poking her head into the kitchen, she noticed that Lily was still outside on the phone. Maybe she hadn't heard the baby. Fisher debated going out to interrupt her friend's phone call or checking on him herself.

Through the glass doors, she could see that Lily was deep in conversation with someone. Probably her husband. She didn't want to disturb the lovebirds, so Fisher decided to check on Brandon. Just to make sure he wasn't in distress.

Carefully, she pushed the door to his nursery open. Brandon was lying in his crib, wailing. He stopped crying when he saw her, reaching his chubby little fists into the air. His sobs lessened with the hope that she'd rescue him from his misery.

With her heart hammering in her chest, she approached the crib. She could do this. She could pick him up and take him to his mother. Her hands shook as she reached down for the baby.

His face broke into a wide-open grin. His blue eyes sparkled with sheer joy as she lifted him from the mattress. He was heavier than she'd anticipated, and soaking wet. She held him out away from her, praying he didn't start to squirm and make her lose her grip. He just giggled, kicking his little feet and laughing as if it was some kind of game to be held at arm's length, as if he was a bomb that would go off if she made any sudden movements.

Somehow, Fisher managed to get him to the changing table. He continued to smile at her, shoving a fist into his drooling mouth. He lifted his legs in anticipation of having his soggy diaper mercifully removed.

She put her left hand on his chest, hoping to steady him as she unzipped the cotton pajama thing he wore. She tried to tug the footed part off his squirming legs, but the material didn't quite stretch enough. So she wrestled one arm out and then the other. She shoved the material down his back. Then she was able to get the feet off and undo the flaps on the diaper. No wonder the kid was so heavy. The diaper must have weighed five pounds.

The diaper pail at the end of the changing table looked like some kind of space capsule. She didn't have the first clue as to how to open it. So she just wadded the diaper up and pushed it as far from Brandon's kicking feet as possible.

The clean diapers were in a cloth-lined basket on a shelf just below the changing pad. She grabbed one and was thankful for the Mickey Mouse designs that helped her determine the front of the diaper from the back.

After what felt like an eternity, she managed to get the diaper on, the flaps fastened, and she was actually starting to feel like she'd pulled this off. But then she wondered if she was supposed to put baby powder down there. Or diaper cream. Should she have used the baby wipes to clean him up first?

Well, she'd just have to confess her incompetence when Lily came inside. Until then, she thought about trying to put clean clothes on him but then thought better of it. So she grabbed one of those little flannel blankets and wrapped it around him like a beach towel and then she carried him into the kitchen.

Maybe she wasn't completely hopeless when it came to babies. He wasn't crying anymore. And she'd managed to make it to the kitchen without dropping him. Kyle would be proud of her.

Kyle.

A tear slipped down her cheek and Brandon reached up with his little baby hand as if he was trying to comfort her.

Then he shoved his fist down the top of her dress.

"Brandon. No. You do not put your hands on a lady without her permission." Lily stepped into the kitchen in time to witness her son grasping at Fisher's chest.

"He's just a baby. He doesn't know any better." Fisher laughed and handed him off to his mother.

"Yes, but if he hears it enough as a baby, when he is old enough to know better, he'll have the idea ingrained in his subconscious." Lily looked at the blanket wrapped around her son and smiled.

"Now, Brandon, would you like your breakfast?" She opened her blouse and began to nurse him.

"He probably needs a bath." Fisher glanced away to give them some privacy. "He woke up soaking wet so I changed him as best as I could, but I really have no experience with babies."

"It's fine." Lily shifted in her chair, settling in for a long nursing session. "I'll give him a bath after he eats. He doesn't usually sleep this late."

"I didn't want to disturb your phone conversation. I think it's great that

you and Carson have so much to talk about even after he just left you."
Fisher wondered if her friend could hear the longing in her voice.

"It wasn't Carson on the phone. It was Cody."

"Cody?" *Why would Cody call here?*

"Yeah, he told me you would probably ask me to cut a final check for
Kyle. And he also told me not to write it."

"Then I guess you could make my final check out, because I can't work
with a man who would betray his own brothers."

"But he didn't," Lily calmly pointed out.

"He would have." How could she love a man like that?

"But he didn't," Lily repeated.

"Only because I warned Cody."

"No. Cody told me everything that happened after you left. About how
Kyle told his old boss to leave and Cody backed him up by threatening to
call the sheriff."

"Wait. Cody had Kyle's back?"

"Yeah. He does."

"But Kyle was going to cheat him out of his business." All she'd wanted
was for the two of them to become friends. Brothers. No. That wasn't
all she'd wanted. She wanted to be able to trust Kyle. To love him with
her whole heart.

"For two million dollars." Lily calmly switched the baby to her other breast.

"No way." Fisher stood up. She didn't know what to think anymore. Two
million dollars was a lot of money. Was she in charge of a multimillion-
dollar company? She felt dizzy. "I think I should go home now." Fisher
gathered the empty coffee cup and plate and carried them to the sink.

"Just leave them on the counter," Lily said. "I'll give Brandon his bath
before I clean up. Unless you want to stay and help."

"No. Thank you." Fisher was confused. She needed to think. "And thank
you for the coffee and muffins. They were delicious."

"Anytime." Lily offered a warm smile. "And, Fisher, I hope you can
work things out with Kyle. I really do."

"Thanks." Fisher walked slowly to her Jeep. She was surprised by how
much money Kyle was going to offer for Swift River Adventures. So maybe
he wasn't completely out to ruin his brothers. But she realized there was
too much she didn't know about the man.

And she wasn't sure if she was strong enough to find out.

Chapter 20

As Fisher drove home, instead of things becoming clearer, she became more and more confused. She had so many questions she couldn't answer.

Who was Kyle Swift?

What did they have together?

Was it just a summer fling that had run its course?

Could it have been more?

The miles whirred by, her thoughts blurring like the trees on the side of the road. Not just about Kyle, but also about baby Brandon. He was awfully sweet. And trusting.

She blinked back more tears, shaking her head at the silliness of her overwrought emotions.

Out of the corner of her eye, she thought she saw something in the ditch. She slowed down, wondering if on top of everything else, she was imagining things. But no, she'd definitely seen something. A nagging feeling caused her to turn around and slowly drive back to where there were indeed tire tracks in the grass. No skid marks, just bent grass leading to an old car sitting in a ditch.

Fisher parked and carefully got out of the Jeep, wishing she had at least a pair of flip-flops for the trek down the gravel- and dirt-lined ditch.

A man was slumped over in the driver's seat, but she didn't see any damage on the windshield. The small scratches in the driver's side door were slightly rusted, as if they had been there awhile.

The man's head rolled to the side and she noticed the slight rise and fall of his chest. He was alive. Her training kicked in and she carefully tried the door, which was, fortunately, unlocked.

The hinge creaked as she opened it and the man jerked awake.

"Who? Who are you?" He looked disoriented, but at least he was conscious.

"I'm Fisher." She kept her voice as calm as possible. "It appears you've been in an accident. Do you remember what happened?"

"I was driving back home. I drove all night but my sons, they... Well, can you blame them?"

"Do you know your name?" she asked hopefully.

"Yes. Joe. Joe Swift." He looked up at her with weary eyes. Eyes every bit as blue as his sons' and his grandson's. "I must have fallen asleep."

He started to get out of the car and Fisher extended a hand.

"How is your head? Did you hit the windshield or the steering wheel?"

"I don't think so. It's just that I am tired." He fell back against the car. "It's a long drive from LA. Especially when..."

He raked a hand through his thinning hair and let out a weary breath.

"I forgot how pretty it is here." His voice was thick with emotion. Sorrow. Regret. Pain. "I never should have left. I shouldn't have come back."

The man was hurting, but she couldn't tell if it was from the accident or thirty years of grief.

"Well, we're going to need some help getting your car unstuck." Fisher could do it herself if she wasn't worried about him wandering off. And if she wasn't barefoot and in a dress. "And maybe we should get you to the emergency room and have you checked out."

"No need for that. I'm fine. I just fell asleep, that's all." He did sound more coherent. And a little bit agitated. "Besides, I don't have any health insurance. I still got a few more years before I can get Medicare."

He seemed much older than sixty-five, but life hadn't been kind to him.

"I don't trust most doctors anyway." No, life had definitely not been kind to him. "Nothing a strong cup of coffee can't cure."

"I know just the place, then." Fisher looped her arm in his and led him carefully back to her Jeep.

Once he was buckled in, she put the Jeep in gear, using her four-wheel drive to keep from spinning out in the loose gravel. She drove carefully back to the resort. If she'd had her cell phone she would have called Tyler or Ross or whoever was around to come get Mr. Swift's car unstuck. Instead, she'd just have to wait until she got back to the house.

The man dozed on the short drive back home, and she made a note to keep a close eye on him. If he showed any signs of a head injury, she would take him to the hospital and worry about the cost later. She'd put out a tip jar at the store if necessary.

When she pulled into the parking lot, she noticed Cody's truck was missing. Carson's too. But he could have been returning tables to the party rental store.

She led Mr. Swift into the kitchen of the guides' house and started a fresh pot of coffee. "Are you hungry? We have plenty of food here. I could scramble some eggs and make some toast."

"You sure you won't get in trouble with your boss?" He must have noticed where she'd brought him.

"I am the boss. At least, when the owners aren't around. Besides, this is my kitchen. I just let the others use it." She gave him a wink and was rewarded with a tentative grin.

Soon she was serving a hearty breakfast with plenty of strong, dark coffee. The color returned to the man's cheeks and he ate with an enthusiasm she hadn't seen since, well, since most mornings around here. The physical demands of their job gave most of the guides a hearty appetite.

"I'll bet you could use a nice hot shower, and maybe a nap."

"Oh, you've done enough, young lady." He wiped his mouth with the napkin he'd placed on his lap. "I should get out of your way."

"Tell you what, if you give me your keys, I'll have your car brought over while you get cleaned up."

"Well, I can tell you're the kind of woman who is used to getting her way. I guess I'd better not argue with you." His blue eyes twinkled with that unmistakable Swift family charm.

"That's right." She smiled and extended a hand to help him up and lead him to the upstairs bathroom. The shower was at one end with a sliding door partitioning it from the dual vanities in the center. The toilet alcove was at the opposite end. It worked out well for the communal nature of their home.

"There are towels on that shelf there, and I'll bring a change of clothes and set them on the sink for you."

"Thank you." He took her hand, holding it a little longer than needed for a simple thank-you. "I can see now that I didn't need to come all this way. I was worried that he'd been blinded by the lifestyle, the fast cars, the easy money. That he couldn't see how that all came at a price."

"What price?" Fisher dropped the man's hand, a sick feeling sinking into her gut. What if Kyle was in danger? The man who'd arrived this morning didn't seem like the kind of guy who would walk away from a million-dollar deal—no, a two-million-dollar deal—with just a shrug of his shoulders.

"I'm proud of that boy. I'm proud of all my boys, but Kyle? He's had it rough. He never had anyone he could count on. Especially me." Joe Swift looked her in the eye. "I can see why he was seduced by Wilson's flash and his cash. He didn't stop to ask where all that money came from; he was just happy to get a piece of it.

"Do you want to know the first thing he bought when he made his first

big deal?" Joe didn't wait for an answer. "He bought his mama a house.
A nice little home, like the kind I should have been able to provide. I've
never been so proud—and so ashamed—in all my life."

Tears pricked the man's eyes.

"I should have taken better care of her. I should have been stronger.
Like my boys." He placed an unsteady hand on her shoulder. "They're
good boys. All of them. No. They're good men. Maybe someday, I can be
more like them."

"Maybe you should stick around awhile. Get to know them." Her voice
had a catch in it, and her eyes felt prickly. "And your grandchildren."

"Grandchildren?" His eyes widened with hope, and then despair. "I don't
know if I can risk disappointing another generation."

"I don't know if you can risk not trying." There. She told him.

"Okay. I'll give it another shot." He looked her square in the eye, the
Swift look of determination shining bright. "If you will."

When she just stared at him, with her jaw dropped open, he chuckled.

"I know about you, young lady. You're the one who ran off on my boy
this morning. Maybe you had good reason. But I can see that you love
him. And I know he loves you."

She started to deny it, but what was the use?

"Listen to an old man who learned the hard way." He placed a gentle hand
on her shoulder. "Regret is not something you want to get involved with. It's
worse than any drug. Any disease. It's the worst kind of heartbreak there is."

With that, the man took his towel into the shower and shut the door.

* * * *

"Wow, I'm surprised you were able to get the Realtor to meet us on such
short notice." Kyle was still a little cautious when it came to Cody's sudden
acceptance of him. There was a small part of him that wondered if maybe
Cody was going to lead him off into the woods where his body would be
dragged off by mountain lions after he succumbed to the elements.

But instead, they pulled up to a very nice custom home right on the
river. There was something familiar about the place, but he couldn't put
his finger on it.

"My buddy from high school has the listing on the property. But since
there's no access from the main road, he's going to meet us at my place."

"This is your place?" Kyle looked up at the cedar siding, expansive deck,
and large picture windows and felt a slight twinge of the familiar envy.
When Miranda came out to greet them, he felt even more of a tug. But

instead of jealousy, it was more a push for him to go after what he wanted. Fisher.

He turned away while Cody and Miranda greeted each other as newlyweds would, by wrapping themselves around each other. Not bad for a couple with two small children.

They broke apart when a car pulled into the driveway. It was actually an SUV and out stepped a gentleman dressed in jeans, work boots, and a polo shirt with a Prospector Springs Realty logo on the chest.

"Thanks for giving me a call." The man shook hands with Cody. "It's been too long."

"Yeah. I've been busy. This is my wife, Miranda." He introduced her first. "And my brother, Kyle."

Both Miranda and the Realtor looked surprised.

"Dave Meyers. Nice to meet you both." He shook hands with Miranda and then Kyle. "Are you ready to take a look around the property?"

"Sure." Kyle was anxious to see if it would meet his needs. If it was good enough for Fisher and the life he wanted to make with her.

He followed Dave to his SUV, wondering if he'd need a four-wheel drive vehicle to access the property. Both Cody and Carson drove 4x4 trucks and Fisher had a Jeep. And like most things around here, it wasn't just for show. He'd bet they all spent a good deal of time off road.

Cody slid into the backseat and Kyle made himself comfortable in the front passenger side.

"Now, this is a real fine piece of property. Almost twelve acres. Mostly level, but with some elevation changes. There is private river access and a nice little beach." Dave was working the sale. "The main reason it hasn't been scooped up yet is that there isn't direct access from the main road. If you were to purchase the land, you'd have to apply for an easement from the public land adjacent on the northwestern part of the property, and it could be a little tricky to get a road in that corner."

Kyle assumed tricky meant expensive.

"Now there is a neighbor to the east." Dave glanced in the rearview mirror at Cody. "He's been reluctant to give access. I think mostly because he had his eye on the property. Or maybe it was his brother."

"What am I missing?" Kyle turned around to find Cody with a big cocky grin on his face.

"Yeah. I had thought about buying the place someday, but when Carson moved in with Lily, I didn't see a need."

"So the biggest drawback of the place would be having you as my neighbor?"

"Yeah. I guess you could say that." Cody chuckled as they bumped over uneven ground and came out on a flat spot overlooking the water.

Dave put the SUV in park and they got out. "Let's take a walk, shall we?"

Kyle looked around. It was a beautiful piece of land. And the river access was just about perfect. The spot they were parked on would be just right for a staging area for commercial trips. It was level enough to build a large equipment shed. There was even room for picnic tables and barbecue pits.

"Now, if you take a little walk up this way"—Dave started to climb a small hill—"I think this would be a terrific spot for a homesite. You could put a two- to three-thousand-square-foot home without having to remove many trees."

"And you'd have plenty of space for a play structure for the kids," Cody added hopefully.

"Well, I don't know about that." Shit. He shouldn't have said anything. Really, Fisher's feelings about babies were the least of his worries. "I mean, I'm several steps away from needing a play structure."

"So what are your plans, then?" Dave asked. "Cody mentioned you might want to start your own rafting company."

"Yeah. They've got more business than they can handle and sometimes a little competition can actually increase business for both companies."

"Is that so?" Dave sounded like he was just going along. Being friendly. Or salesmanly.

"Yeah, you know how as more and more wineries popped up in the area, the wine industry really started booming," Cody added helpfully.

"Maybe I should grow grapes instead," Kyle joked. He knew nothing about the wine business, other than people liked wine.

"Well, this property isn't zoned for agriculture," Dave mentioned. He was a straight shooter. Kyle liked that about him. "It's currently zoned for residential or commercial use only."

"Good to know." Kyle stood on the top of the hill, where it was indeed a terrific spot for a home. He tried to envision what Fisher's dream home would look like. He knew it wouldn't be fancy. But it would be of top quality. He'd make sure of it.

The only thing he required in a dream house was his dream woman.

His strong blonde.

Chapter 21

Fisher finally crawled into the shower a little before noon. Joe was sleeping soundly in her bed, and Brooke had wanted to hear all the details about what he was doing there. In all the excitement, no one seemed to notice that Kyle was nowhere to be found. His RV was still parked behind the house, but she had no idea where he'd gone.

Maybe he had gone back to LA. If he was rich enough to make two-million-dollar deals, he could always send for someone to drive his RV back home. If that was the case, she'd just have to focus on her new mission. Getting her friends, her true friends, Cody and Carson, to get to know their father. She'd like to help them find forgiveness, and she wanted that for Kyle, too.

Because she knew that if she did stand a chance of continuing a relationship with him, he'd need to heal his childhood wounds. Or at least make an attempt.

Fisher found Brooke in the kitchen sipping iced tea.

"I'm still impressed you rescued Carson and Cody's dad." Brooke set her glass on the table. "You are like a superhero, aren't you? Saving your boyfriend from a snake, pulling old man Swift out of a ditch. What can't you do?"

"Well, until this morning, I…I had never changed a diaper." She started to tell her that she'd never even held a baby, but that was a little deeper than she wanted to dig into her own issues.

"What I still don't understand is what was Dad Swift doing here?"

"He came up to try to warn Kyle about someone he used to work for."

"The guy in the limo?" Brooke must have seen him pull into or out of the parking lot. "But why would Cody and Carson's dad want to warn Kyle…? Oh my God. They're related, aren't they? They're brothers. Of course.

How did we not see it? Those eyes. Did you just find out this morning?"

"No. I knew they were brothers. Kyle told me. But he wasn't ready to tell them."

"Why?" Brooke stirred the ice in her glass. "Does it have something to do with their dad?"

"Yeah. I think so. They've all got some serious baggage there." Fisher sighed. Her heart ached for all of them. "And they've got it tied down so tight, it'll take some time to unravel it."

"Or you could just cut through it all with one sharp slice." Brooke placed her hand over her heart and made a slashing motion as if she were freeing the knife the guides all kept attached to their life jackets in that spot.

"I'm not sure how."

"Get them all together. In one spot."

"What, like in one boat?" The river did have a way of working its magic on people.

"Or maybe you could start with something simple. Like lunch."

"I could get the wives involved."

"You definitely need to get the wives on board." Brooke grinned. "And maybe a few beers, some wings, and those killer onion rings they serve at the Argo."

"Stop, you're making me hungry." But a public place was maybe a good idea. That way no one could just storm off or make too much of a scene.

"Tell me about it. And I'm going to have to settle for leftovers."

"You're not coming with me?"

"No. It's a family thing."

"I'm not family." Fisher wondered if she was going too far. Maybe she should just butt out of it.

"Oh, come on. You didn't need to catch the bouquet last night. It's pretty obvious that you're next."

"No. Far from it." Just hours ago, Fisher was certain she'd never see Kyle again. And now here she was plotting a forced family reunion for the Swift men.

"Oh please. It's inevitable." Brooke shrugged and offered a knowing smile.

"Yeah? What about you and Tyler?"

Brooke blushed a deep pink. "Yeah, I know. I'm equally doomed. He's talking about going to South America together over the winter. Either that or getting a place in Tahoe."

"Well, good luck with whatever you decide." Fisher couldn't imagine either of them making such a commitment.

"Hey, but we've still got this summer, right?" Brooke's grin widened and then Tyler entered the kitchen.

"Hey, babe." He dropped a kiss on Brooke's neck. "You still want to go on a picnic?"

"Yeah. I hear Lost Mine Winery is pretty this time of year."

"It sure is." He stared lovingly into Brooke's eyes.

Fisher was ready to leave the two lovebirds alone when he stood up and asked, "Who's the old dude in your bed? You stepping out on Kyle?"

"No. It's their dad," Brooke interrupted before Fisher could answer.

"Fisher's dad?" Tyler sometimes played the part of the clueless dude.

"No. Kyle's dad. And Carson and Cody's dad."

"Oh. Cool." Tyler shrugged and then pulled Brooke to her feet, patting her on the fanny as he led her out the back door.

* * * *

"So what do you think? Are you ready to make an offer?" Dave held open the door to his SUV for Kyle after they'd thoroughly inspected the property.

"I'm considering it." Kyle thought it was perfect. But what would Fisher think? "I'm definitely considering it."

Cody had taken a phone call and they were waiting for him to finish his conversation before they drove back over to his house.

"Hey, why don't we head over to the Argo and discuss it over a couple of burgers and beers?" Cody hopped into the backseat, awfully cheerful for a guy who hated his guts just a few weeks ago. Now he was hoping they'd become neighbors?

They made small talk on the way to the Argo. Or rather, Dave made small talk, pointing out the various amenities of the area, offering to make recommendations on local contractors, and basically acting like it was a done deal.

Kyle had been confident like that, many times over the last few years. But he'd always known going in that he had a buyer. A buyer with unlimited funds. He shuddered when he thought about why he'd never wondered where those funds had come from.

He'd just blindly followed the money. Thinking it would make him happy. Believing he had been happy.

But in the last few weeks, he'd discovered true happiness. Fisher had taught him that money wasn't the most important thing in the world. It was love. Friendship. Family.

"So before we get down to figures and paperwork"—Dave had insisted the first round and lunch was on him—"why don't you tell me what your misgivings are, and I'll see what I can do to address any issues moving forward."

The guy was good. But he also seemed genuine.

"Cody says you went to high school together." Kyle decided to let the man do his job. "Have you lived here all your life?"

Dave leaned forward, grinning like he thought he was the luckiest guy around. "Yeah. Except for college. I can't imagine living anywhere else. People first came here for the gold, but they stayed for so many reasons. The land being one of the main ones."

"And the river," Cody chimed in. "Although I suppose that's part of the landscape."

"Yes. The climate is almost perfect. Not too hot, except maybe one or two weeks of the year when it doesn't cool down at night. The winters, even the wet ones, are usually mild. The snow levels are higher up, so you can enjoy winter recreation without having to shovel your driveway." Dave continued to sell him on reasons that didn't matter too much to Kyle. He had one reason to buy the property.

But she was also the reason he hesitated.

"So what are your concerns?" Dave sat back in his chair, not quite tipping back against the wall. "Besides having this guy as your neighbor? It's not so bad now that he's married. No more epic parties, huh?"

"Well, wait until the twins start school." Kyle couldn't help but razz his brother a little bit. "I imagine there will be some major birthday parties. Times two."

"Yeah, be careful. Apparently twins run in our family." Cody razzed right back.

"Well, maybe I won't have kids."

"Does Fisher know how you feel about it?" Cody dropped the casual, just-joking-around demeanor, and he sat up with genuine concern.

"Maybe Fisher is the one who doesn't want kids." He really didn't want to discuss it in front of a stranger. Especially not a stranger who had something he wanted.

The waitress appeared with their food and Kyle was grateful to have a reason to stop talking, at least for a few bites.

He dug into his burger, savoring the juicy, delicious treat.

When he looked up, he noticed Lily and Carson walk into the restaurant, with their baby in tow. Lily gave a quick wave and they walked over to join them.

"What are you guys doing here?" She had an almost too-surprised tone in her voice.

"Hey, Dave." Carson gave a nod to the Realtor. Of course, he would have also gone to high school with the man.

"Carson. Nice to see you out with the family." Dave stood to be introduced to Lily, and then he helped pull another table over. "I've been getting to know your younger brother."

"Does this mean you're planning to stick around?" Carson gave Kyle an assessing glance. He hesitated, as if giving the idea a chance to sink in before he broke out into a welcoming grin.

Kyle stood and extended a hand as a peace offering. Carson pumped once and then pulled him into a hearty embrace. Kyle was the first to break away and then he looked up to see Fisher walk through the door. Followed by Miranda, the twin girls, and his father.

Mixed emotions flooded him.

When Fisher offered him a tentative smile, one emotion rose to the surface. Love.

He loved his strong blonde. And she must love him back. Why else would she bring his father here? His whole family. Well, almost his whole family. Hopefully, before the summer ended, his mother would have a reason to come north.

Kyle stepped forward, pulling Fisher into his arms. It had only been hours since he last held her, but it had felt like a century.

"I missed you." He buried his face in her hair, taking in her sweet scent. Then he whispered in her ear, "I love you, Fisher. I do."

She held him tightly, telling him without words that she felt the same. Words would come. He had a feeling there would be a whole lot of words before the day was through.

Finally, all too soon, she released him.

"Look who I found on the side of the road." She stepped aside so his father could offer a steady handshake. He'd showered and changed into one of Kyle's shirts.

Fisher.

"What do you mean you found him on the side of the road?"

"Well, as I was driving home from Lily's after having a much-needed girls' talk"—she smiled at her friend—"I saw a car in a ditch, just before that one curve."

He glanced over at his father, but he didn't see any cuts or bruises. In fact, the man looked better than he had in years. Fisher had that effect on people.

"I guess I fell asleep at the wheel." Dad looked down, briefly. "But then this lovely lady came to my rescue. Don't you let this one get away, son."

"I won't. Dad." He had that same hesitation in his voice as Kevin Costner in that baseball movie. The one where he wanted to have a catch with his dad. "I'm sorry I didn't have time for you this morning."

"Oh, well, I can see why you were in such a hurry to go after her. I'm glad she caught up to you." There was a warmth in his father's voice. A twinkle in his eye.

"Yeah. Me too."

"I'm glad I got to meet her. And this lovely lady." Dad smiled at Miranda, who gave him a warm pat on the arm. "And my…" His voice became unsteady. "My granddaughters."

Carson stood up then. He introduced his wife and his son. The look of sheer joy transformed his father's face, making him look taller and younger, and for the first time since he'd known the man, fully alive.

Fisher quietly slipped her hand in his and he knew he'd do whatever it took to make her his family.

More tables were pushed together and another round of drinks came out. It was like Thanksgiving and Christmas and Sunday dinner all rolled into one afternoon. Everyone was on their best behavior, and any discussion of past hurts was put aside in favor of "pass the salt, please."

Their family problems didn't just go away, but somehow he knew they would all do a better job of communicating. Maybe even work up toward having the kind of extended family Kyle had only seen in movies.

When Fisher stepped away to use the ladies' room, Kyle slid over to Dave. "About that offer. Where do I sign?"

"You can come down to my office or I can meet you wherever, whenever is most convenient to you." Dave extended a hand, an offer of goodwill and welcome.

"Could you meet me back at the property? Say an hour after we finish up here?"

"Sure. You remember how to get there? You probably need four-wheel drive."

"Yeah. I remember, and I'll take Fisher's Jeep. I want to make sure she's as in love with the place as I am."

"Gotcha." Dave gave him a wink. "Always good to get the woman's approval. Especially when it comes to putting down roots."

Chapter 22

"Give me your keys." Kyle wrapped his arm around Fisher and whispered in her ear, sending shivers down her spine.

"I can drive. I only had one beer." She was too nervous to have any more than that. But it seemed like the day went well. Sure, there would be a lot of work ahead of them. All of them, but baby steps had been taken. Well, not literally, the three infants were months away from walking. But somehow, she sensed healing waters start to flow between the Swift men.

"I know, but I want to show you something."

"If it's your RV, I've seen it." Not that she wouldn't mind crawling into that bed she'd spent some of the best nights of her life in. "And it's still early."

"Well, we might need to make use of the RV for a few more months." He had an odd sound in his voice. Like he was up to something.

"Does that mean you are planning on sticking around for the summer? You're not just here to make a deal and run back to your fancy lifestyle in LA?"

"No. I'm through with that life. I'm here to stay. If you'll let me?" He smiled tentatively, hopefully.

"I'm sorry I got so upset this morning."

"I should have been more up front with everyone. Especially you."

"Hey, I was supposed to be just a one-night stand." She shrugged, trying to act like her heart wasn't shattered in pieces just a few hours ago.

"I never expected you." He stopped next to her Jeep, brushing a strand of her hair off her face. "I never expected to feel like this. It's like you showed me a whole new world. A whole new way of life."

"Yeah, this is the glamorous life." She looked down at her worn shorts, her faded T-shirt, her well-worn river sandals. "It's not just about running the rapids and showing off your muscles."

"I know. It's about scrubbing the dishes and keeping the raccoons out of the lunch. Filling the water bottles and emptying the groover. It's about making sure everything is picked up, packed up, and put in place for the next trip. Being ready for anything, whether it's high water, low branches, or rattlesnakes." He took both her hands in his.

"Yeah. We try not to mention the snakes." She shuddered just thinking about that snake. "But there are also girls in bikinis."

"There's only one girl—one woman—I'm interested in." He brushed a kiss across her forehead. "The one who charms snakes, rescues dads, and—"

"I changed a diaper today."

"You did?"

"Yeah. I picked up Brandon, changed his diaper, and lived to tell about it."

"I love you." He rested his forehead against hers and she knew she didn't need to be afraid anymore.

"I love you, too." She barely got the words out before Kyle pulled her closer, covering her mouth with his, devouring her with one of his bone-melting kisses.

"Good. Now I want to show you something."

"Oh, I've seen it. Seen it. Touched it…" Tried to taste it.

"Not that. Although, if you're a good girl, maybe later." He opened the passenger door to her Jeep and helped her up before going around to slide in behind the wheel. "No. I want to show you something that I hope you'll really like."

"A surprise?"

"Yeah. A big one. But I think it will be something we can build on. Literally."

She looked over at him, but he just shook his head, chuckling softly as he started the engine.

They drove over the river and up Cody's driveway. But instead of stopping and parking behind Miranda's Prius, he took a sharp turn through the dirt and onto the adjoining property. In a wide meadow with fresh tire tracks, he stopped. He turned off the ignition and grinned at her.

"Well, what do you think?"

"I'm not sure." She sat back, wondering if he'd lost his mind. They'd just had a large lunch. Surely he didn't think a picnic was a good idea.

He hopped out and came around to her door. "Come on, let's look around."

"Um, this isn't part of the resort. Or even Cody's land."

"I know. But it could be something special."

He led her down to the water.

"We could start our own company. Launching daily from right here." He sounded excited. He turned and pointed to the meadow. "And we could set up picnic tables and maybe even a small campground here."

He started walking up a small hill.

"But this is the best part." He led her to a flat area overlooking the river and the meadow and the wildflowers. "I thought we'd put our house here."

"Our house?" Her heart thudded, drowning out the sound of the river below.

"Well, we'd probably have to stay in the RV for a few months, during construction, but yeah. I thought this would be a good place to build a house together. A life together."

Her legs gave way and she slumped to the ground. Kyle dropped down next to her.

"We can do this." He pulled her onto his lap. "We can make all our dreams come true. What do you say? Are you ready to dive in with me?"

She wanted to say something. Words stuck in her throat. Tears sprung to her eyes. Her heart hammered even harder. How did she go from being the girl no one even noticed was female to this? This man offering up the whole world, and the river below?

* * * *

He'd blown it. He'd gone too far. Too fast. Instead of joyful acceptance, Fisher had slunk to her knees and become mute.

"I'm sorry." He leaned back, expecting her to run off. Instead, she slid off his lap and sat in the dirt next to him. "I guess I haven't changed all that much. The first sign of trouble and I go waving my checkbook trying to buy my way back into your heart."

"You'd really buy all this? For me?"

"For us." Kyle had made a plan. And it was a good plan. He couldn't work for his brothers forever. Not if he wanted to give Fisher more than just a good time.

"So instead of buying your brothers' company, you want to start your own?"

"Yeah. I mean, our own company." Kyle exhaled. "Look, I talked to Cody about it, and he's the one who told me about this place. Sure, there would be some competition, but we would also work together. Helping each other out with overbookings or borrowing guides in a pinch."

"It wasn't that long ago the two of you could barely tolerate each other."

"You were right. I just needed to give him a chance." Kyle gave her hand a small squeeze. "And he needed to give me a chance. But he will kick my ass if you don't fall in love with this idea."

He grinned wildly and she punched him playfully in the shoulder.

"So what do you say?" Kyle hoped for the best.

"I don't know." She looked around, as if it was a lot to take in.

"I've been told I can be a little impulsive."

"You think?"

"Look, Fisher, I just happen to be the kind of person who sees what he wants and goes after it. Especially when I know how amazing it can be."

"And I'm the kind of person who puts off making a decision for fear of making the wrong one." Fisher leaned forward, resting her forearms on her knees. "I only went to grad school because I didn't know what kind of job I wanted after college."

"I thought you have the job you want."

"I do love the river." She sighed. "But a lot of people think I'm wasting my education."

"Do you feel like you're wasting your time? Because your opinion is the most important one."

She looked down at the river.

"Fisher, what if you ran your own business? Would that make you feel like you were putting your degree to good use?"

"It's not a business degree. I don't know anything about business." She was still hesitant.

"I don't have a degree, but I do know how businesses work. You know the river and this area and the clientele. Let me worry about things like permits and advertising and start-up costs."

"You really think we'd make a good team?" Hope bubbled up in her voice.

"I know we would."

"You're willing to move here, away from your old life? Away from your family?"

"Yes. Besides, most of my family is here. And I have a feeling my father will be spending more time up here. Thanks to you."

"Do you really think you guys can all get along? I mean, I know one lunch isn't going to fix everything, but I do hope it's a step forward."

"It will take time, but that's okay." He had a good reason to try. "We have time. It will take at least a year to get the business up and running. Probably several months to design and build our dream house."

She was quiet for a long time. Almost too long.

"You'd give me this?" Her voice was thick with emotion. "A house? A rafting company of my own?"

"Yes. All of it." He'd give her more if he could. The entire Sierra Nevada mountain range, all the rivers and lakes and the whole damned Pacific.

"What could I possibly give you?"

So many answers floated through his head. A life. A family. A future.

Before he could narrow it down, she pushed him down on his back and reached for the zipper on his shorts.

"I know what I can give you." She gave him a devilish grin and then put her mouth on him.

Oh dear sweet heaven.

"Fisher. God. Stop. Stop." She was killing him.

"What?" She lifted her head, uncertainty in her voice. "Was it really that bad?"

"No, baby, it was good. So good." He owed her, big-time. "It's just that the Realtor guy will be coming by so I can sign the paperwork. He could drive up any minute."

She sat bolt upright and looked around, but there was no sign of Dave. Thankfully.

Kyle zipped his shorts and sat up. He reached for her, cupping her face in both hands.

"Fisher, you are the most amazing woman I've ever met." He meant it with all his heart.

"How many of those Strong Blondes did you have?" She teased him, even now, when he was pouring his heart out to her.

"I only need one. I only need you."

"Oh, please." She blushed and tucked a strand of her long blond hair behind her ear. She rose to her feet and turned once more toward the river.

"I'm the one who's begging." He stood next to her, admiring the view, but admiring the woman even more. "You warned me the first night we met that you'd knock me flat on my back. You also told me that this was a good place to find myself."

"I didn't realize you were lost." She turned and met his gaze, so much love shining in her eyes.

"Neither did I, but you helped me realize that I'd spent so many years trying to make a living that it didn't occur to me that I didn't have a life."

"And now?"

"Now, I want to build a life with you."

"I suppose we could build a life together and make a living while we're at it." She put her arms around his neck and pressed her luscious body against his. "It could be pretty good."

"Life with you will be very good." He kissed her then, kissed her with everything he had, knowing that this was just the beginning.

In case you missed it, here's an excerpt from book one in the Swift River Romance series:

SWEPT AWAY

Carson Swift may look exactly like his twin brother Cody, but they're as different as tie dye and camouflage. Reliable, responsible, and usually the designated driver, Carson is also over being his brother's keeper, but suddenly his plans to break free are complicated by the woman they fish out of Hidden Creek . . .

Lily Price is not your typical damsel in distress. Infidelity, infertility, and downsizing provide a triple threat to her ego, but falling into the swollen river nearly ends her life. If not for the handsome stranger—make that two handsome strangers—she might not have had a chance at having a baby by any means necessary . . .

As Carson helps Lily overcome her fear of the river, she helps him save his rafting business from going under. She also saves him from abandoning all that is important to him in order to get a taste of freedom. Together they find that love is the ultimate adventure.

A Lyrical e-book on sale now.
Learn more about Kristina at
http://www.kensingtonbooks.com/author.aspx/30540

Chapter 1

"Man this water's really pumping." Carson Swift hiked a few steps ahead of his twin brother, Cody. His feet landed firmly on the familiar trail to Hidden Creek, but his thoughts were a million miles away. Make that eight hundred miles, give or take, depending on whether he took Highway 50 or Interstate 80 through Nevada. "With the water this high, I don't think we'll catch a lot of fish."

"Good thing we have steaks in the fridge." You'd think he was nine, not twenty-nine, by the way Cody trotted along excitedly, skittering small bits of gravel along the well-worn path. He was too damn happy with his life. "We're not pulling anything out of the river today."

"At least it's finally warming up." What a coward. Carson had dragged his brother out here to have a serious conversation. Instead, he was discussing water conditions. The weather.

"I thought winter would never end." Cody would probably still catch a fish or two. He had that kind of luck. Women and trout landed at his feet without much effort. "But summer's coming and it's going to be a hot one."

Another summer stretched out in front of them. Long, hot days on the river. Longer, hotter nights at the Argo—throwing back a few beers, shooting pool, picking up pretty strangers. Who wouldn't want the easy life of a whitewater guide?

"June bookings look pretty solid." Carson tried to look at the sunny side of the creek. Business was good. That wasn't why he wanted out.

"We should get quite a few bachelorette parties." Cody had suggested advertising in the regional bridal magazines. His idea was to offer Girls' Weekend trips, complete with a selection of local wines and discounted cabin rentals. It was one of the few times he'd taken an interest in the business itself.

Most of the time Cody was all about the fun. Hot babes and cold beer on a warm summer night were the only things he seemed to care about. Except in winter, when he'd head up to the mountains to ski. Leaving Carson to take care of repairs and maintenance.

"Plenty of family trips too." All those intact families. Smiling. Laughing. Bonding. Being there for each other. Reminding Carson of what he didn't have.

"Don't forget bachelor parties." Cody was always up for a good time. The man lived his life as though it was one big party. A lot of guys would give up their flat screen TVs to walk in his sandals. "Man, we've got the best job in the world."

"Sure. A day's work for us is a vacation for most people." Carson still loved the heart-stopping rapids and Zen-like calm stretches on the river. He still loved helping people connect with nature and discover a little something about themselves along the way. And he still loved the constant, yet ever-changing force of the river.

It was the change that called to him now. He might as well be guiding the jungle boats at Disneyland. He was seeing the same sights, telling the same jokes over and over again until he felt like one of the automated characters. He needed a change of pace. A change of scenery. A change of company.

"Yeah, we've got it made." Cody trotted along like a kid on the first day of summer vacation. He had no idea his brother didn't share his enthusiasm for the status quo. Carson was afraid of becoming stagnant. A breeding ground for bad blood.

It wasn't that Cody was a bad guy. He was just there. Always. They lived together. Worked together. Ate together. The only thing they didn't do was sleep together. Although there had been women who would have been willing to take on them both. Cody probably could have been talked into it, but it was bad enough sharing breakfast and small talk with his brother's dates. Carson wasn't about to share anything more.

He should just get it over with. Say the words. *I'm leaving.* But the lump in his throat rose like the spring runoff, drowning out his voice. If he could think of another way to get Cody to grow up already, he'd take it. But the only way to get him to change would be to force it on him. He had to toss his brother overboard and hope he'd come up swimming.

"What the hell?" Cody skidded to halt. "Is that woman actually swimming? In this high water?"

* * * *

Damn. This water is cold.

Lily came up for air, sputtering and spitting out a mouthful of river water. She grasped for something—anything she could hold onto. But the current was too fast, too strong for her to grab hold of anything. She tried to find her footing, but the force of the river kept her from getting her legs underneath her. Quickly she realized that it was probably for the best. If anything, she could end up breaking a leg if she slammed against a rock. Or worse, her foot could become entrapped and it wouldn't be long before the river pulled her under, drowning her.

She wondered how long it would take to find her body. Would some fisherman stumble upon her days, weeks, or even months from now? Or would the current eventually pull her downstream, where she'd wash up lifeless on the shore?

For the first time in her adult life, Lily was thankful she was childless. There was no baby to leave motherless. Left to be raised by her rat-bastard ex-husband.

Water shot up her nose, and Lily coughed. She tried once again to regain control of her body, but she was caught in a force too powerful to fight.

The movies were all wrong. Her life didn't flash before her eyes. Nothing but water and sky and regret rushed past her as she was carried downstream.

Lily didn't want her last conscious thought to be about her ex. About her failures.

As a wife. A daughter. An employee.

A woman who hadn't been able to conceive.

She tried to think of something positive. Relaxing her body, she willed her last thoughts to be about something beautiful. Like Hidden Creek. She'd always loved it here. The smell of the pines and the whisper of the wind through the trees. How the night sky was so clear and the stars shone so brightly she felt as if she could reach up and touch them. Blackberries that would be ripe in another month. She could bake a pie in the cozy kitchen of her cabin.

Her cabin. The one thing she'd fought for in the divorce. The place where she'd hoped to raise a family.

But now it would go back to Brian.

Over my dead body.

With a new sense of urgency, Lily fought back against the current, flailing about as if her life depended on it.

* * * *

Carson turned his attention to the river. He expected to see the slow, graceful movements of a woman out for an afternoon swim. He expected smooth, easy strokes and efficient flutter kicks as she propelled herself through the water. He expected to pass her by without another thought. Instead, he felt his muscles tighten, his heart rate accelerate, and his vision narrow as the realization that she was in trouble hit him like a flash flood.

Instinct kicked in. He dropped his rod, pulled his keys and phone from his pocket, and raced into the raging river. He dove into the waist-deep water, swimming aggressively toward her. The current was strong. He had to be stronger.

"Just relax. I've got you." He kept his voice steady, projecting strength, confidence, and competence. He couldn't let her panic. *He* knew he was trying to save her, but there was no way of knowing what was going through her mind.

She struggled briefly, mumbling something, as he wrapped his arm around her waist and pulled her against his chest. The buzz of adrenaline flooded his system, blocking out the cold, the current, and everything but the need to keep her head above water and bring her to shore. He kicked hard to propel them away from the strongest part of the current. Working with the flow of the river and not against it was crucial in getting them both out alive.

The river slowed as they approached the eddy. Carson adjusted his grip and his hand slid up over the smooth curve of her breast. He corrected his hold on her, but not before his thumb grazed her nipple.

Focus.

Get her out of the water.

All the hours of training drained from his head. This wasn't the first time he'd rescued someone from the river. It certainly wasn't the first time he'd touched a woman's breast. He should be able to get his mind back on track. Once they made it back to dry land, then he could think about her perfect breasts. When she was safe, he could let his mind wander in the direction his fingers had wanted to go. Not to mention his mouth.

"I've got you." He tried to sound calm, in control. Like someone who knew what he was doing. Her life was still in his hands. "Trust me."

Her body relaxed against his as she wrapped her arms around his neck. Relief flooded him as he realized she wasn't going to panic and try to fight him. He still had to get her out of the water. Then get her somewhere warm. The image of his bed flashed through his mind and he brushed it away like a pesky mosquito.

Cody stood downstream, holding his rod case over the water. A rope would be better, but they'd left the hoopi in the truck. The tubular nylon webbing, often used by climbers, was one of their most valuable pieces of river gear. Almost as versatile as duct tape, and Carson wished he had some with him. He did have his brother. Cody might not remember to pay his cell phone bill on time, but get him on the river and he was one of the most reliable men around.

"Hold tight." Carson reached for the case, and grabbed hold as Cody pulled them toward the shore, reeling them in like a couple of steelhead. Carson got his feet under him and helped the woman stand.

"You're okay. You're going to be just fine." His legs felt like wet beef jerky now that the adrenaline drained from his system. His heart rate should be returning to normal, but he'd just felt her up in the middle of the river and he didn't even know what color her eyes were. Let alone her name.

"Thank you." She shivered.

Hidden Creek would be a very different river in another month. Once the runoff slowed, it would be marked with gentle riffles, calm pools, and some of the best trout fishing in Northern California. Today, it was a surging flow carrying a winter's worth of snowmelt as it merged into the South Fork of the American River. Not as cold as it had been a few weeks ago, but still cold enough that twenty more minutes might have led to a different ending.

Carson tore off his wet shirt and pulled the woman against his bare skin. "I've got to get your core temperature up." He massaged her arms and torso briskly, hoping she wouldn't think he was some kind of perv. But, damn, she felt good pressed against him, soft in all the right places and naked except for her bikini bottoms. The idea was to warm her up, but he was the one on fire.

"Cody. Give me your shirt." His words came out harsh and demanding. His brother obeyed, pulling the dry T-shirt off and tossing it to him in one swift motion. Carson slipped it over her head, breaking the contact but not the impact of her bare skin against his.

"What's your name?" Carson asked.

"Lily Johnson." She held her hand out, but quickly retreated. "Sorry. It's Price. Lily Price."

She shook her head before extending her hand again. Her grip was firm and surprisingly warm. Had she recently changed her name or was her confusion because of injury? He glanced down at her left hand. Bare. But that didn't mean a thing. The river was a thief. She'd been known to take jewelry, sunglasses, and bathing suits. Even lives.

"I'm Carson Swift." Carson dropped her hand, but he still felt the charge as if he'd been struck by lightning, and the water only intensified the conductivity. "This is my brother, Cody."

"Oh, so there are two of you." She let out a sigh of relief. "I thought I was seeing double."

"We're twins." Cody reached out to shake hands. "Identical."

"Nice to meet you both." Lily glanced from one brother to the other. The glazed look in her honey-gold eyes told Carson she'd have to work at telling them apart. They were too much alike. On the outside.

"It's our pleasure." Cody emphasized the last word, letting her know that he was interested. Then again, Cody rarely met a good-looking woman he wasn't interested in.

"Well, thank you both for…" Lily held her breath just long enough for Carson to suspect she was not as calm as she pretended to be. "Saving my life." She flashed them a fake smile to let them know she was fine, thank-you-very-much.

"Hey, no problem." Carson wanted her to believe it was no big deal. All in a day's work.

Except it was a problem. A big problem. He couldn't just walk away from her now.

Physically, she'd recover. She'd be sore for a few days, but the color had already returned to her cheeks. She stretched her arms overhead and rolled her head from side to side. He almost expected her to throw a few jabs in the air just to prove she was a fighter. But she kept casting glances at the river as if it might reach up and swallow her. Carson worried more about her emotional state. Fear could creep in like an unwanted vine and if left unchecked, it would take over, choking the life out of her.

"Let's get you someplace warm." Carson took her arm to lead her back up the path. "My truck is just down the creek."

"Oh, that's okay." Lily eyed the water again with mistrust. "My cabin is right on the river."

"Cedar shingles? Green trim?" Cody asked. They had fished this stretch of the river enough times to know the place she was talking about.

"That's the one." Lily's face lit up with pride. There were only a few residences along the way and hers was by far the most welcoming.

"Trust me," Carson said. "My truck is much closer."

She shrugged and then bent down to pick up his keys and phone.

"You might need these then." She handed the keys to him and their fingers brushed, sending a shiver down his spine.

"Is there someone we should call?" Carson asked as he took the phone.

"No." Lily shook her head. Sadness flickered across her face, disappearing almost instantly. "I'm enjoying the solitude of Hidden Creek."

"So you're all alone out here?" Cody's voice dripped with invitation. Could he be any more obvious? The woman had just been plucked from the river and Cody was trying to get her into bed.

"I'm taking a much-needed vacation." Lily's voice held a hint of defiance. "The first since my honeymoon seven years ago."

"So will your husband be joining you?" Carson's voice cracked like a thirteen-year-old boy. He half-hoped she was still married. Then he could just forget about her.

Yeah. Right.

"My *ex*-husband can go to hell." Lily's voice shook a little. As if she wasn't used to using such strong language. Or maybe she wasn't used to standing up for herself. "Did I say that out loud?"

"You did." She made him laugh, in spite of everything.

"I am so embarrassed." Lily blushed, a deep, dark pink. "I'm not really the bitter ex. I swear."

"What, did the guy cheat on you?" Cody asked. Leave it to his brother to use a woman's divorce as an opener to hit on her.

"Yeah. Among other things." Lily looked down at the trail, as if it was the most interesting thing in the world. Obviously she didn't want to talk about it. She marched forward, but stumbled on an exposed root.

Carson grabbed her arm. Just to steady her. The sooner he got her back to her cabin, the better.

"Let's get you home. Get you warmed up, and we'll be on our way." Carson would sleep better knowing she had no lasting effects of her ordeal. Besides, he already felt responsible for her.

He needed someone else to worry about like he needed another Swift River Adventures T-shirt.

Maybe he could use another shirt. His was dripping wet and covered in dirt. Lily was the only one of them wearing a shirt, dry or otherwise. And damn, if she didn't look really good in it. Her hips swayed ever so slightly as she walked. She wasn't very tall, but her legs stretched long and lean beneath the faded blue shirt. Her damp hair fell just below her shoulders. Carson couldn't tell if it was light brown or dark blonde, but either way it would look great spread across his pillow.

He didn't need to peek at Cody to know he was thinking the same thing. They were way past the age of acting like horny teenagers. Or they should be. Besides, Carson wasn't going to stick around; he had no business lusting after her.

She was just something else he would leave behind.

* * * *

"So, Lily, what were you doing swimming in such high water?" one of the brothers asked. The one who'd pulled them both from the river. He'd also given her the shirt off his back. Literally.

"I wasn't swimming." Lily didn't like the defensive tone in her voice. "I... I fell in."

"Well, it's a good thing we came along when we did," the other brother said. He tried to keep his tone light, but Lily sensed an undercurrent of worry. They all knew what might have happened if the brothers hadn't been there.

Some Mother's Day this turned out to be. Not that she was fortunate enough to be a mother. And instead of being a good daughter, spending an uncomfortable day not talking about her divorce with her mom, she'd decided to relax in the sun, finally diving into that novel she bought for herself last Christmas. With everything that happened to her in the last few months, Lily hadn't had time for small pleasures. Now she had all the time in the world. The next few months, at least. She planned on taking the summer off before looking for another bookkeeping job, or even landing clients of her own.

Lily had felt a little reckless sunbathing on that rock like a teenager. She'd even switched to SPF 15 instead of her usual 50. UV rays had turned out to be the least of her worries. She should have waited for the paperback or gotten an eBook. With the bulk and weight of a hardcover edition, the book had slipped out of her hands and as she reached for it, she'd tumbled head first into Hidden Creek.

She was a strong swimmer, an experienced swimmer, but the swift current had taken her by surprise. She'd tried swimming back toward the rock, but there was no way she could fight the force of all that water. Disoriented and a little ticked off at the twenty-seven dollars she'd spent on that book she'd never get to finish, she'd started flailing about, reaching for something, anything to grab onto so she could get her feet back under her.

She'd been in the water ten minutes, maybe longer, when she'd heard a deep male voice, felt strong arms around her, and realized she wasn't alone in the water.

The rest happened so fast. She was in the water. Then out. Somewhere along the way, she'd lost her bathing suit top and this man was holding her close. There was a second man, identical to the first. He gave up his shirt and flirted with her. The first guy seemed worried about her. But she was fine. Really. They were making too much of a fuss over her. "Sorry to interrupt your fishing trip." Lily tried to steady her voice, to sound like a woman who could take care of herself.

"Hey, it's okay," one of the guys said. "The water's a little high for good fishing, anyway."

"We caught something much better." His brother smiled and spoke with a light-hearted tone. He was definitely flirting with her. She remembered flirting. It's what her ex had done with every woman but her.

"Tell me again who's who." They'd reached the end of the trail. Lily was trying to keep them straight, knowing it must be hard to be constantly mistaken for your twin.

"I'm Cody, the good-looking one." The first brother flashed his dimples and smoothed back his blond hair in an over-the-top, I-know-I'm-good-looking way.

"Yeah? When was the last time you got a haircut, you hippie?" His brother gave him a friendly shove. Lily's gaze strayed to his wet shorts. He'd been the one to jump in the water after her. He'd been the one to really save her life. She shivered at the thought. And at the way the damp fabric clung to his muscular thighs.

"At least I don't look like an escapee from boot camp, like Carson here." Cody snapped to attention and offered a salute.

"I like it short." Carson sounded a little offended. "Besides, my hair's so thick if I go more than four or five weeks without a trim, I have to put stuff in it."

"And it would just run out into the river, poisoning the fish." Cody recited the words like scolded schoolboy. "Lighten up, man."

"So I care about what gets washed into the river." Carson shook his head and chuckled. "You only care about what you pull out."

"Hey, at least I catch something once in a while."

"I'm not talking about the fish."

They teased each other, but there was genuine affection in their banter. Lily envied their closeness. As an only child, she'd envisioned a large family of her own someday. Three, maybe four kids running through the house. Walking down to Fairy Tale Town or the Sacramento Zoo. Baking cookies and hanging their artwork on the refrigerator door. The only thing hanging on her refrigerator now was an appointment card for Foothills Fertility Clinic.

She followed the twins to a white double-cab Toyota truck. Carson clicked open the locks and held the front passenger door for her. He offered his arm to help her climb up into the cab. A jolt, almost as startling as the icy-cold water, shot straight through her.

How long had it been since she'd been touched, really touched, by a man? For the last few years, sex had been entirely clinical. An act of procreation—and desperation—that had nothing to do with intimacy.

But he hadn't really touched her. Not like that. He was only trying to help. Like he'd been trying to help when he pulled her against him. And he was only trying to help when he'd touched her breast. Lily wasn't going to read anything into it. She didn't need a man. She definitely didn't need two of them.

Carson went around to the driver's side and Cody slid into the backseat. Lily clicked her seatbelt in place. If only she could restrain her nerves so easily.

"So tell me." She turned so she could converse with both of them. "What do you two do when you're not rescuing topless women?"

Masculine laughter filled the cab. The deep, rich sound warmed Lily from the inside out. Carson started the ignition and turned the heater on full blast, to warm her on the outside.

"We run Swift River Adventures, a rafting company out of Prospector Springs." Carson's smile showed a man who took pride in his work.

"It's not far from where gold was first discovered in California." Cody leaned forward, inching closer, making her aware that there was entirely too much testosterone in this tiny space. They were big men. Strong men. Very good-looking men.

It took twice as long to drive to the cabin as it had for her to float downstream. At last, she was home. *Home*. Even if it was only temporary.

"Nice place." Carson shut off the engine and turned toward her. His eyes were as warm, and as blue, as a summer's day. "Are you renting for the summer?"

"Nope. It's mine." She was still getting used to the idea. "All mine."

"Is it a vacation cabin?" Cody asked from the backseat.

"Not exactly." Lily turned to find Cody's eyes were just as startling and blue as his brother's. "My house in Sacramento sold a lot quicker than I anticipated. So this is home. Until I figure out where I want to end up."

"Well, I'm glad you're here now." Carson's voice was slightly lower than Cody's, without the teasing note. She just hoped she'd be able to find other ways to tell the two of them apart. They both wore faded khaki shorts, complicated athletic sandals, and nothing else. Carson had tossed his wet shirt in the back of his truck and she was still wearing Cody's.

"So, Lily." Cody didn't seem to want his brother to get the last word in. "What do you do when you're not charming the shirts off a couple of fishermen?"

"I'm an accountant." Or she had been.

"No way." Cody leaned forward again. "You're much too interesting to be an accountant."

"I think that was supposed to be a compliment." Carson shot his brother a disapproving look. "What kind of accounting?

"I don't have my CPA license." Lily was making excuses again. Focusing on what she lacked, not what she could do. "I do general bookkeeping, payroll, just about anything except income taxes. But my company decided to outsource my duties, so here I am."

She exited the truck and approached the front porch steps. Both men followed her across the wraparound deck and through the front door of the two-story cabin. The place had been built in the 1940s, when things were made to last. The floors were well-worn oak planks, the fireplace had been built with rocks gathered from the area, and a large picture window overlooked the river below. Three bedrooms, plus a loft, would provide plenty of space for the large family Lily still hoped to bring back here someday.

They entered the bright, spacious kitchen, with its knotty-pine cabinets, butcher-block counters, and a large cast iron sink big enough to bathe small children in. Lily had so many dreams for this place. None of them involved being divorced, jobless, and alone.

"Do you have any tea?" Carson eyed the kettle on the back burner of the gas stove. "Or hot chocolate? Something to warm you up?"

"How about some whiskey?" Cody suggested. His grin made her somehow think of those old cartoons with the big St. Bernard lumbering through the snow with a barrel of whiskey on his collar.

"Um, yeah. Tea bags are in the cabinet over the stove. There's beer in the fridge." Lily pointed to the old-fashioned Frigidaire. Not the most energy efficient appliance, but it reminded her of a simpler time. Back then, fresh fruits and vegetables replaced microwave popcorn as a snack. Cupcakes were made at home, not ordered online and delivered to your door. And families were created when a man and a woman loved each other very much and wanted to share that love with a child. It didn't take a credit check or a series of lab tests. "Make yourselves at home while I go change."

"You should take a long, hot shower," Carson suggested. His voice warmed her and made her shiver at the same time.

"Are you offering to wash my back?" The words just slipped out. She wasn't the kind of woman who traded suggestive comments with a man she'd just met. She'd never even made that kind of statement to her ex-husband.

"He doesn't have the skills." Cody stepped closer, invading her space. "But I'm very skilled." He lowered his gaze to her chest and licked his lips subconsciously. Or maybe it was on purpose. He seemed like the kind of man who knew exactly what he was doing when it came to women.

"Sometimes it takes more than skill." Carson shot his brother a disapproving look. Oh dear, they were fighting over her. Not fighting really, just competing for her attention. She should warn them that she'd vowed to go the rest of her life without ever having sex again. She'd spent the last few years with pillows propped under her hips every Tuesday and Friday from 10:15 to approximately 10:27. All for nothing.

Water under the bridge. Over the dam. Spilled out into the ocean by now.

She closed the bathroom door and slipped the oversized T-shirt over her head, catching a glimpse of herself in the mirror. A large bruise bloomed along her left side, stopping just below her breast. More bruises appeared along her hip and back. Tears stung her eyes as she realized just how lucky she was that Carson and Cody had decided to go fishing that day.

"I'm going to fix you a cup of tea," one of the twins said through the door. "Do you need any help in there?"

"No, I got it." Lily tried to make her voice as strong as possible. She didn't want whoever it was to think she was weak.

"Just checking." His voice was strong, steady, and very sexy. "Let me know if you need anything. Despite what Cody says, I'm very good at washing backs."

It was Carson. Her heart fluttered as she remembered the feel of his arms around her. His hand on her breast. The way he'd pressed against her, trying to warm her up. He was so solid, rock hard arms, chest, and well, if that was shrinkage…

She turned on the shower. It would take a few minutes to warm up. The water, that is. She was already warm in all the wrong places. Maybe she should take a cold shower instead. Like that would help get her mind off the two hunks in her house. Either one of them was twice the man Brian was. And put together? She shuddered as she stepped under the hot water.

The warm spray did wonders to release the tension in her body. It wasn't just the day's events, but the last eight months of stress that she needed to wash down the drain. She had turned thirty wondering why it was such a big deal. She had a good job, a nice house in a desirable neighborhood, and a smart, successful husband to share her life with. The only thing missing was a baby. They had been working on that.

But then she'd lost her job. No big deal. They didn't need the money. She was going to quit when she got pregnant anyway. But they had been trying for three years. Two years longer than most people waited to get tested. The results were more than disappointing. It had been the final straw that had broken the overstrained backbone of their marriage.

Damn. She must have gotten shampoo in her eyes. The stinging sensation couldn't possibly be tears. She had nothing to cry about. She was alive. That had to count for something. She still had plenty of time to have a baby. She had options. Maybe even right there in her living room.

Stop. Don't go there.

She wasn't desperate. Gone were the days when only a married couple was given a chance at having children. She could probably even adopt, if it turned out that Brian wasn't the only one with fertility problems.

With a little effort, Lily managed to dress after her shower. A bra was out of the question, considering the bruises on her side. The guys had already seen her girls in all their glory, so she slipped on a dark green T-shirt, hoping she wasn't asking for trouble. She'd just have to go out there and be herself. If only she knew who that was.

That's what she'd come up here for. To live life on her own terms. And that meant taking one step at a time, starting with marching into the kitchen where her rescuers were waiting.

"Oh, good. You're both still here." Lily put on a brave smile. "I'm not sure how to thank you. For everything."

"Don't worry about it." Carson handed her a cup of tea. "We're just glad we could help."

"I could make you dinner. Or something." Lily tried to think if she had enough food for three.

"No. That's okay," Carson was quick to decline. "You should get some rest."

"We could light your fire," Cody offered, and his brother gave him a quick elbow to the ribs. "In the fireplace. To make sure you stay warm."

"Oh, that's not necessary." She wasn't sure if Cody was trying to be funny, but the way Carson glared at him made her suspect that Cody's over-the-top flirtation was a sore subject between them.

"Is there anything else you need?" Carson's concern was a little overwhelming. She needed to get a grip on her emotions. Her hormones. All she had to do was finish her tea and thank them for saving her life. She wasn't looking to create a new life with either of them.

Meet the Author

Kristina Mathews doesn't remember a time when she didn't have a book in her hand. Or in her head. Kristina lives in Northern California with her husband of twenty years, two sons, and a black lab. She is a veteran road-tripper, amateur renovator, and sports fanatic. She hopes to one day travel all 3,073 miles of Highway 50 from Sacramento, CA, to Ocean City, MD, replace her carpet with hardwood floors, and throw out the first pitch for the San Francisco Giants. Visit her on the web at kristinamathews.com.

Printed in the United States
by Baker & Taylor Publisher Services